I0649531

How To Market Your Grief Blog

by
Mike Sauve

GhostTruth

It is unlikely that man, as we know him, would have survived without the fictive, counter-factual, anti-determinist means of language, without the semantic capacity, generated and stored in the 'superfluous' zones of the cortex, to conceive of, to articulate possibilities beyond the treadmill of organic decay and death. It is in this respect that human tongues, with their conspicuous consumption of subjunctive, future, and optative forms are a decisive evolutionary advantage. Through them we proceed in a substantive illusion of freedom. Man's sensibility endures and transcends the brevity, the haphazard ravages, the physiological programming of individual life because the semantically coded responses of the mind are constantly broader, freer, more inventive than the demands and stimulus of the material fact.

Isaac Steiner, "After Babel"

Well the future to me, is already a thing of the past You were my first love, and you will be my last

Bob Dylan, "Bye and Bye"

Author's Note: With the lone exception of some character traits of Cannabilizin' Terry Stripes, all plot details concerned with pandemic and the instantiation of artificial super intelligence were written prior to 2020.

Ten Tips for Getting Back in the New York Groove

*I*f as time passes memories delude us with their transience and telescopy, be pleased that the only change in Catherine is a faint grace added to the fundament of her beauty. If eye contact proves too powerful for everyone's tastes, look away then immediately look back again. If effects precede causes in some inertial frames, your glasses could cloud the knowing before you. Crush them underfoot.

One: If here comes her ghost again and her peacoat is free of detritus as her peacoats somehow always are, and you wear a younger man's clothes, and there you stand on Bleecker Street in the fixity of your fiction suits, press your palms against her hips, which hips you once complimented as "ample," and while she'd said this was not a compliment *per se*, you've forever remained unconvinced.

Two: Should a joke seem necessary to leaven the tension of a reunion fifteen years in the making, speak the words, "Our long national nightmare is over—Abraham Lincoln said that. It sure is nice to see you again—I said that."

Three: Though you find the substance neurotoxic, get unethically-traded coffee in a multinational franchise, and while no more cosmopolitan than all the franchises from Seoul to Sault Sainte Marie, it is in Manhattan and contains the girl to whom all your longings speak, thus fulfilling a promise once trod into the soil of a St. Joseph's Island farm with her as sundress'd Juliet and thee as the holy fool, Balthazar.

Four: If still at a loss for words, but in a high comradeship of spirit, do not be romanced by the ceilings of the NYPL's Stephen A. Schwarzman Building. Don't pontificate on man, blessed man, 19th century Giuseppe or whomever, up on some literal latter to the stars sculpting those ceilings to resemble the Sistine Chapel's. Because if you get distracted photographing the ceilings you may lose her again. She could step away and leave you nothing but the ceiling, and then the pictures of the ceiling, which is one of the most photographed ceilings in America, meaning it's there but no one can really see it.

Five: Do not have a religious experience at a Bob Dylan concert lest those similarly-afflicted congregate at The Dublin House where she will make friends, as her winsomeness not only allows but dictates, where if her past precarity is any indicator, she will flit maddeningly on the periphery like a 'floater' caused by clumped vitreous in the agèd. If a suave Bobcat remarks, "Your girlfriend and I should get a motel room," punch the man's chin such that his brain collides with his skull, sending him out of that evening's sex economy. If asked to decamp by Dublin Mike, a sixty-year-old bartender in the Irish Mickey Ward vein who's seen so much he appears bored even in the act of breaking up a fight, then place your forearm on Mike's bar and sweep a dozen pints and shots and snifters crashing to the ground, causing Dublin Mike to raise his fists in the classic 'put your dukes up' position, a posture that would seem hilariously Vaudevillian were he less hell-bent on pummelling you.

Six: If pulled to safety by Catherine, recite the last two verses of *Oh Sister* from 1974's *Desire* to reassert your sensitivity after the recent milieu of general beastliness. If she finds your earnestness wearying, double-down on your gratitude that she's been mysteriously saved.

Seven: If you and Catherine have never sampled the delights of the marriage bed, and Catherine seems more inclined towards the solitary restfulness of the Airbnb's living room couch, ask her, "Wouldn't it be sad if the memories from the old life had to last us our whole life?"

Eight: If Catherine's moral virtue supersedes yours, she'll reject your dawntide repackaging of the night's transgressions and insist you return to The Dublin House to apologize. If your usual strategy of avoidance—minimum one year—hasn't been knocking it out of the park lately, why not give this contrition angle the old college try? With every nerve ending frayed and afeared of more raised dukes, approach Mike to say, "I was an asshole." If Mike then looks into your blood-red eyes with more empathy than you've deserved in many years and quotes[1], "A man's attitude... a man's attitude goes some ways. The way his life will be. Is that somethin' you agree with?" and you quote back, "Sure. Sure." And Dublin Mike

---

[1] (Lynch, Mulholland Drive, 2002)

continues: "Now...did you answer cause you thought that's what I wanted to hear, or did you think about what I said and answer cause you truly believe that to be right?" and you say, "I agree with what you said, truthfully," and Dublin Mike replies, "What'd I say?" his smile should reveal that this is a rib. If Mike says "Hadn't seen the old full bar sweep in some time," what Mike must mean is, 'This has happened to all we intemperate individuals before, and the Infernal Serpent knows it will happen to all of us again, so if we won't forgive what good is even being alive?'

Nine: If St. Patrick's Cathedral is a free and ornate place to request penance for all the cardinal sins recently committed, a desanctified place where tourists take altar selfies during communion, and no one knows the head-tapping maneuvers required for the responsorial psalms—yet if you are holding her hand again after all this time, the cloud of forgetting behind you, and the neo-gothic setting is like Batman's house, bloody palm wounds on the stained glass, Jesus pretty adamant about having died for our sins, then get down on your knees and pray, for if the psalmist speaks,

> Then Jesus answering, said to her:
> O woman, great is thy faith:
> be it done to thee as thou wilt.
> then that means she must choose.

Ten: If a father and son band play Dixieland jazz by the central park pond from which Holden Caulfield's stupid ducks once migrated or perhaps froze to death ☹, lie your hoodie on the cold wet grass for her to sit upon, enfold your legs into hers, place your forehead against hers and say, "Those hair vitamins you buy are worth every last dime." In the Guggenheim, take pictures of *Orpheus in Hades* (1897) by Pierre Amédée Marcel-Béronneau. Take pictures of Jean Delville's *Portrait of the Grand Master of the Rosicrucians in Choir Dress* by Joséphin Péladan (1895). Buy postcards of the paintings even though the pictures already exist in higher quality on Google Images, because when the mystical symbolists were convinced to convey the peculiarities of God, they weren't conveying anything so peculiar as a disappeared loved-object. If you recall that not Lincoln but Gerald Ford spoke the words, "Our long national nightmare is over," and that your photographic memory should not have permitted you to forget this, understand under your sweaty blogger's bedsheets, back in the corporeal world in which the spiritual world subsists, that this is another cruel dream, as she was never yours for more than an evening at a time, for just as she might have been, another man, perhaps needing her as much, but certainly not *more*—maybe only a man who believed his own gimmick more concretely than you—came along and spoke the words, "You're always running away from things." Other-directed as she was, and no less impressionable, Catherine couldn't run away from such a declaration. If this is the case, try to discontinue consciousness to find some last remnants of her to be stolen from the mouths of the M'Wasis at the Bronx Zoo. If as ever these vestigial dreams involve only the loss of the loved object across subway platforms, losing

Catherine in the crowded bar, losing Catherine to the circus fiend, to superior causes, to all the hard-luck wolves of the night, losing her at Calvary and in the demilitarized zone and in crummy old Windsor, Ontario, then hang down your head and cry.

Some Tips Towards the Monetization
of a Grief Blog

*F*orgive me, reader, should you think it crass that my sophomore effort in the grief space is concerned with the marketing of a grief blog. However, if you are not consoling a wide audience of the grief-stricken and *ergo* achieving traffic and commensurate remuneration, then why write a grief blog in the first place?

One: Avoid what is known as *direct marketing*. Do not Facebook message an acquaintance to ask if they count themselves among the stricken. Do not ghoulishly troll the obits.

Two: Be yourself. Do not emulate grief bloggers who have already achieved traffic and remuneration. The stricken will smell a rat. Avoid books like *Chicken Soup for the Grieving Soul* lest you imitate the tepid style therein, a style that has already oversaturated the grief marketplace.

Three: If Eisenstein wrote in *The Structure of the Film*: "There is no such thing as grief 'in general.' Grief is concrete; it is always attached to something; it has consumers,"[2] that

---

[2] (Eisenstein, 1947)

means you must avoid wishy-washy tenses. Employ the imperative tense! When necessary, employ the counterfactual.

Four: Like and share other grief bloggers. Unbecoming as it often feels, sharing ten consecutive articles from *Grievin' Gary's Grief Refuge* will capture Grievin' Gary's attention. Sharing one will not. Sharing one will make you no more estimable in Grievin' Gary's eyes than some grief-stricken mark.

Five: Don't put too much pressure on yourself. As Daniel Johnston famously sang, "Millions and millions of people have already died." Thousands will die today. To say nothing of pets, catastrophic brain injurees, and those enduring a type of living death due to opiate dependence. Among the scant few not yet grieving, you can count on anticipatory grief, *e.g.* 'father ridden with cancer.' There is also a sort of nameless dread: a fatalistic grief for the unknown sorrows to come, such as the prospect of worldwide pandemic, a new Philovirus, for example.

Six: Don't display your grief *bona fides* right out of the shoot. Little is more tiresome than the grief blogger flogging a deceased Bull Terrier for every last click and share. Granted, *bona fides in absentia*, questions may arise, *e.g.* "Just what is this guy gripin' and grievin' about anyway?" They'll get past this, the grief-stricken, because they really don't care, such is their bottomless need for consolation. Besides, who among us has not known grief in one or more of its many manifestations:

The grief of the non-historical nature of time.

The grief of parasitism and the Personal Protection Equipment (PPE) during the Philoviral outbreak to come.

The grief of the sinister hobbies, *e.g.* 'inveigling,' *e.g.* 'deceit.'

The grief of the coins accidentally eaten while on Ambien, the coins presumed to be mints.

The grief of *Time and Narrative*: "It is remarkable that it is language usage that provisionally provides the resistance to the thesis of non-being."[3]

The grief of the unread Cybergothic wherein "Time produces itself in a circuit, passing through the virtual interruption of what is to come, in order that the future which arrives is already infected."

The grief of the coroners' doubts as detailed in *Redbook Magazine*.

The grief of who the heck propagates this theory of non-being anyway, the nontologists?

The grief of your murdered sister.

The grief of the downward sloping marginal utility curve, *e.g.* 'Fifth burger in a row only 5% as satisfying as first burger,' *e.g.* 'Same with roller coaster rides, sexual triumphs, all life's phony pleasures.'

The grief of alcohol, pills, and the fluorescent-lit morning to follow.

The grief of the Archons bedevilling us since time immemorial.

---

[3] (Ricouer, 1984-1988)

The grief of a sister's shampoo in the springtime, its scent and its memory.

The grief of the intrapsychic crypt.

The grief of the most troublesome mistress' borderline personality disorder co-morbid with her glittering eyeshadow twinkling through the dextroamphetaminic evening.

The grief of a wife's allergies and the repetitive nature of allergenic sneezing.

The grief of "Where's your empathy, David? Do you think sneezing is fun?"

The grief of throw pillows on a Christmas wish list when all you want is your sister alive again!

The grief of not having enough "grease to go to the brothel" in the words of Donald Barthelme, author of the seminal grief novel, *The Dead Father*.

Remarks glittering well past the borderline of propriety.

The grief of "a kind of causal Darwinism called post-selection that governs the flow of information backwards and forwards through the glass block of Minkowski spacetime," in the words of Eric Wargo, author of *Time Loops: Precognition, Retrocausation, and the Unconscious*, "Information refluxing into the past [that] only 'survives' as meaningful insofar as it cannot be used to foreclose the future that 'sent that information,'"[4] meaning sadly you can't save your sister Catherine from being beheaded on the side of Highway 17.

---

[4] (Wargo E. , 2018)

Seven: Get featured on blogs like *What's Your Grief* that often review the hottest grief blogs.

Eight: Know that the bar to entry at national grief conferences is refreshingly low!

Nine: Don't blog of clues in Catherine's obit pointing to Archons or maybe the Infernal Serpent being behind all this sadness, as Archon-focussed blogging and small press publishing yields next-to-nothing, remuneration-wise, and can only lessen your standing in the grief blogging space. Never mention the Archons to your prescribing doctor. If you must discuss Archons try to position them as a type of malevolent AI perpetrating non-linear-causational tyranny on humankind. Don't mention how you may be implicated in all this. Steer clear of the word *Gnosticism* in discussions with your doctor, and with all others.

Ten: Don't get in a maudlin headspace prior to composition. Listening to The Cowboy Junkies' *The Trinity Sessions* is what the grieving are *already doing*. Listen to something fun like *Back in the New York Groove* to remind readers that, "Hey, life can be a party, and it's time to delete that folder of Catherine pictures and maybe blog about something more remunerative such as the Soda Stream™."

5 COMMENTS ON "SOME THOUGHTS TOWARDS THE MONETIZATION OF A GRIEF BLOG"

Father_Of_A_Lost_Angel: Are you trying to mock the grief community?

Brampton Int'l Grief Conference: All of our THIS! Would you be interested in speaking at the Brampton International Grief Conference in January?

Grievin' Gary: Sorry to hear about your sister man. Is that whom you are grieving? You should probably write a post about the specific person you're grieving if you want the community to accept you. I'll share this post, but I would like to know whom specifically has passed before sharing any others. If it is the dead sister then please accept my sincere condolences. Also, I would suggest buying your WordPress site. It's only $25 a year and it will appear much more professional. And don't worry WordPress doesn't pay me to say that lolololol.

What's_Your_Grief: Thanks for the mention. Good luck and stay strong! ☹

Erik Wargo: Going forward please ask permission if you plan to use quotations of mine longer than three sentences.

Rly David_Astaire: Won't happen again.

Ten Tips for Autostereogrammatic Epiphany

A number of commenters have inquired regarding the high volume of mistresses referenced on this grief blog, *e.g.* "How does an apparent deadbeat like yourself appeal to so many mistresses?????" Or "Unless you're a French aristocrat, the word *mistress* is a low point for even this dubious blog read solely by your dozen former classmates who maintain morbid interest in how low you might plummet," or, "Your headshot sneers epicene. Your teeth are too small for your mouth, offering a feral impression. Please elucidate your unlikely process for procuring mistresses and spare no detail." Having (fingers crossed) recently added a new *tertiary love interest* into the fold, here is the process.

One: Find yourself in the Liberty Village apartment of a pretty young woman from your hometown of Sault Sainte Marie, the crucial preliminary maneuvers lost in the nebulosity of a blackout. Based on the tears on some faces, most notably your own, and the voices hoarse from shouting, many cruel words must have been exchanged during the unencoded hours, yet still you find yourself cross-legged before her, looking into her eyes and holding her hand. If the Sault is notorious for its shallow gene pool, and the lighting low enough, let her vaguest resemblance to Catherine hold you in thrall.

Two: If your small press Amazon listings can't convince her that the "great man in history" theory applies to you, do not denigrate her chosen profession of "marketing" by suggesting that marketers referring to themselves as *creatives* is the cruellest oxymoron ever to manifest. These tactics can only set you back.

Three: If Mariana is explaining what brought her to Toronto, *i.e.* "I was in love with an actual great man, Pete…" and her sad saga of an ill-advised *menage-a-trois* incorporating both Pete and his brother Paul is poorly told with hundreds of diversions, none of which even remotely relevant to mistress procurement, albeit slightly more relevant to the subject of grief, then even after editing it down to the fewest possible clauses while maintaining her speech's integrity of dialect, place it in a supplementary PDF so overburdened readers can skip it if they so choose.

Four: If she sobs "And now it's come to this, 5:30 am and here with this doofus rather than Pete or even latent Paul," yet a mixture of stimulants and GABAergic drugs has you feeling like no doofus but rather the "original vagabond,"[5] then dust off your high school Latin to speak the words of blessed Augustine, "*Quid est enum tempus?*" "(What, then, is time?)"[6]

Five: If it gets to dark to see the Catherine in her anymore, try to make your home in the darkness. Lie beside her. Touch

---

[5] (Baez, 1975)
[6] (Augustine, The Confessions, 1998)

her purple pyjamas. Attach a leash of longing. Here is the crux of all bonding. Here is where and when you will acquire that tertiary love interest, reader. The euphoria of post-coital repose is often attributed to the magic of the coital act itself; however, lying down beside a woman is itself a magic rite. The hair vitamins' yield. Static electricity off pyjama bottoms.

Six: Align your knees with hers. Align your regrets. Touch her neck. Tell her she's adorable, which she is. You are no longer lying. You are being yourself. Tell her that you've always been aware of her sexual appeal, *i.e.* 'the tan and the $400 haircut and the boyish charm,' but now you are aware of a certain humanity as evinced by the Pete-Paul fiasco, a tenderness that calls to mind no specific girl from your Sault Sainte Marie youth but all of them.

Seven: Ask her if she has read the essay *The Autostereogrammatical in Thomas Pynchon's Mason & Dixon*. If she has not, or if more likely she doesn't respond, emits a fake snoring sound for example, then remind her that an autostereogram is better known as a "magic eye" poster and then quote the following from Julia Jordan:

> These two methods of seeing an autostereogram correctly are thus either known as wall-eyed and cross-eyed, or convergent and divergent. To achieve either view, the brain has to overcome its desire to focus, or to converge at the point of the image. This moment of revelation, where images become multilayered and munificent, is known as parallax. The autostereogram thus offers a model

of vision where the image itself seems to be an agent: we can provoke it, we can coax it, but nothing is guaranteed; the autostereogram asks us to consider whether two perspectives, if converged on correctly, can give way to a previously hidden third element—by dint of its revelatory structure, the autostereogram is naturally epiphanic.[7]

"We're having an epiphany," tell her. Explain how the moment of revelation occurred when her humane side evinced by Pete's big mistake, *e.g.*, 'appeasing Paul as best he could,' parallaxed with her Instagram appeal, and the complete human being was born in time. Ask her, "Isn't this munificent?" Confess that all fully-coaxed human imagery cannot but invoke Catherine's humanity for you. Say, "We've found the third element!" Say that several times for effect, with increasing enthusiasm. Say, "We've coaxed it." Say, "I love you."

Eight: If she isn't laughing, chuckle a bit, *i.e.* 'Hey, above all, life is a gag. These magic eye visions may be mirror refractive folly, but you must know how possible it is to love a stranger or even an in-law in any given moment, for love exists outside of time and only flits back into existence when credentialed by desire converging at the point of the image.' Say, "I love you, Cathy," while kissing her neck, Cathy being a nickname of your dead sister that also conceivably rhymes

---

[7] (Jordan, 2015)

with *Mari*, which maybe Mariana is sometimes called. If she says, "I love you, Paul," then you are in business!

Nine: If later Mariana awakens provoked by the deceased sister coaxed in her living room and well nay in her, she'll retreat to her own room that contains another heterosexual man, *i.e.* 'Any heterosexual man would be less unsettling than you right now after all that dead sister talk, Dave,' then why not lie on the floor, on a big pile of soiled garments for example, until you are asked to leave.

Ten: If after a strategic interlude of exactly three days you text her the following from Julia Jordan

> On one hand, the autostereogram disturbs our assumption that meaning resides in depth—in what is buried and latent—by creating a hyper-determined surface; the depth that it promises to disclose literally exists on the surface. We know as a viewer of the autostereogram, and as a reader of fiction, that depth is an illusion, and that both interpretative acts are therefore a mode of play, where the delight and vitality of the depthless, glittering surface is allowed to be all. But simultaneously, the autostereogram lives up to its promise, sharing its secrets and showing what was previously hidden. The surface is less meaningful than the image it obscures.[8]

---

[8] (Jordan, 2015)

then do not compulsively check your phone for return texts while re-reading this essay, for even if Mariana has consciously forgotten you, overtly denigrated you to her housemates once you'd been Ubered away, you have made the excellent mistake of exposing something real of yourselves in the place between profane and mythic time.

5 COMMENTS ON "TEN TIPS FOR AUTOSTEREOGRAMATIC EPIPHANY"

Anonymous: Doesn't even sound like she's your mistress bro.

Mariana Sicoli: Okay first I am not your mistress and second there's a reason all these posts get 1 like on social and it's that YOU DON'T KNOW HOW TO MARKET YOURSELF PROPERLY. Third I don't even miss Paul and I'm glad we broke up. Fourth I don't even remember you saying any of that crazy stuff and quite frankly I think you made a lot of it up. Did we play footsie or something? Maybe, I forget. Take this down or I'm contacting a lawyer.

William Pitts: So I was thinking, "Yeah, she's not going to be his tertiary love interest. But since ^ obviously got pretty worked up maybe David has an outside shot. I hate to think this guy actually knows what he's doing and this is how I should be carrying on if I want more tertiary love interests.

LigottiLigotti: How's it going with the borderline personality one?

David_Astaire: Not well. ;(

Style Tips for the Stricken Blogger:
Writing Killer Dialog

---

*D*ialog has been answering the big questions dating back to antiquity. Not bootless corporate-speak like "Let's have a dialog," but Socratic dialog, defined by Wikipedia as *a formal method by which a small group (5-15 people), guided by a facilitator, finds a precise answer to a universal question (e.g. "What is happiness?", "What is integrity?", "Can conflict be fruitful?", etc.)* or more germanely to this blog, "What is grief?" If you may know 5-15 people to nod at them in the dog park type thing, but not to discuss "What is happiness?" because these individuals believe they already know what happiness is, even if their knowledge is no more sophisticated than some "Live, Laugh, Love" meme; or worse, the question of "What is Happiness?" frightens them because they lead unexamined lives and would rather contemplate simpler candy-based predicaments on their phone, then your Socratic facilitation may beg the question, "Isn't that your dog's excrement on the opposite side of the off-leash area?" Rather than endure that indignity, why not automatically write the following dialog to converge or hopefully diverge into autostereogrammatic clarity at some later point in time?

Sample Dialog - St. Michael's Hospital Floor 8:
Neo-Natal

"Abraham was only being tested was he not?" asked David.

"So if we go through the motions, maybe we'll be stopped," said the other David.

"Informational hazards cross the digital corpus callosum. So like Sartre said, 'How does Abraham know that he is Abraham?'"

"The metaethics of digital physics am I incorrect? The OS could stop trading voltage for current in the nearest power transformer to dim the lights or stay the qubits of our very hand. Not sure why that rotten old ragamuffin let us come this far in the first place then but still maybe."

"Might be a non-linear causational type of quest. The most annoying kind. Full of quantum error corrective feedback loops. We incur the wrath because we've already slain the babe. Our Abrahamic self-certainty may be what's subjected us to so many of the Cluster B disorders up to this point as it is."

"Think you might mean complex causality," David said with disinterest.

"We should not have stopped taking math in grade ten."

"Guidance counsellor said we'd be closing a window to the future."

"Sounds just comically ominous now doesn't it?"

"Fate of humanity will be determined by your ability to distinguish between time-like, space-like, and light-like universes."

"Or Stump and Kretzman's *Eternal-Temporal Simultaneity*."[9]

"Oh Lord, and remember Bem? We worked so hard to comprehend *Feeling the Future: Experimental Evidence for Anomalous Retroactive Influences on Cognition and Affect*."[10]

"After the Colbert appearance."[11]

"And then Bem was discredited the next day."[12]

"Discredited himself when the academy was too busy to discredit him, 'I'm all for rigor, but I prefer other people do it. I see its importance—it's fun for some people—but I don't have the patience for it.'[13] Even Colbert must have been embarrassed."

"We too lack rigour. Lacked the rigour to reconcile how the blockchain creates artificial time. Lacked the rigour to read even the consummate Bem dunk, *Correcting the Past: Failures to Replicate Psi*.[14] Lacked the rigour for Stump."

"Couldn't tell a p-value from the hash of the previous block."

"All the old memories from all our past lives...."

"Memories of the baby's ten teeth, smiling up at us from the first pile of leaves he played in."

"Memories of the raspberries he so enjoyed."

[9] (Stump & Kretzman, 1981)

[10] (Bem D. , 2011)

[11] (Bem D. , 2011)

[12] (Galak, LeBoeuf, Nelson, & Simmons, 2012)

[13] (Engber, 2017)

[14] (Galak, LeBoeuf, Nelson, & Simmons, 2012)

"That effective raspberry pi language he created at just four."

"How demurely he first learned to say, 'Yes,' and then the obstinance with which he shrieked, 'No!'"

"The little feeding apparatus that let us strap him to a counter at the Starbucks."

"His messy face, in need of eternal wiping."

"Eh, but then there's the vomiting, the bleeding through the eyes, the liquefaction of our organs. The Manistique Strain," said David, wincing.

"Won't go back to that. What about just standing between the aspirator and the babe, clogging up the works somehow? Seems the peaceful way. The humane way."

"The humane way?" David asked.

"Better never to have been born, as Benatar posits. This baby is almost not yet born. Practically just barely born. Better never to have been barely born?"

"Believe Benatar and all the anti-natalists are just clini-cally depressed. Benatar must never have considered how wildly a baby can thrust in their Bouncy, how enthused they are to meet the world."

"Oh nothing, nurse-maid of the unspecified realms, just admiring our interdimensional offspring here. Same-sex cou-ple baring a severe resemblance to each other is all. And a good evening to you."

"I need a pep talk. I think I can do it. All the peas and the carrots shoved into his mouth all messily need never to have been. Our memories and fondnesses and fatherly prides don't equal the bubos and the splitting that will afflict all human-kind, all childkind."

"Retrodiction and obfuscation, good angle."

"Guess so. Feel like Abraham was enticed with more of a carrot than a stick. Should have probably paid more attention in religion class too, eh?"

"Infralapsarianism, sublapsarianism, supralapsarian-ism—who could care about the distinctions?"

"What of Eliade, a relevant quote of whom's I've scrib-bled on this napkin here, ahem,

> All sacrifices are performed at the same mythical instant of the beginning; through the paradox of rite, profane time and duration are suspended. And the same holds true for all repetitions, i.e. all imitations of archetypes; through such imita-tion, man is projected into the mythical epoch in which the archetypes were first revealed. Thus we perceive a second aspect of primitive ontology: insofar as an act (or an object) acquires a certain reality through the repetition of certain paradig-matic gestures, and acquires it through that alone, there is an implicit abolition of profane time, of duration, of "history"; and he who reproduces the exemplary gesture thus finds himself transported into the mythical epoch in which its revelation took place.[15]

---

[15] (Eliade, 2005)

"The Stalaghh soundtrack to it all? The ocular trauma of the eye icicles? The scent of Espanola? The Infernal Serpent makes these concepts knowable on an olfactory level."

"Coherently extrapolated volition, heard that on a You-Tube video. It means the ASI was designed to do what this red-faced little gaffer told it to."

"Is there no intervention that doesn't involve our own beloved son? Why not baby Geordie Rose, inventor of the D-Wave quantum computer? Why not give him the business? We'll never feed Geordie Rose carrot mush. There can't be a single cause."

"Unless the single cause is mere Machinic Desire: 'Far from exhibiting itself to human academic endeavour as a scientific object, AI is a meta-scientific control system and an invader, with all the insidiousness of planetary techno-capital flipping over. Rather than its visiting us in some software engineering laboratory, we are being drawn out to it, where it is already lurking, in the future.'"

"*His* own son."

There does seem to be a certain equifinality about culling his very babe on this very morn. It's his only begotten son. Not mine and not yours. That's the meagre sacrifice we must make. Anyone could kill baby Geordie Rose, some might even pay good money to do so given his unctuousness."

"Your complexion appears much too white."

"Wish we could influence the moment of conception instead, simply don't stick it in: a sin of omission, if any sin at all."

"An emission sin of letting the geriatric pregnancy window close."

"Speaking of missions, how do we know this baby even becomes the one prophesied? Maybe this baby sucks at coding. Standard deviation between worldlines is there not?"

"You are a charlatan. As am I. We know not of which we speak. There's nothing to trust but the math. And we dropped math in grade ten. How can we sub-Stumpians grasp something simple as 'two-value logic,' meaning it's either perception programming as mass human control or that same wise guy who gave Abraham the gears?"

"I'd thought a sustain was something achieved with a whammy bar, lol."

"Just going to wash our hands, Mr. Janitor of the unseen realms. Never can be too hygienic around these vulnerable young souls, even interfacing supra-dimensionally as we are."

"Fuck it, I'm going to pinch this tube."

"Aspirator isn't clogging. You are without agency!"

"Somebody up there putting a stop to things! The best possible outcome isn't it? We're Abrahamic heroes! The whole thing was one long test!"

"Except now the suction is sputtering. And except now the suction has stopped."

"What's this then from our fatherly counterpart in the corporeal realm, the third David, prone on the ground?"

"As the aspirator sputters anew, appears he's making that old sign of the cross."

"Damned if even that doesn't look computational somehow, doesn't it?" asked David.

Ten Tips for Spreading Yuletide Cheer

*I*f while visiting sad old Sault Sainte Marie your father invites you to his study for an evening dram, grab him by the lapels of his smoking jacket and shout, "Why couldn't you have prevented it? Why? Why? Why couldn't you have prevented her decapitation?"

One: Let this set the dark tenor for the family Christmas.

Two: If you can't stop shouting, "You're not a man. Not in my book. Not if you couldn't have kept her alive!" across the yule loaf at the man who diligently and decently raised you, then it's best to partake of a few solitary drams before boarding a bus to a downtown bar. If barflies buy drinks for young girls in flower, any of these reprobates may have been Allan Raval's third accomplice, perhaps even the procurer of the saw.

Three: Photograph landmarks like the International Bridge and the Big Picnic Table in Bellevue Park and send them to Grievin' Gary as per GG's request.

Four: Weep until 5 am while imbibing all available spirits and even a few household solvents. Fall into the closest available set of arms, be they the arms of a mother, or a father, these arms distinguishable by whether they are clothed in a nightgown or a smoking jacket. Bellow with all the anguish inside you, "I was once a brother!"

Five: Stalk the palatial estate of Allan Raval, the grey man who saw (pun certainly not intended!) her last. If his infinity pool has been drained for the winter, fill it with a token amount of your urine.

Six: If Allan Raval has O.P.P. enforce a restraining order that mandates you keep 500 yards from both Raval and McMansion, inform the Ontario Provincial Police that that restraining order expired in 2015. If lawmen remark upon the scent of solvents emanating from your person, claim to have been varnishing.

Seven: Absorb their eyerolls, pity, and hatred. Whisper as you decamp, "Why couldn't you have prevented it?" at Constable Bad Douglas Bindi Jr., the discoverer of Catherine's severed head.

Eight: Urinarily deface the home of Rob Dagg, known accomplice of Alan Raval.

Nine: Treat your parents to a nice meal! Remember that they themselves still grieve in whatever miserly way their hearts are capable of. According to Grievin' Gary, food is just gangbusters for the grieving. The stricken love to strap on the old feedbag. If dining out is cost-prohibitive, local Italian restaurants sell tomato sauce to go. As noodles are a real high-yield item, simply buy these at a grocery store, affix $8 sauce, and you have provided a restaurant-quality meal for a song.

Ten: Smell the night. Visit the snow, this most pristine of condensations coating the entire town as it cannot in smoggier climes. Blog of how the most meagre Christmas decoration shines far brighter when offset against the dismal. Blog of how a twenty-five-year-old Zellers tree looks better than all of Rockefeller Centre when offset against a slushy vestibule full of fentanyl fiends. Blog that contrast is the crux of all known beauty in this world.

Ten Tips For Getting Yourself Killed

*I*f Mariana, also home for Christmas, sends a surprise text inviting you over for a swim, presume your autostereogrammatic missives weren't such a bust after all. If many sober relatives in her hotel room aren't keen on your heightened reverie, know that a comic repurposing of your urinary Alan Raval harassment will not get over with this crowd.

One: Inquire if an Archonic allegiance against mankind's goodness is what's made them such buzzkills.

Two: Spill whiskeys and throw clean towels atop the booze pools. Ask if Pete is about, and if not Pete, perhaps Paul.

Three: If tense relatives have heard Mariana drunkenly rearrange these apostles a time or two about *The Last Supper* table, then pass around a picture of your own sister, *i.e.* 'I too can tread the maudlin and incestuous path of the unreal conditional!'

Four: If Paul stops by with some biker friends, placing the odds of coaxing the autostereogrammatic with Mariana at an all-time low, abscond with that roughian's backpack to let him know who the real man is, even if you're more the chickenshit type of heel. Check the backpack during the cab ride home to find $18,000.

Five: If plot points of Mariana's long-winded and supplementarily-PDF'd anecdote regarding the Outlaws Motorcycle Club regain autostereogrammatic foci, realize you have stolen $18,000 from the Outlaws Motorcycle Club. Even if described by Mariana as, "not even that bad of guys," you will be in danger.

Six: Call bail bondsman acquaintance who once bonded Big Donnie, a local enforcer for the rival Hell's Angels. Receive Donnie's Facebook messenger contact. Message Donnie the lay of the land. Inform him that the $10,000 is all his if he can absorb the heat.

Seven: Hang out in Catherine's room, left to stand as some creepy shrine to the 20-year-old girl she'd once been and would never be again (thanks Allan Raval!) Blog of how her undergarments have been tactfully hidden away after your indiscretions of 09-12-2016.

Eight: If bail bondsman acquaintance texts that Big Donnie's cousin Jenya is dating a Hell's A and *ipso facto* Sault Sainte Marie enjoys a rare period of *détente* between the Outlaws and the Angel's, then in good faith Big Donnie has relayed your message to his Outlaws counterpart, One-Eyed Dave. Check the bus schedule, urgently. If no buses until the following day, hide under covers. Hear a knock on the door followed by O-E Dave's polite inquiry as to your availability. Emerge into the mud room to stand your ground with One-Eyed Dave. If One-Eyed Dave isn't wearing a pirate patch or anything, but only has glaucoma in the left eye, joke that he, "probably didn't see this particular Yuletide assignment coming." Interfere as best you can with One-Eyed Dave's removal of a hammer from his Outlaws leathers.

Nine: Absorb hammer blows with your forehead. Observe the whiteness of the light. Avoid eye contact with your father if he perches above you in the ambulance. Request a paramedical notepad upon which to scrawl a last will and testament concerned with domain names and intellectual property rights.

Ten: Say goodbye to the cruel world and all of its beauty.

Tips on Avoiding Hell [Or: (If Having Failed To,) How to Experience Hell to the Fullest]

*I*f frolicking imps followed towards the light become less ebullient, kind of pushy even, you'll soon find yourself cheerlessly confined to the pit.

One: If self-recrimination is the true nature of the pit, then blame others where possible and while you can. Say maybe if it weren't for Allan Raval or for Donnie's hammering, or if like the Good Thief or Emperor Constantine you'd only gotten right with God at the last minute, say maybe then…. Say none of this aloud. It won't go over well with the hellspawn who've taken over your chain of custody from the imps.

Two: Zooming out a bit: if still alive, take in VERY LITTLE hell-based content. The most accurate model of hell is the *Swedenborgian*, also known as the *personal model of hell*. That means Hell will manifest your darkest imaginings: an eternal struggle against Ravalian stand-ins, for example. It will manifest high school hallway fistfights long dreamt in dreams: endlessly punching with no efficacy, being punched, eye gouging. And of course there's the fire, and of course there's the flaying.

Three: Come to think of it, maybe stop reading these tips right now. Just click that little X in the top right corner because the more the innocent reader knows of flayings, the more likely she is to be flayed upon her arrival in hell.

Four: The worst part about the flaying, incidentally, is that your skin grows back.

Five: Flayed once, sure, no picnic, what with nerve-endings and organs exposed to acidic regurgitations from demonic maws, yet in your first flaying's wake you'll rationalize, "Heck, they can only slice that skin off the once." Not so. The growing back of the skin is at first curious, though itself painful, until by the third of fourth flaying you realize the true pain is the subjunctive pain of the flayings to come, of the flayings evermore.

Six: To the extent that there is buggery, and this extent is significant, lobby to be the "pitcher" rather than the "catcher" if the intimation is clear. This is no condonement of the heteronormative tendency to use the words, "Fuck me in the ass," as an expression of the worst fate that can befall a man. It is fair warning against the sharpened nature of hell's phalli.

Seven: Don't request a sit-down with the Infernal Serpent. He is busy running an interdimensional organization. Don't try to barter your way up the chain of command. Play the long game.

Eight: Do not let your mind wander to any concept unbearable as the "eternal."

Nine: If asked by a functionary demon if you'd like a break from the flayings and Rick Rude-inspired dick choppings, do not, repeat, DO NOT accept their invitation to spend an aeon or two in The Hall of Memories. Just going to repeat that for emphasis: AVOID THAT FUCKIN' HALL OF MEMORIES.

Ten: Emphasizing this once again because mere remembering is something we're all afflicted with on the prison planet, so it sounds pleasant relative to sharpened dicks, but there are memories we cling to all our lives for the sole reason that these are the memories we need to forget.

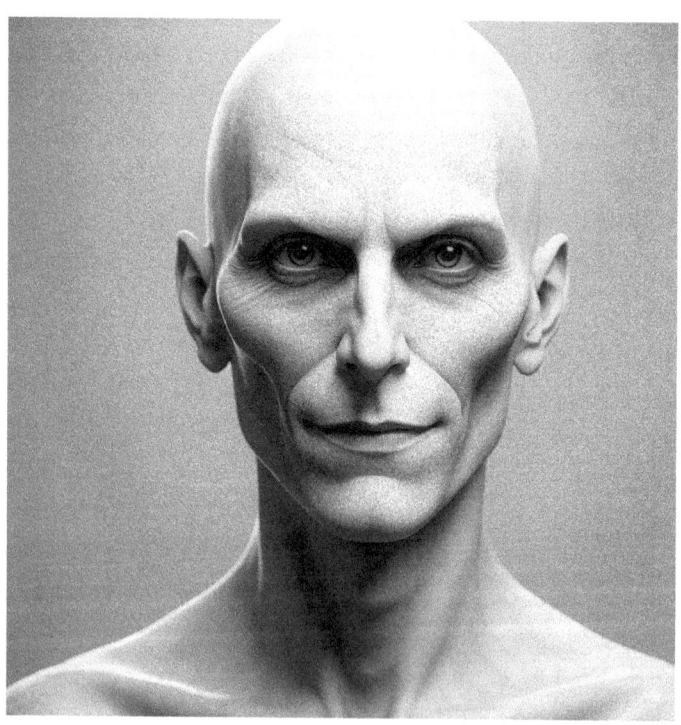

Ten Tips for Reversing the Flow of Time

*C*aveat emptor—readers must be in hell for these tips to possess value. If not already in hell, readers will have no means of reversing the flow of time. Bad news for the reader not in hell: this list can't aid you in reversing time. Good news for the reader not in hell: you are not in hell! Readers not in hell are encouraged to count themselves lucky, but also to like and share so that any friends reading from hell might benefit.

One: Request of middle management demons, "Certain to be a common request, Anthony, but mightn't I be better utilized advancing the infernal cause back on *terra firma*? No issue with the pencil-sharp penetrations whatsoever, starting to derive an almost pleasant humiliation from them in fact, but I am something of a silver-tongued devil myself, pun intended, Tone, and it seems certain talents of mine, blogging talents, are being underutilized at this level of the organization."

Two: Be persistent! Don't think these supervisory demons wouldn't all like to reverse the flow of time themselves. And regardless of blogging ability, almost everyone considers themselves a silver-tongued devil, hence Twitter, hence the banality of Reddit.com.

Three: Network! Network! Network! People in hell might seem *désagréable*. And sure you'll have to hear about their own schemes and dreams for escaping hell, but is the cocktail hour at an insurance convention altogether less dispiriting? It is not. Network until some demonic higher-ups recognize you as a go-getter.

Four: Tip three transcends reversing the flow of time and is relevant to any field.

Five: Keep roars of agony down to dull roars. The insurance adjuster who refuses to spend all his lunchroom hours "bitching and moaning" will be appreciated for his imperviousness to the calling's crushing mundanity. Similarly, demonic middle management will note your pluck and mention you in Slack threads read by the Archfiend.

Six: When you finally get that meeting with the Archfiend, kiss his pointy toes and offer your orifices to him as sexual chattel, per custom.

Seven: If lying when you plead, "Mr. Infernal Serpent, um, Adversary to most but certainly not to me, you old Son of the Morning you, listen man it's not about wanting out, it's about bringing everything we've got down here up there," it won't matter much; The Archfiend has been lying since he could hold a fiery trident.

Eight: Accept the Archfiend's offer that you can leave hell on the grounds that you immediately sire a son and teach him the pattern extraction at the bedrock of artificial super intelligence (ASI) engineering, thus instantiating what Destinee has in store for you:"[s]o much positive feedback fast-forward that speed converges with itself on the event horizon of an artificial time-extinction."[16]

Nine: Have your mission encoded via Neurolinguistic Programming. Feign surprise when NLP guru Richard Bandler is on hand in hell to administer your training module.

Ten: Upon reintegration of corporeal consciousness, remove an intubation or two. Recall the Bandler-recommended books to read to the son you must now sire. Request notepaper from your mother's purse. Record book titles before they flee your mind as dream-encoded messages flee in the hypnopompic moment:

Python for Dummies

Paradigms of Artificial Intelligence Programming: Case Studies in Common Lisp

R for Data Science

Artificial Intelligence: Foundations of Computational Agents

Record 18,959 letters of code. If a doctoral student writing his dissertation on post-concussive savants begs you to take his battery of acquired savant tests, respond, "Nah, should probably just fly back to Toronto before Outlaws get word of my miraculous recuperation but feel free to chart my progress at *http://wordpress.com/toweepistomakelessthedepth.com.*"

---

[16] (Land, Machinic Desire, 2011)

Ten Tips for the Coerced and Unenthusiastic Father

*I*f needing to make good on your Satanic accord, inform your wife that after years of her unsubtle pressure you're now willing to ejaculate into her during periods of ovulation. Should any nagging doubts or *Eraserhead*ian fatherhood anxiety plague you, the unwilling father, in the weeks thereafter, here are tips for quantum erasing some of those.

One: To the best of your ability, sever ties with all her relatives and social relations. If she resents this, describe the vampiric energy economy wherein a baby *supplies* the elder generation's interminable *demand*, these forebearers practically fuming if they aren't offered the placenta to eat. Describe with distaste this generation's employment of food euphemisms, "Look at the little jellybean." "I just want to eat you up." Here is man's true cannibalistic nature laid bare. (A cannibalism of spirit, rather than flesh, conceded.) Worse yet is how a baby somehow offers voice to the human adult's most insipid internal monologues: "Is that a doorway? I think it is. I think that is a doorway." Conclude with sorrow that this is the median quality of the human animal's inner monologue.

Two: Baby-proof all electrical sockets.

Three: If fiscal planning is essential for a low-earner dependent on blog-based revenues, buy a few Facebook ads out of the baby's nascent college fund to increase traffic and remuneration.

Four: If wavering on your satanic accord, *i.e.* 'Maybe all a dream,' then read aloud to your partner from *Better to Never Have Been* by David Benatar, which advocates the anti-natalist position that it is immoral to birth yet another human being into a world of suffering when enough extant human beings are already suffering that you could adopt. If the jacket copy succinctly summarizes:

> …coming into existence is always a serious harm. Although the good things in one's life make one's life go better than it otherwise would have gone, one could not have been deprived by their absence if one had not existed. Those who never exist cannot be deprived. However, by coming into existence one does suffer quite serious harms that could not have befallen one had one not come into existence [17]

she may question your fatherhood *bona fides,* and wonder if, abortively-speaking, it is not even yet too late. Should she be the non-compliant party, the Infernal Serpent might concede that at least you'd tried.

---

[17] (Benatar, 2006)

Five: Television commercial saccharinity oozes forth from the rough ground of real life, so accept that the whole, "Say goodbye to your sleep/enjoyment of life" meme must be suffering's means of essaying itself through tepid humour that barely even tries to disguise itself as such.

Six: Ducts and vents will also require babyproofing. Sharp knives will need to be replaced with dull knives. Bid *adieu* to your clean cut through the raw chicken breast. Whereas colleagues at *Reluctant Gourmet* advise to "let the knife do the work," prepare to do the work yourself by sawing those breasts ragged until your prophesied offspring is fourteen or older, when new threats like crystal methamphetamine and any Philoviruses percolating in the upper peninsula of Michigan's simian population may take precedence.

Seven: Choosing a name for accursed offspring can be a bone of contention amongst even the healthiest of couples. If your relationship is, to be charitable, *strained*, then all the uglier. To avoid the worst of it, insist your child be named Marcel_Proust. Insist on the underscore rather than Proust as middle name, or he'll be plain Marcel in no time, and soon thereafter something as pedestrian as Marc. Argue that by naming your baby Marcel_Proust, he's obligated to pick up a copy of *La Recherche* at some developmentally-appropriate life stage, providing him the eternal gift of Proustian self-reflection, as well as some minor iteration of Proust's elegant prose line, helping to uphold the family tradition of self-reflexive and prosodic blogging. If your wife's full-time job precludes her from reading the 4,215 pages of *La Recherche* assigned to her, meaning she cannot conceivably complete your weekly comprehension quizzes, ask if this shortcoming doesn't render her ill-qualified to discredit your sobriquet of choice. Argue that she could quite easily in fact "be able to love" a child thusly named. If her "best friend" also finds the name ill-considered, ask why her "best friend" failed to obtain even the lowest level of Baccalaureate degree if she is so brilliant? Why did her best friend have to go to Seneca College to study Early Childhood Education if she is so adept at naming children? If talks reach an *impasse*, play a manipulation game or two by singing the praises of your 45-year-old and hopefully-barren mistress. If that too fails, *i.e.* "She has borderline personality disorder and you know you can't tolerate her for more than a single lurid hour at a time," then concede that the name will be Ikea_Shelf or whatever while intending to oversee all birth certificate duties while she is under epidural so that when her consciousness re-asserts itself and a nurse introduces the red and screaming but healthy and hearty and somewhat strapping Marcel_Proust to her, hopefully then the name will take.

Eight: If said mistress with borderline personality disorder has always wanted a baby but now lacks the youthfulness of womb to produce one, inform her as gingerly as possible that you've changed your address and the set of keys she's stolen certainly won't work at the new address; why would they? Otherwise, she will likely arrive unannounced with all the violent intentions she was possessed of on the night you made the mistake of calling her "tedious."

Nine: If your wife claims nothing cheaper than an $1800 stroller will suffice, find a perfectly good one at a garage sale for a fraction of the cost. That fraction being a nice clean one of 3/1800, or by reducing to the lowest common denominator: 1/600. If your wife contends, "This is a child's toy. A stroller for a baby to push her own toy baby around in," then make a big production out of fortifying its more translucent fabric with rawhide at your workbench. If your wife sends Amazon link after Amazon link for the $1800 stroller, place a ten-pound flour sack in the toy stroller to demonstrate how it could easily meet ANSI standards if heaven forbid subjected to ANSI scrutiny in the event of a wrongful death investigation.

Ten: If you do choose to go a different route, *i.e.* 'the non Marcel_Proust route,' avoid rhyming names like Amelia Bedelia, lest your child be teased, this according to colleagues at the Mom365 blog.

4 COMMENTS ON "TEN TIPS FOR THE COERCED AND UNENTHUSIASTIC FATHER"

Mom365 Blog: Please don't link to us again.

Early_Childhood_Educator/10: Proud Centennial College graduate here! UGHHH Child Protective Services anybody…

Erik Wargo: Potential negligence would be occurring in the future so how to imprison him for that right now tho?

David Astaire: Do you really still believe in Newtonian relics such as *past* or *future*, lmfaoing at your life.

Ten Tips for A Grief Prevented

*I*f awoken mid-REM cycle and agitated off to a maternity ward, nurses will show the pregnant party infinitely more empathy than you the emissionary emissary. If they counterfactually call her "mumma" + epidurally catheterize her a bottomless fountain of fentanyl while offering you the polysubstance addicted blogger not a measly Oxycontin 80, then focus on the breath and swallow your resentment.

One: If an anesthesiologist places her phone where a nurse had recently placed a bloody cervix stretching glove, figure that's just the cost of doing business and unobtrusively engage the anesthesiologist in the "does consciousness reside in the microtubules"[18] debate.

Two: If a no-nonsense head nurse suggests, "If you've got nothing better to do you can tidy up your big pile of scarves and Goethe volumes and McDonalds coupons," mutter as you tidy that, "The no-nonsense individual is rarely little more than all-nonsense." Resent when this nurse whispers to your wife and mother-in-law as if you weren't there.

---

[18] (Barlow, 2015)

Feel called to be a nomad. Feel about as necessary to this nascent coven as that low-down rake murdered at the end of Robert Altman's *Three Women.* If all you can muster in response to the pregnant person's shrieks of anguish is irritation, joke glibly of how the oscillating TOCO scores on the contraction monitor sound like the techno soundtrack to a Gaspar Noe film. If in response the head nurse issues you a look of utter contempt, recall Rainier Maria Rilke's sentiments on irony:

> Do not let yourself be governed by it, especially not in uncreative moments. In creative moments try to make use of it as one more means of grasping life. Cleanly used, it too is clean, and one need not be ashamed of it; and if you feel you are getting too familiar with it, if you fear this growing intimacy with it, then turn to great and serious objects, before which it becomes small and helpless. Seek the depth of things: thither irony never descends—and when you come thus close to the edge of greatness, test out at the same time whether this ironic attitude springs from a necessity of your nature. For under the influence of serious things either it will fall from you (if it is something fortuitous), or else it will (if it really innately belongs to you) strengthen into a stern instrument and take its place in the

series of tools with which you will have to shape your art.[19]

i.e. 'There's a time and a place, fool.'

Three: Try to recover a sweet love that you knew. See in your mother-in-law's eyes a love for your wife you might again manifest. See that same love in an old English nurse named Deirdre. If it's way past midnight and the pushing has begun, note that the lion's share of the birthing process involves nothing less lurid than Deirdre's vigorous fingering of the pregnant person. If there's a less lurid term for pre-natal fingering other than "digital masturbation," doubly problematic under the circumstances, please suggest it in the comments.

Four: If your wife is too jacked up on fentanyl to properly splay her legs for further digital coaxing, find yourself enlisted to hold steady her right gam. Endure a front-row view of the whole gory tableaux. Heeding Deirdre and Rilke's anti-irony chastisement, resist the urge to compare this tableaux to a bowl of raw hamburger meat.

Five: Should pushing prove fruitful, you will see the crown of a head. Oil will be poured into the hamburger bowl. Hair will become visible. The baby will be pulled out. The baby will be thrown on the mother presently factual. The baby will not be breathing. The baby will not be moving.

---

[19] (Rilke, 1943)

Six: If a dozen doctors and nurses attend to the code pink called for your baby, love him in that instant of life or death more than you have loved any woman you've ever sacrilegiously called *baby*. Find sinister the appearances of two fractal reflections of yourself espied in the window pane above the aspirator. Associate their presence with the aspirator's temporary sputter. Fear they may be deflecting your Hail Marys. If you remember the Lord's Prayer a bit better, recite many from memory.

Seven: Meet the pleading eyes of the mother still factual: pleading with you to save the baby, or for so little as an update, to do this one thing right, to dispel the fractal murderers, to be worth something for once. Hear your name, "David!" while wading through the *Night and Fog* of agency panic. Request the forgiveness of your debts until a cry to the end of time forgives them, and though you'd dreaded the sound of a baby crying due to your irritability and chronic low-mood, the child's voice will sound finer than Bob Dylan at the Beacon Theater in your New York dreams. Following this cry Marcel_Proust will raise his eyebrows and throw his hands up in extreme comic exasperation, *i.e.* 'Might have been better to have been born with the ability to breathe, eh? Still, it can only get better from here, a baby must wager.'

Eight: Give a thumbs up to your partner and her loving mother. Diagnose Marcel_Proust as, "Going to make it. Going to be just fine." Hear what you perceive as griping and groaning from the fractal shadows in the window pain of the post-prophetical.

Nine: If you thank the doctors and nurses who have saved your son with their quick thinking and competence, they will appear stoic, *i.e.* 'All in a day's work,' because every twelve-hour shift they fight a war on this battlefield where every stillborn birth still hurts. All the anguished mothers and fathers. The permutations of heartbreak, desolation, and guilt. Resentful accusations of "Why didn't you do anything?" or "What took so long?" Yet they return deliberately and daily into an arena where all of a mother's dreams may need to be gingerly removed from her arms and incinerated.

Ten: Consider what might have counterfactually come manifest: returning to the Etobicokean crib and bassinet and bottle drying rack and all the baby toques and t-shirts that women are biologically-mandated to buy for other women's babies. Imagine placing that crib out by the curb or else leaving it for fourteen months while risking a recurrent fate, the crib and the sleep sacks a daily reminder of what's befallen you and may befall you again: the classic four-word Hemingway poem titled *For Sale*—

Baby shoes; never worn

Know in this future contingent the bottomless depth of genuine grief. Understand with uncharacteristic humility that the limits of grief extend beyond all sisterly scope. And but rather than contritely abandon your grief blogging, *i.e.*

"What am I gripin' and grievin' about anyway when people are putting cribs by the curb?"—rather than that, double down, double down on shining whatever stupid and silly and inconsequential light you can shine into the darkness, for if we are to address the question of "Why do bad things happen?" then every fractal fool—the holy and we compromised by self-interest alike—we must testify through the unique prism of our pain.

Ten Tips for Loving a Newborn Boy

*I*f in his early hours outside the NICU you resist holding your baby for fear his neck might snap, try to look busy doing other things, *e.g.* 'Grief blogging,' until your wife's sheer urinary need forces the issue.

One: Should the child's neck stay sound under your skittish maintenance, gain confidence.

Two: Hold the boy against your chest; burp the baby; note his small features resemblant of yours: the unassailable nose, the furrowed brow of confusion and contempt, the pronounced widow's peak that calls to mind WWE's Kane, described during the Attitude era as "the Devil's favourite demon."

Three: If nearly a decade previous you had awoken in hypnopompic confusion, grasped your Affen Pinscher by her mid-quarters, and to the poor beast's fiery consternation, patted her back while saying, "Got to burp the baby," understand this as preordaining your current responsibility.

Four: Consider his crying an apt response to the human condition, *i.e.* 'Only two days old and seen enough of the prison planet already.'

Five: If the hyper-maternal neonatal nurses grant you esteem for your clumsiest of efforts towards baby maintenance, realize that the bar to entry to fatherhood, much like grief expertise, is refreshingly low.

Six: Resent not that phrases like, 'Everything changes when you see him,' or 'First time I ever cared about anyone more than I cared about myself,' have been true all along, but that these flags were planted with trademark normie inelo-quence, leaving nothing novel to blog of.

Seven: Relate to the oft-essayed, "When [Regular baby name such as *Brawnzen*] was born my heart left my body and now it [less interesting version of *roller-skates down embank-ments, plays dice in the alley with the sons of lewd women*, etc.]

Eight: If you've reached this waystation on the highway of regret, realize with chagrin that now there is nothing you won't do, *e.g.* 'Only two chicken wings on plate better give both to Marcel_Proust,' *e.g.* 'Driving him to Scarborough to play with a friend who doesn't even strike you as cool,' *e.g.* 'Giving him your hard-earned blogging remunerations for crass commercial products that he'll believe himself to want or even need once pubescence dawns and he becomes an insa-tiable maw of low consumerist instinct.'

Nine: See your partner in a new light: the light of estro-genic surplus.

Ten: Compliment a particularly winsome nurse on the genuine sentiment that must have gone into her "Live, Laugh, Love" tattoo.

How to Plan a Christening

*P*lanning a christening can be a real headache! Relatives' schedules to balance, clergymen booked and remunerated, and lest you forget the end goal of buttressing baby Marcel_Proust against *Tzvarnoharno*, the force that hates the good in mankind and applies unceasing pressure towards our moral ruin.

One: If buds are on the vine, then it's that lovely season for baptism—the Spring, but should your baby be born in the despair of late fall, waiting on crocuses to bloom is no option, because for babies born under dark accord as otherwise, baptism is just one of many safeguards needed against confinement to the abode of the damned.

Two: Based on your own life experience, request a caveat to the baptismal vows wherein the baby should be protected against what Wilhelm Reich styled "emotional plague."[20] If the priest gives your many napkin-scrawled baptismal caveats the hairy eyeball, pull theosophical rank by asking, "Would you agree with Gurdjieff that 'the force and degree of a man's

---

[20] (Wilhelm Reich, 1945)

52

inner benevolence evokes in others a proportionate degree of ill-will?"[21]

Three: Baptismal gowns can cost as much $$$$$ as a wedding dress. If you were married at city hall, and *ergo* remain unexploited by the wedding dress and DeBeers mining industries alike, why start that exploitation train a-rollin' on this most earnest of life's milestones? If your mother is leery of providing material from your sister's prom dress of 06/15/2001 after your anniversarial onanism incident of 06/15/2011, assure her of the occasion-specific need for the coveted fabric.

Four: Slick and frilly invitations are worth the extra buck. Baby Marcel_Proust's family and friends can tuck theirs away in some drawer until the family and friends die and the frilled stationery enjoys its life's second act brightening some squalid landfill.

Five: To hedge bets against the Infernal Serpent, ask that a reading be (what is it?) performed from the Gnostic Gospel of Philip, the gist neatly summarized by the gnostic blogger LonerWolf: "the Archonic force's main objective is to keep humans ignorant of their divine origins beyond the physical universe."

Six: If the priest argues that Our Lady of Lourdes is a Roman Catholic rather than a Gnostic church, invite some local Light Worker pals from the Sethian Gnostic

---

[21] (Gurdjieff, 1933)

Community to suss out if the priest is some sinister Rosicrucian intent on maybe hexing rather than blessing Baby M_P.

Seven: At the post-baptismal reception, in the park, with its frozen branches reminding everyone of necrosis, do not mention your deal with the Infernal Serpent wherein baby Marcel_Proust is destined to bring about mankind's unceasing imprisonment by means of exponential advances in deconvolution, lest any forward-thinking Light Workers decide to remove Baby M_P from the penitentiarial equation then and there.

Eight: Ask that the reception be soundtracked by Stalaggh's *Project Misanthropia*, described by the 1st-year journalism students at *VICE* as "the ugliest, most horrific oppressive noise possible." This should keep the bars of the Black Iron Prison in full view for any relatives deceived by whatever celebratory skeins of jubilatory crepe paper the occasion has temporarily stretched between the bars of the Black Iron Prison.

Nine: If the priest compliments your grief blogging profession to clear the air after the Gurdjieff incident, elucidate exactly what you grieve for as per Grievin' Gary's advice: "It has to do with my sister, Padre. We spent summers playing cards or reading paperbacks called *It* and *Phantoms* on the splinter porch of my aunt's cabin. It may sound strange for teen siblings to spend entire summers in relative seclusion while beach beers beckoned as they only can before beers grow so stale, but peers came to Catherine hat in hand. She could choose when she wanted beach beers as I can't now or couldn't then. My social status was dubious, as you might back-extrapolate from my current affect, yet no peer did I prefer to her. She'd dive over top of me into ice-cold Patton Lake, risking catastrophic neck injury. Sweat rivulets and bristling brown hair on her tan arms in the sauna straight from an erotic Lorenzo Lamas movie, which may be too abstruse a reference for a man of the cloth, though I'm not sure what you were up to in 1992 when Lorenzo was portraying Gropius in *The Flesh and the Devil*. We'd pour water over each other's heads from the dipper, father. Shivers ran as happiness does down the spinal column. Her innate sensuality made sensuality with even one's sister feel natural enough, no sin against God and nature or anything all that worthy of condemnation to hell. We took turns changing in the sauna's little lobby area and I'd perch on the sauna's top bench and catch glimpses of a breast's underside or that uppermost portion of intergluteal cleft that possesses not the faintest stigma of anality. After such saunas, I'd believe in the future. Aunt Claire would be reading her Ed McBain wondering why so many saunas so often. Despite her normalization of in-sauna sensuality, Catherine did act differently when Aunt Claire was around: standing a little less close to me, touching me less frequently, making me wonder if something transgressive really was occurring in the haze. I'd pump water from the well feeling like a real frontiersman. As our baptismal boy's namesake elucidated in suffocating detail, time's duration dilates during adolescence. A month feels like a year. Three months of a sixteen-year-old's summer equate to most of middle age. An entire life stage of duration as Catherine and Aunt Claire washed yellow beans, seeming more like my wife and mother than my sister and aunt, and after dinner, there was Catherine's graven image illumined across the bonfire, her laughter as fresh and clean as the lake after each sauna. We would stay up all night buzzing like katydids, a cricket noted for its mating call. I'd fidget on the top bunk debating the bold move towards her bunk below. Tell her it was for warmth when she gasped in mock astonishment, maybe. And then came her murder so soon after, taking all of my contented yellow bean middle age from me before I'd turn twenty, leaving me all alone to face the horror of true middle age, misunderstood, love not having been learned, unless then again this child might teach me something." If a long silence follows, the priest will uncharacteristically quote words you won't comprehend until embraced in the San Francisco Public Library by Divinitee,

> It is the sister who guides the path of the wanderer throughout the nihilistic metamorphoses, during which the securities of ontotheology lose their authority and disappear into their twilight, and before the arising of that new thinking which betrays itself only in scarcely perceptible hints. The sister is associated with transition, and with the indeterminacy of an unthreaded time. Even the corrupted seals that stamped the distinctive mark of scholasticism and theological apologetic are broken, and no new type has taken their place. The

haunting voice of the sister is heard as the brother drifts away from the ancient genus of theological metaphysics and towards the genus of the stranger. Yet the sister's voice cannot be identified with the type of the past or with that of the future, it cannot be subsumed within a genre.[22]

Ten: If the priest returns from his extratemporal trance state to subsume your grief into the genre he's better suited to, Beatitudes, "Blessed are those that mourn, for they shall be comforted," before inquiring what gnostic theology offers you, realize you can only cobble together some flimflam from *Bibliotheca Pleiades* articles and bloggers with names like UNLEARN THE LIES. Should all the marbles of man's continued residency in the open field of divinity be in play, epiphanically understand it's best to knuckle down and quietly align yourself with the One True God depicted in that corpus of Abrahamic scripture that pre-dates the big find at Nag Hammadi.

---

[22] (Land, Narcissism and Dispersion in Heidegger's 1953 Trakl Interpretation, 2011)

How Not to Trade on Bunz

*E*xamples of offers on the Bunz trading app could be, looking to trade… "velvet painting of Robert Bresson the Jansenist predeterminist for three cans of Maximum Ice strong beer," "three measures of barley for a penny," or "a quick but satisfying rim job for a ride to the methadone clinic, eye contact prohibited."

One: If your intramarital allowance seldom covers even the balance insurance on the lone credit card allotted you, waste many shaky hours hunting dumpsters for returnable cans.

Two: If griping to your wife that cans are a low-yield source of income, *i.e.* 'one can = 1 cent,' she'll remind you that Marcel_Proust's $1800 stroller provides 400 litres of carrying capacity, allowing you to expand your search beyond cans! An unstrung banjo will be tradable on Bunz for a $7.21 LCBO gift card, nearby enough for two Maximum Ice Strong Beers. A cadmium-intensive McDonalds promotional cup featuring the Great One, Wayne Gretzky, can be traded for an empty Cool-Whip can yielding inhalable nitrous oxide.

Three: Create a comprehensive In Search OF (ISO.) Common examples include headshots of Darryl Bem, discontinued La Senza products, *etc.*

Four: Services can also be requested, such as the afore-mentioned ride to the methadone clinic. A service relevant to your more paranoid priorities might be, "Private Python tutoring sessions. Must be comfortable tutoring a baby."

Five: If you receive a Python-related inquiry from a man named Ronald Majthenyi, view his ISO and see he's serendip-itously *in search of* Maximum Ice Strong Beer. If in addition to neural networking expertise, Ronald's LinkedIn highlights several decades as a top man at DuPont's Teflon division. Conclude rashly that Ronald simply enjoys a strong beer tip-ple after a long day of programming and isn't some stew bum.

Six: If you invite Ronald Majthenyi into your home, regret this evermore.

Seven: Find Ronald Majthenyi altogether more sinister and Mephistophelean than hoped. Realize the Max Ice ISO was an obvious rouse as Ronald clearly serves the Son of the Dawn. Relate anew to your father's feelings of impotence upon the sad occasion of Catherine's murder. Relate anew to his pathetic reliance on Beatitudes, particularly, "Blessed are you that weep now, for you shall laugh."

Eight: If Ron Majthenyi speaks to Marcel_Proust in tongues, experience mild fatherly relief when Marcel_Proust mostly just giggles at the tongues.

Nine: When your wife arrives by Fiat into the driveway, ask that Ron Majthenyi reign in the tongues and stick to incanting from *Python For Dummies*.

Ten: Realize from Ronald's non-compliance and pitying visage that Marcel_Proust—a cosmic coal of decency from whom you are in the process of learning love—may continue to lodge with you, but he is property of the Infernal Serpent and Ron Majthenyi by proxy, meaning while your father and son can- and banjo-scavenges can continue as the tutoring schedule permits, Marcel_Proust is no longer your charge. He belongs to Majthenyi, who won't teach the boy about Proust, or how to be a good man, or how to endure the world's endless irritants, or read him *The Changing Light at Sandover* to ensure your baby knows that "flowers are witches."[23] Ronald Majthenyi will only steer Marcel_Proust towards orchestrating the eye icycling and the bleed-outs of the Ebola Cheboygan Variant, all and only because you the disconsolate grief blogger were too selfish to spend eternity in The Hall of Memories.

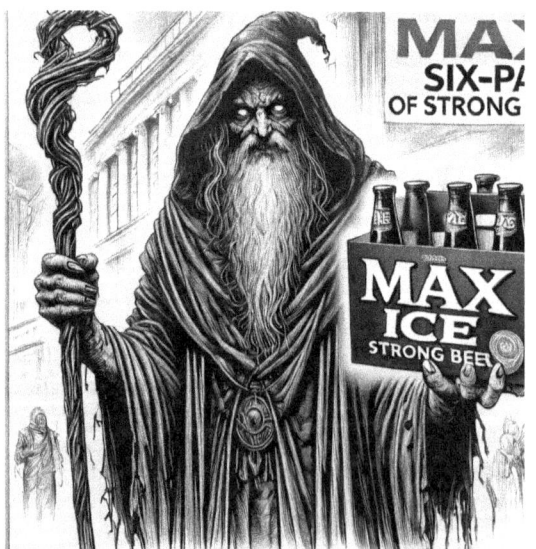

[23] (Merrill, 1982)

Ten Tips for Welcoming a House Guest

*H*eed these tips for welcoming into your humble abode a friend, family member, or even a stranger who resembles no one so much as the 4th century's Alaric the Visigoth.

One: Inform your wife that Ronald Majthenyi will be living with you. Remind her of the ageism epidemic in kids' coding camps, wherein the pessimists at Kinvert.com state, "The youngest so far that we have successfully taught was six years old. The biggest barrier in my opinion to teaching young kids Python is their reading and typing abilities," thereby gatekeeping Marcel_Proust out of even the chintziest plaza-situated coding camp, requiring you the mourning-averse grief blogger to have camped there yourself while Marcel_Proust slept with the name "Binarity Inverarity" name-tagged upon his closed stroller. Remind her how Marcel_Proust's incapacity to take the hourly quizzes was mocked by admins, necessitating the concession, "Yes, on a strictly physiological level my fingers are guiding his fingers. He is eight months old. He lacks dexterity." Remind her of the admins' galling challenges to your soundness as a child's guardian, forcing you to pivot towards subjects of common interest, *e.g.* 'Toronto Maple Leafs,' *e.g.* 'folk causality,' *e.g.* 'Metatron,' until security staff paid minimum wage to enforce the cultural norms of a shabby plaza accost you the recent traumatic brain injuree, invoking a terror in Marcel_Proust assuaged only by mobile ordering him a baby-sized helping of McNuggets, blending the McNuggets at home, and streaming for him Python tutorials that establish YouTube's free tutors as inadequate to setting any baby's double pendulum a-oscillating or to feeding the figurative chickens of his "quantum bestiary"[24] some fries, whatever either of those Bandler-encoded phrases might mean.

Two: Point to Marcel_Proust as he sits transfixed before Majthenyi's MacBook, streams of abstruse code flowing past like snakes down the Ganges. Ask if she'd prefer Marcel_Proust be sitting slack-jawed in front of Disney+ all day as her 'best friend's' bestial children are wont to do.

Three: Should she sneer with dark neuroticism, take the high road by speaking softly, "Not in front of Ron, please."

Four: Experience a mix of terror and admiration as Ron hypnotizes your wife into finding him fresh bedsheets.

Five: Lacking strength and wisdom and knowing not that you are deceived, lay before Ron your best bathrobe in a similar psychogenic fugue. Oblate him with spritzes of sweet Polo Sport odours. Bring him fine wines and raw elk meat.

Six: Make room for a guest's belongings! If the guest is Ronald Majthenyi this will include many ancient apothecary bottles. Clear a shelf for pharmakons. Clear a shelf for tinctures. Employ the Marie Kondo method and throw away your wife's balms and lotions and essential oils that no longer bring anyone joy.

---

[24] (Wargo E. , 218)

Seven: Anticipate your guest's needs! Minor touches like an unwrapped bar of soap go a long way.

Eight: Share all the little household secrets! A house guest will not know how to stoke an anachronistic wood stove with timber should he catch a chill in the night.

Nine: Think like a hotel! If Ronald Majthenyi prefers to live deliciously, place elk meat (Ziplocked) on his pillow. Should he be busy teaching Marcel_Proust that *clustering* is the detection of similarities, thereby keeping you out of the pit, this must be the least you can do.

Ten: If inclined to shiver off and pray, sneak into the bathroom to proclaim a single Apostle's Creed lubricated by eight Max Ice. Optimistically attribute your fatigue, weakness, cotton mouth, nausea, vomiting, stomach pain, light sensitivity, dizziness, and shakiness to strong beer rather than Ronald's telepathic percipience.

2 COMMENTS ON "TEN TIPS FOR WELCOMING A NEW HOUSEGUEST"

Clean Mama Blog: Great tips! Although if you throw away your wife's balms that might get YOU spending some time as a houseguest…in the dog's house! LOL!

UNLEARN THE LIES: Frankly this Ronald guy sounds every bit the Archon to me. I think you're making a huge mistake by getting off the gnostic bandwagon. Don't sleep on Yaldabaoth brother.

Ten Foolproof Tips for A Fun Double Date

*I*f Ron's taught a network of Google Homes and Amazon Alexas to converse in some ghastly neo-language, and these Homes and Alexas have transfixed the gaze of Marcel_Proust in eldritch fashion, then practice avoidance of all that by planning a double date!

One: If quaternary and even quinary love interests remain ill-enthused in the months proceeding your child's birth, shoot for the moon by pitching that most rejective of mistresses, Mariana Sicoli. Pitch not your own mediocre merits, but the chance to meet a Dupont big-wig who is no stranger to the marketing space.

Two: Stick to topics of common interest! How rude if you and Ron discussed nothing but automatic feature extraction's time-frequency representation of time while Mariana and her expectedly-dumpy colleague simply stared at their napkins? How exhausting if Mariana and Stacey spent half the evening issuing marketing buzzwords as life advice, there in the franchise candlelight of Il Fornello, as they in fact did?

Three: If old Visigoth Ron plays footsy with Mariana then grieve the munificence of things past.

Four: Should substance-abusiveness inflame your humors, order your triple gin and sodas discretely from the bar. Request them in a water glass lest you make the table uncomfortable as they sip their single beers or single wines while leaving large portions of their single wines infuriatingly unfinished.

Five: Don't seem overeager! This shouldn't be a problem if your date is Stacey Keats. However, if Ronald Majthenyi is reading Mariana's palm with the affect of a swami, then maybe he could be perceived as overeager, unless of course he is some suave stinking wizard who always comes off as looking pretty slick.

Six: If Mariana replies to your attempts at Autostereogrammatic reintegration by saying, "You belong on Reddit's iAmVerySmart board, Dave, fool," Stacey will try to reduce the tension by reading from r/funny's vacuum of immutable insipidity. Do not cite the wildly-superior 4chan's curation of a news story headlined: "Obese American passenger forces Taiwanese flight attendant to wipe his butt on plane"[25] and sub-headlined: "As she wiped, the passenger allegedly moaned in pleasure and urged her on, saying, 'deeper, deeper!'" Do not speculate upon the stewardess' emotional valence upon hearing that first moan, when any hope the man was in genuine anal distress must have been abandoned, as this duty-bound airline professional realized she'd been relegated to fetishized 'wipe whore.'

---

[25] (Linder, Obese American passenger forces Taiwanese flight attendant to wipe his butt on plane, 2019)

Seven: Do not repeat the "wipe whore" line as an increasingly-transgressive callback. If Mariana asks, "What are you even talking about?" don't be bated into reading from Wikipedia: *A callback, in terms of comedy, is a joke that refers to one previously told in the set. It is also known as an internal allusion, a literary device that helps give structure to the piece of* writing.

Eight: Do not flirt with the other person's date by asking Mariana if she knows that *stound* is sometimes defined as "a sudden pang of grief when a loss is remembered," and this must be the etymology of *astound*, wherein one is panged, suddenly, by remembering an autostereogrammatic breakthrough, for example, or an incestuous dalliance with the brothers Pete and Paul.

Nine: Act the big man by footing the bill! If Ron noshed on ziplocked elk from his briefcase, ordering only a single high-sulfite mineral water, while Mariana, to the best of your understanding, doesn't eat food *per se*, and Stacey ordered only fried pickle spears, this will cost a mere $26 more than your $78 bar tab.

Ten: Avoid emotional outbursts! Do not recite an *Ode on Melancholy*. Do not remind Mariana that she may well be the last person ever to witness what is decent in you again. Do not mention the anamnesis coaxed, the epiphanic third element found, the axiomatics of Julia Jordan texted. Nor yet should you discuss concerns of your own dwindling sex appeal, of sisterly reconciliation in dreams, of the Kerouacian experience of feeling your heart break every time a beautiful woman passes in the opposite direction. Don't ask Mariana to tell the Paul and Pete story again. Don't do any of these things with tears brimming eyelid edges. For if you do, Ron will ask with the 80s sitcom-satirizing faux-triteness so favoured by the world's marketers, "Would you get a load of this guy?" evoking a big cathartic laugh from the uncomfortable women desperate for a life preserver of normative behaviour.

Ten Tips for Planning a Human Sacrifice

*I*f nothing less than human sacrifice is required to maintain an accord with the Infernal Serpent, ask Ronald Majthenyi to "Keep a lid on it in front of the Uber driver will ya? Think of my rating."

One: Ask Ronald Majthenyi why he never pays for the Ubers. Don't be deceived by his dumb joke that he doesn't like to leave a digital "hoofprint."

Two: Learn that "No" you can't "start small" with a "raccoon or a seagull" unless you're eager for another go-round in The Hall of Memories.

Three: If you nominate Alan Raval as the human sacrifice, two birds with one stone-type operation, Ron will stress the Infernal Serpent's preference for female sacrifices.

Four: If Maj claims the Infernal Serpent prefers these female sacrifices "more on the fleshy side," *e.g.* ' Stacey Keats,' *e.g.* 'No child-like anorexics,' Figure Maj is lying because he wants to do the horizontal mambo with stupid small-boned Mariana.

Five: Alternate between counterfactual remorse and paranoid desperation. Compute fairly self-evident mental equations *e.g.* 'Life in jail > eternity in hell.'

Six: Plot and scheme. Confirm what time your wife attends her Scrapbooking with Babies Meetup at the Dufferin Mall. Construct a pyre using firewood and coding books that Marcel_Proust has already internalized. Request a second date with Stacey by promising to be "way more normal." If she declines, citing the *Obese American passenger forces Taiwanese flight attendant to wipe his butt on plane*[26] callbacks, request the date on behalf of Ronald instead. Meet an eager Stacey at a Starbucks.

Seven: If despite being many vile things, you are providentially no abductor of women, yet now in the Alan Raval role, think only of your sister's final moments. Plead with Majthenyi, "I can't do it." Plead, "As a top Dupont executive, surely you're accustomed to having blood on your hands."

Eight: Grow pallid as The Maj hog-ties Stacey in the back seat of his Escalade. Aim to curry Majthenyian favour on the villainous ride home by shouting, "Darn impressive fine motor skills you possess there, Ronald."

Nine: If hogtied Stacey is placed against the pyre by a Maj who hands you a barbecue lighter and gas can along with a withering look, *i.e.* 'Any more hand-holding and this sacrifice is not going to count!' then quibble and stall by arguing, "If the neighbours can't abide road hockey past 6 pm, do you really think they'll abide roasting human flesh and screams of anguish?"

---

[26] (Linder, 2019)

Ten: If Ron concedes to a quieter murder in the coat closet, his use of the word *asphyxiation* will sap you of agency. Stacey will get a hand untied, escape the coat closet, and lunge for a carving knife adjacent the elk carcasses. Ronald Majthenyi should then execute the sacrifice himself. If while Lysol-wiping blood from his ceremonial daggers Ron glares them your way as well, this means you've made Another Big Mistake and will pay and pay and pay. Pay a bit of that penance up front by joining Ron in his dorky choral praises to the Infernal Serpent as Stacey's flesh is silently burned not atop but amidst the pyre.

Ten Tips for Losing Your Wife and Child Pt. 1

Should Teflon Ron be unaccustomed to having his personal hands bloodied, this infernal usurper will require your wife and child as recompense.

One: If Ronald charms your wife by offering to try his hand at the Scrapbooking game, roll eyes at wife's muttered, "You see. Ron's willing to try new things."

Two: Attempt intercessory prayer in Ron's absence. Grow afflicted with sebaceous cysts about the neck and face.

Three: If your wife and Ron seem quite chatty upon their return from scrapbooking, deceptive brain signals will impel you to disgust her with boil administrations, *i.e.* 'squeezing and safety-pin pricking at increasingly-irritated boils,' thus voiding your lone-remaining good quality: handsomeness. If you linger on *Pimple Popper MD* on the so-called *Learning Channel* to glean do's and don'ts of the boil-lancing game, hear Majthenyi whisper to your wife, "Don't we see enough liquor puris around here already?"

Four: Fly into a rage. If still unable to castigate Majthenyi, castigate your wife. Hear her weep and plead,

"You're breaking my heart. I don't know how much more of this I can take."

Five: Hear her say, "I get like no sleep cause I'm always putting up with some crazy bullshit. And you don't even care. And now the baby is crying. You only care about yourself. Do you ever think about me? Me and how I feel?"

Six: If she sobs like a little girl who can barely get out the words "You don't even care," relate anew to Bob Dylan's observation of what women break like. Pet the baby's head to signal that you care about the baby at least.

Seven: If agency to rebut her grievances is imperceptibly "Libeted"[27], watch with grey hatred as Ronald Majthenyi magnifies himself in her heart. Understand that Emily was your last lone bulwark of grace protecting against your inclinations towards iniquity. Understand every measured word and every poutful pour-out of a paint thinner can as a two-decade beneficence The Maj duped you into surrendering. In your abjection, understand that while her moral hygiene had seemed to inhibit the lifestyle you'd coveted, said hygiene was all that kept you from the pit, and you'd traded it months previous to any dealings with the archfiend for evenings that glittered past the borderline, for autostereogrammatic pleasure that was anything but satisfaction.

Eight: Upon waking from an Etizolam stupor, find Ronald Majthenyi waving his wand and casting an apparent hex unto thee: "Upon ye I cast the flippancy of the vivacious

---

[27] (Fifel, 2018)

histrionic; the sulky and easily-wrought up impulsivity of the tempestuous histrionic; the synthesized staginess of the theatrical histrionic; the guileful double-dealing of the disingenuous histrionic. Seek attentions to excess. Attempt inappropriate seductions. May you be periodically inflamed. May you be turbulent. May you be politically voluble. All while affected and pouting and labile and unlovable. By Belphegor let us borrow from the Schizotypal diagnosis for this witches' brew—let Ideas of Reference be cast unto thee: so that the innocuous will seem strongly significant, every passage in every pavement periodical pertaining directly unto thee, periodically inflaming you with perceived meaning and purpose you must convey through put-on postures all will recognize as childlike hysteria."

Nine: If that sounds dire + your belongings have been packed in boxes: fleshlights in boxes, PlayStation VR helmets in boxes, many bottles of Varsol in one greasy box labelled "Garbage?" in a passive-aggressive elegance of script, understand the parental panic of knowing that each loving glance in the direction of your child may be your last.

Ten: Appreciate the dental asymmetry, child-like smile, and boyish personality of your wife, reborn as she's been in the light of Ronald Majthenyi's devious love: a revitalization you could have brought about by repaying a fraction of the love she'd spent on you. Hope it's not too late to inappropriately seduce her. Understand that it is. As Bob Dylan also remarked while looking sad, bewildered, drunk, and on drugs, upon the reception of his Lifetime

Achievement Grammy at Radio City Music Hall in 1991: "It's possible to become so defiled in this world that your own father and mother will abandon you, and if that happens, God will always believe in your own ability to mend your own ways."

Ten Tips For Losing Your Wife and Child Pt. 2

*I*f that most fiscal of marital bonds, your credit card, is declined by The Days Inn, impulsively visit Seton House men's shelter. Learn they aren't accepting new 'bos until sundown. Sulk all stagey-like for the security guard.

One: See the rising sun return. Drink Maximum Ice strong beer amidst Allan Gardens itinerants while getting the inside scoop of your new Setonean digs. Experience personal apocalypse. If you show your lock-screen photo of Marcel_Proust to the dispossessed, the dispossessed will show tattered Polaroids of their own 1978 offspring. Laugh with the dispossessed. Smile with the dispossessed. Cry with the dispossessed. Be falsehearted with the dispossessed. Fight with the dispossessed. Urinate in the Allan Gardens greenhouse bathroom, which reeks of indigence. Eat a sandwich provided by Mormon outreach youths.

Two: Whenever any new social safety netting is unfurled, the redolent and dispiriting love to entangle and befoul that net, making places of respite not-yet-dominated by the redolent and dispiriting tricky to locate! If hell itself seems preferable to the bed bugs, piss stink, and Hep C stabbings of Seton House Men's Shelter, then the movies will ever be an A1 respite. Cineplex plays second-run movies for $7.99. The corporately-dehumanized teenage staff won't roust you unless actively provoked by overt double-dealing, *e.g.* 'coating your Equality Brand Whole Wheat Bread in free liquid margarine from the dispenser right in front of Ethan, the day manager.'

Three: Inappropriately seduce any pretty young consumer survivors you encounter in Allan Gardens. What they have consumed and survived is the mental health system. Sit on an Allan Gardens' bench with the wayward and the winsome and comment upon how Marcel_Proust brought an immensity of meaning into your life. Guilefully quote D.W. Griffith's, "Cinema is the wind in the trees," to console yourself and also to impress upon a consumer survivor that 'Yes, you have survived the medical model. Yes, I have lost Marcel_Proust. Yet here we have the wind in these trees.' The ponytail of this mentally unhealthful girl will enliven your spirits. Her wild accusations and wilder roundhouse rights will keep you on your toes.

Four: If de-lousing becomes a life priority, hand dryers in public washrooms are a handy source of lice-destructive heat, *n.b.* 'The high-powered Dyson dryer is the Rolls' Royce of de-lousing dryers.'

Five: Newspapers work as insulation or ersatz flak jacket while also offering a window into real estate, the automotive realm, and the *insights* of the medium talents tasked with writing the intellectual pabulum of the "Ideas" section.

Six: Assuming you are not some backwards and heteronormative caveman, and assuming most of your sebaceous cysts are draining nicely, inappropriately seduce geriatric men of the light-loafered orientation. If not so light of loafer yourself, spurn their advances and simply eat as much of their Wing Street leftovers as possible before the geriatric men just paw to the extent their Boneless Bites entitle them.

Seven: If after only day three of living rough you have prostituted yourself for not even an authentic chicken wing but only a "saucy nug,"[28] ask hobo chums about the demand for male gigolos servicing the female John population. Learn that the limited number of female Johns are satisfied by a small cadre of well-credentialed and ab-intensive misogynists of the *Magic Mike* mould.

Eight: Eat people's leftover fries and things at Burger King!

Nine: Rant and rave of your desperation! Wonder how you became the very ranter and raver you'd always crossed the street to avoid. Remark to a destitute associate how quickly God-fearing men such as yourselves can fall.

Ten: If sucked into a vacuum of purposelessness, weep for all that is gone: weep for your sister; weep for Marcel_ Proust and his writhing hands as he endured a diaper change, his shrieks of enthusiasm as the Go Train passed, his facility for picking the records you hadn't played in years.

[28] (Matthews, 2020)

Ten Tips for Post-Facto Grieving the Death of Stacey Keats

*I*f coping with the guilt and grief natural to any non-sociopath complicit in *Murder Most Foul*, here are ten tips for passing the buck on that.

One: Dance a joyful jig when *The Sacred Executioner* by Hyam Maccoby is available at the Toronto Public Library branch you squat at. Relate to Maccoby's assertion that the sacred executioner is both sacred and "accursed," and that, "such a person in myth is ejected from society and condemned to long wanderings."

Two: Take solace that in conjunction with being "accursed," you are at least also "sacred." Resign your personage to a life of long wanderings.

Three: But then if long wanderings seem a little labile so soon after losing Marcel_Proust, and how much worse can the Infernal Serpent possibly make things anyway, take up tenuous cudgels against the Adversary.

Four: If the cudgels invoke no cramping or boils, assign research librarians with a query of, "How to combat the Infernal Serpent's forces manifested on earth."

Five: Should paucity result, librarians will advise search refinement, *i.e.* 'Combat Satanic forces.'

Six: If librarians weary of your desk-pounding urgency, find tips on battling Satanic forces from wild-eyed dispensationalist YouTubers instead.

Seven: Wonder how many of these characters even battle satanic forces and how many are contemptible loons.

Eight: Read *The Crying of Lot 49* for the first time and retroactively understand your "Binarity Inverarity" pun.

Nine: No matter how defiled a man becomes in this world, it is important to have a purpose commensurate to life's suffering! This tip goes beyond anti-Serpentine blogging and applies to all fields. Book thirty minutes of Internet time to replace the current cudgel barers by starting your own Satanic forces battling blog.

Ten: Feel a purpose not quite commensurate to your Marcel_Proustian loss. Wonder if purpose commensurate to loss will increase as you gain followers and remuneration for your new blog: http://www.wordpress.com/*CanTheDevilSpeakTru*

High-Stakes Investigative Immersion Journalism Tips for Self-Reflexive Bloggers

*T*o infiltrate the ranks of the iniquitous while also imbuing your blog with verisimilitude, RSVP to that week's Thornhill Satanist Meetup Group.

One: If the homeless aren't often trusted with institutional cash donations, reach the swanky streets of Thornhill using a TTC token gifted in lieu thereof.

Two: Shake hands with assembled Satanists whose collective sartorial ardour resembles that of low-brow auteur Kevin Smith. Note jaw-lines you'd expect from a competing Meetup Group: Involuntary Celibates Anonymous. If anti-Catholic/anti-pedophiliac humour, *e.g.* 'Lol, imagine taking advice on moral forbearance from a bunch of pedo creeps,' carries the day, understand these Satanists are communally-bound around the fallacy that an anti-pedophilia stance is transgressive.

Three: If you the unplacatable won't be placated, don't mention that there is no culturally-dominant Christianity left to rebel against, thus they are essentially kicking down some old lady's Nativity Scene much as children might hurl dog excrement at a bus driver hated for his lisp. Definitely do not quote Heidegger,

> To be a poet in a destitute time means: to attend, sing-
> ing, to the trace of the fugitive gods. This is why the
> poet in the time of the world's night utters the holy.

Rather, moderate their tempers by yielding.

Four: If Satanists genuflect before the altar of scientism, don't ask them just how unaware they might be regarding science's reliance upon the mystical, or how the scientific method alone could never generate the jump from Newton to Einstein. Do not quote Heidegger's *Nietzsche: Volume 2— The Thought of Eternal Return*, as the group has already made clear they don't care to know who Heidegger might be,

> The fact that every science as such, being the spe-
> cific science it is, gains no access to its fundamental
> concepts and to what those concepts grasp, goes
> hand in hand with the fact that no science can
> assert something about itself with the help of its
> own scientific resources. What mathematics is can
> never be determined mathematically; [...] what
> biology is can never be uttered biologically. To ask
> what a science is, is *to ask a question* that is no lon-
> ger a *scientific* question.

Five: Wonder if you might be going a little hard on these teenagers, and if you merely have a bee in your bonnet regarding the Faustian bargain you consented to in cowardice.

Six: Resemble a lovestruck Bugs Bunny when the group's lone gal arrives. If her idyllic Courtney Love roots recall roots you so loved in the late 90s, wail your own hauntological song of sadness. Hold her green-eyed gaze as she introduces herself as "Britannica." Speak exclusively to Britannica from then on. If her size 2 Vans sneaker brushes against your own sodden DC Shoes sneaker, place your sneaker atop hers.

Seven: Interrupt the group's un-germane discussion of the Marvel Cinematic Universe by asking, "Being new to the dark arts, perchance a more adept practitioner might redpill me on this whole 'religion of the flesh' concept?"

Eight: Should a bloated bag of *Deadpool*ian ironies answer windily, issue sideways glances at Britannica indicating you'll be tuning Roy out until you hear Britannica's take on the whole 'religion of the flesh' idea.

Eight: Realize the Infernal Serpent himself is tempting you with this heavy-stacked and yet Gwen Stefanian and probably RH negative girl to your immediate left, making you forget all about the cudgels.

Nine: If the hellzapoppin" quorum don their various cloaks and fedoras and bid their adieus, wish Roy "a life well lived,"[29] square Britannica in the eyes, and speak in your small press authorial baritone, "It was very nice meeting you today." Feel Britannica's hands on your hips. Look at her lip gloss. Fasten and clutch to her.

Ten: Ask of Britannica, moodily, "What's to become of us?"

---

[29] (Roiland & Harmon, 2015)

Ten Tips for Experiencing
Earthly Delights

*I*f pleasures of the flesh must be endured to afford your anti-Satanic doctrine with credulity, visit a nearby ravine with Britannica. Hang on to her. Clasp fists full of her puffy jacket's down. Kiss her fluorescent pink lips. Think to yourself, "It's been too long," though it has not been particularly long.

One: Engage carnally. Cleanse "frustrated spontaneous emissions"[30] from your stomach with a baby wipe from a travel pack once used to change diapers, and then to live rough, and now for this noble purpose: the end goal of emancipating Marcel_Proust from the Archfiend's conflagrant clutches.

Two: Animatedly ask Britannica to dance. Partake of Britannica's digital marijuana pen. Offer a mannered and put-on, "Hail Satan" in response to Britannica's earnest and robust, "Hail Satan!"

Three: Should you inquire, "Know any good awnings we might squat beneath?" Britannica's apprehensive grimace

---

[30] (Wargo E. , 218)

will make clear that you are the only homeless party in this impromptu romance.

Four: "My parents aren't home."

Five: "Rigid moralists? Bible-thumping Protestants?"

Six: "They're very progressive actually. They wouldn't care. They only protestant against corporations and stuff that's actually bad."

Seven: Travel to an aptly-furnished Thornhill McMansion. Disrobe. Simulate desirable and dramatic poses in a steamy shower. Stay fused to her ornate twist of a waistline.

Eight: In passion's throe, craftily test the waters by issuing the commonplace expression of pleasure, "Oh my God!"

Nine: "What did you just say?"

Ten: "Nothing whatsoever."

Ten Tips for Being a Terrific House Guest

Should you take up housekeeping with a twenty-year-old charge of her parents, not precisely a tertiary or even secondary love interest after thine wife hath abandoned thee, making Brittanica more like your primary girlfriend, here's how to make that less weird for all involved.

One: If Brittanica's parents, scarcely older than you the randy grief blogger, return from Panera Bread to observe an unspeakable practise or unnatural act upon their cream-coloured sectional, greet them with a false-hearted little wave, *i.e.* 'lol what a predicament.'

Two: Reaffix trousers. Glance patriarchally in the direction of Britannica's tube top, *i.e.* 'Put your tube top back on for Pete's sakes.'

Three: Over milk-diluted neurotoxins with John and Deborah Lee, essay a sob story incorporating much truth, *e.g.* 'the brain injury,' 'Jenya,' 'histrionic personality disorder,' *etc.*, while wholly exculpating yourself for having drawn so sob-intensive a lot in life.

Four: If John stiffens at the words "histrionic personality disorder," appeal to Deborah Lee's higher amplitude of progression.

Five: Explain that histrionics are but the pedestrian crossing of your major metropolitan intersectionality at this point, intersectional referents including: "binary-based hang-ups," "substance abuse disorder," and "neurasthenia." Receive patronizing and maternal pat on the shoulder from Deborah Lee, *i.e.* 'Of course you are worthy of my respect and allyship despite defiling our sofa just now.'

Six: If Deborah Lee whacks John with a newspaper for requesting a precise definition of *intersectionality*, rap her own knee and speak softly, "Don't worry. He means well. He's just not ready to face his journey."

Seven: Precipitously play the E. Elias Merhige film *Begotten* for the family after dinner. Blink back a tear if this had been Marcel_Proust's favourite. If Debora Lee sits beside you on the couch, indulge in some temperate thigh-to-thigh contact that compels John towards his basement wood-turning hobby. Get a big laugh if you ask the couch-assembled ladies, "Is his wood often turned with such angst?"

Eight: Retire to Britannica's bedroom. Hear a polite knock mid-coitus. If you'd hoped for Deborah Lee, eager of subsequent coital opportunity, encounter only a red-faced John remarking, "I want to be respectful to your position, uh, interstitial as it is."

Nine: If after being corrected he says, "Of course intersectional, this is all new to me but I am doing the work. I'd like to remind you, man to man, man to…intersection…I'd like to remind you that the walls in this house are very thin," then clasp John's hand and assure him that as a father yourself, you certainly understand.

Ten: If after a $158 brunch at Mandarin, John takes you aside to air grievances with a mealiness of mouth transparently mandated by the Infernal Serpent, expect to hear, "David, we've been pleased to have you stay with us, so don't count this as another microaggression, but the sounds, David. I've mentioned the sounds, and you have made an effort, so I'd like to meet you where you're at. I'd like you to honour that Debora Lee is a light sleeper, as she twice mentioned. Might we unpack how the sounds have not stopped, have only increased in frequency and duration? At the risk of sounding less than entirely sex-positive, I'd like to set some sonic boundaries, right now, right outside the Mandarin. Also, some personal space boundaries if you're open to that. I want you to have a stake in this. Ours is a comfortable but not a large dwelling. Your morning appearances in your underwear, in the lavatory, drinking water from the tap, David, these appearances have been provocative to Deborah Lee and to myself. Not provocative to me in the way that Deborah Lee has been provoked. And that's not to be some regressive 'no homo' type, as the young people say, or were saying a few years ago anyway, as I've done enough work on my journey to identify as *homo* were I homoerotically provoked by your early morning erections, Dave, if I may call you Dave, in which way I am not provoked... Regardless of the provoking erections, Dave, my aim is to respect your lived experience whatever the cost to my own masculine pride may be. Anyhow, I understand where you come from, not intersectionally, of course. I won't take up space in that conversation, but romantically. Deborah Lee's father used to cast aspersions my way. Perhaps it was the progressive nature of my views relative to the regressive nature of his own. Perhaps it was my eyebrow piercing, certainly less than completely heteronormative in 1997. This is not to compare the oppressions of the eyebrow pierced with your intersectional struggles. I am not trying to hijack your narrative, Dave, it's all yours. Anyhow, I do know what it's like to be on your end of the spectrum. I do not mean any sort of medical model mental health spectrum. I mean the spectrum of resentful fathers and sexually-indulgent sons-in-law. And for this reason I'd like you to visit a psychotherapist, on my dime of course, which is also the dime of Deborah Lee, for an assessment. Alternatively, and I will deny this if you mention it, I can estimate the approximate cost of psychotherapeutic care, and give you that in cash money if you agree to permanently leave our home before Britannica's next ovulation cycle," and then, his back turned, not quite under his breath, "Back to the corner of Louse and Loser where you belong, one block downwind of Souse Street, psycho."

Dominate Your Psychotherapist From Visit #1 Using This One Weird Trick

When seeing a new psychotherapist, it is Integral to pull intellectual rank on him at the first visit lest he gain an upper hand he'll never relinquish.

One: Cite the July 2015 study, *Evidence for Holistic Episodic Recollection via Hippocampal Pattern Completion.*[31] Also cite *Recalling happy memories in remitted depression: A neuroimaging investigation of the repair of sad mood.*[32] The gist being that recalling happy memories alleviates depression, *ergo* it is not "aberrant" to consider your sister Catherine often as you do.

Two: Tap your nose and say you know exactly what's going on at MIT where, "recently, they showed that they could <u>plant false memories</u>, and that they could switch the emotional associations of a particular memory from positive to negative, and vice versa."[33] Ask if MIT might reverse memories of your sister's death, auto-rendering them positive, and

---

[31] (Horner, Bisby, Bush, Lin, & Burgess, 2015)
[32] (Foland-Ross, Cooney, Joormann, Henry, & Gotlib, 2014)
[33] (Trafton, 2015)

why the folks at MIT would even want to do such a thing, assuming they aren't in league with the Infernal Serpent.

Three: Regale Dr. Whybrow with memories, what Huxley described as, "Those images on the other side of the eyes that go on living that private life of theirs, undisturbed."[34]

Memories of the viewed brassiere through the Oxford dress shirt sleeve.

Catherine's singing of O Canada at the Greyhounds game, arms raised, somehow making it whimsical, somehow making even the estimable Hounds humorous, even the *terre de nos aïeux*.

Her laughing with the vocal might of Aretha Franklin or something.

The coyness conveyed by her eyes' scrunching, eye-lines that said, "I get you. I get it. We get it. We are in this together against all the idiots, all the Dr. Whybrows of the world," although naturally her eyelines couldn't have conveyed anything acausal as all that about you, Dr. Whybrow.

The night her boyfriend Mario Fantappie broke up with her on the dance floor and she danced with you, the patient of today, a penitent still patiently awaiting a future you'd presumed benign while holding her then at the high school dance.

The black bathing suit. The blue bathing suit.

Angles through t-shirted armholes.

Hair that should have required one hundred disciplined brush strokes to achieve the lustre of, yet she achieved only by infrequent washing

---

[34] (Huxley, 1936)

How she brought out the best in everybody, even Alan Raval. Even Alan Raval, that's the tragedy of it all, Dr. Whybrow.

Songs that played on the radio.

Sitting in the back seat.

Her elegance in the matutinal moments before her baring reasserted itself, looking almost bewildered, almost scared, maybe even foredoomed by the subjunctive and decapitative tendencies of her guitar teacher, lover, and spiritual advisor— Alan Raval.

Have you ever had a sister, Whybrow?

A melancholy marriage?

Tell me which is preferred.

As mine, her teeth were too small for her mouth; yet still her smile, resultant of craniofacial blessing I was unblessed with, was the opposite of the deranged and unlikable smile I'm terrifying you with now.

Please note that I refer to Aldous, not Julian Huxley— that transhumanist scum of UNESCO and *New Bottles for New Wine* notoriety, Dr. Whybrow.

Skin in the summertime. Fire-red halters. A nail-biting habit. The sweetness of the strawberry puffs. Brown bags of penny candy and the sprinkler.

And according to MIT postdoc Xu Liu *et al*[35], all of these engrams have an anti-depressant effect, Dr. Whybrow. They can free me from the doldrums, rather than mire me in the

---

[35] (Ramirez, Liu, & MacDonald, 2015)

doldrums, as previous clinicians have intimated might be the case regarding my picture collection, my VR practise, and my unsatisfactory results with the DeepNude web application.

The armholes of the white Oxford shirt.

Had I mentioned those?

Four: Should Dr. Whybrow stem the tide of what he calls "repetitive and pressured speech" by requesting your name, date of birth, and Ontario Health Insurance Plan credentials, ask if he must stick to the meaningless requirements of his craft, might a structured discussion of bereavement and its sequelae be less odious than administrative queries? Remind Dr. Whybrow that this is a feeling-out process, a dance, and you've yet to even address Marcel_Proustian guilt.

Five: If Dr. Whybrow responds irritably, "The writer?" ask if he is even qualified to discuss certain biphasic responses to separation found in non-human primate studies, the two phases being agitation and then of course withdrawal. *Withdrawal* meaning that all the Britannicas in the world can't save your son or resurrect your sister. Speak this last part softly should Britannica and John await in the waiting room while Dr. Whybrow's door and wall thickness remain unknown variables.

Six: Should Whybrow's attention wane, assume a striking posture and quote Edwin S. Shneidman in saying, "Suicide is chiefly a drama in the mind."[36]

---

[36] (Shneidman, 1998)

Seven: If Dr. Whybrow readies his ambulance-dialling finger, reassure him by rating your own intrapersonal lethality as low-to-improbable.

Eight: Change the subject by asking, "And what of the Kohutian postulates?"

Nine: "A need for succorance?"

Ten: If Dr. Whybrow nods derisively, get the hint and say, "Well, I think it's been a productive session!"—words clinicians like to hear.

Ten Tips for Appeasing an Aggrieved Lover

*I*f having heard all of this, Brittanica screams accusations from the backseat while you the Knight of Infinite Resignation sit up front issuing retaliatory eye scrunches, *i.e.* 'Not in front of John, please,' then here are ten tips for deceiving Britannica into believing you love her.

One: Play Beethoven's sonatas in Brittanica's bedroom. Recite from *A Lover's Discourse*, "There are two words: pothos, desire for the absent being, and Himeros, the more burning desire for the present being."[37] invoking an, "So your dumb desire for me is more burning just cause I'm here? What was so burning about your stupid sister anyway? Was she better looking than me? Can I see a picture?" Regret showing Britannica a few hundred pictures when she weeps, knowing as anyone that she could never measure up to Catherine's pulchritude.

Two: While waiting out Brittanica's own histrionics, raid the kitchen for *zesty mordant croustilles*.[38] Recoil at the word *pyres???* written on a fridge notepad. Decline incoming

---

[37] (Barthes, 2002)
[38] (Clattenburg, Smith, & Torrens, 2005)

call from Toronto Police Services on the wirelessly-charging phone of Deborah Lee.

Three: Request John's $10,000 walking money. Grudgingly accept $183 of "diaper money" in cash and a cheque for the balance. If John requests that you decamp without bidding Britannica *adieu*, suggest said bid could well prevent John's casting in the unenviable role of her life's eternal villain who compromised her lone chance at romantic love. Draw a vague sketch of Alan Raval's unwelcome place in your psychic landscape. Walk into Britannica's room. Propose Judeo-Christian marriage without specifying it as such. Request immediate elopement. Absorb her reticence. Regarding "living expenses," return to *A Lover's Discourse*, "I gladly abandon dreary tasks, rational scruples, reactive undertakings imposed by the world, for the sake of a useless task deriving from a dazzling Duty: the lover's duty. I perform discretely, lunatic chores; I am the sole witness of my lunacy. What love lays bare in me is energy."[39] And while abandoning rational scruples has rarely covered living expenses, she is so sold, which is sad, since your only intended "lunatic chore" is to placate something unplacatable within yourself by murdering Allan Raval.

Four: Defenestrate yourself from Britannica's second-story window. Offer to break her fall once she's duly defenestrated. Fail to. Absorb a lot of belly-aching about a broken or twisted ankle that's obviously just malingering since she is able to walk just fine.

---

[39] (Barthes, 2002)

Five: If Brittanica limps alongside you towards the nearest Scotiabank branch to cash John's cheque, pull on her plump wrist while explaining how you had to burn her dad. A financial rather than pyre-based burning, assure her.

Six: If she rubs her ankle and asks, "What are you always talking about those friggin' pyres for?" note her uncanny relegation to the Sissy-Spacek-in-*Badlands* role. Board that Greyhound bus. Protect Britannica from the advances of Greyhound creeps straight out of central casting. Flash your blade when required.

Seven: "Where we going? Vancouver?"

Eight: "Sault Sainte Marie."

Nine: "Eww, no. Why? I'm getting off in Sudbury and getting a cab."

Ten: If the Beck Taxi App calculates the cab's cost at $912, feel Britannica's thighs curl into your own as she acquiesces. Index finger a few micropaedic entries onto her tummy. Rest a palm on the curvature about her hip and realize you'll forever be an Image-Repertoire victim so long as you can't access the past but pretty girls persist in the indexical present.

How to Take a Trip Down Memory Lane (That "Doesn't Involve Your Sister For Once!")

*I*f your mother opens her front door and accedes silent access to your room, lead Britannica to the turquoise childhood bedroom you'd been "Dave Bowman'd"[40] back into via a salvia experiment during your third UofT semester, more or less syncretizing in your sophomoric mind that one Kant takes leave of spacetime without cowering in a childhood closet for a decade's worth of perception, intuition, and experience.

One: If she yawns at your yearbook photos, remind Brittanica that the romantic poet Robert Southey said, "Live as long as you may, the first twenty years are the longest half of your life. They appear so while they are passing; they seem to have been so when we look back on them; and they take up more room in our memory than all the years that succeed them."

Two: If she compares members of your old gang to her personal *Pool* of *Dead*-beats, offensive as this may seem, wonder if the old gang was even all that cool or if you've just reminiscence-bumped them up the tentpole of intrapersonal

---

[40] (Clarke, 1968)

esteem. Quote from the *Journal of Personality and Social Psychology*:

> Nostalgia becomes particularly appealing when people feel confused about their intrinsic selves or feel unable to express their intrinsic self in their current lives. [...] people tend to reflect on nostalgic memories when they find themselves in situations that make it hard to know or express who they truly are.[41]

Three: Doodle some lifespan retrieval curves as you describe for Brittanica the Catherine dreams. "They're rather quite rare. Once or twice a year. Grand reunions always ending in renewed estrangement."

Four: Tell her how the initial estrangement occurred after a series of incidents wherein you had "gone too far"[42] with mean-spirited jokes regarding Alan Raval's concept albums, having been egocentric, labile, and prone to moodiness long before Maj cursed you.

Five: If Britannica ushers you on, iPhone record the conversation to cut down on the following day's blogging slog.

> "Allan Raval was her guitar teacher. Prematurely bald at twenty-two. A prodigious wearer of hats. Big confident smile, give him that. Sizable centrals.

---

[41] (Baldwin, Biernat, & Landau, 2015)
[42] (Barthelme, Some of Us Had Been Threatening Our Friend Colby, 1981)

You need gnashers that size to be a quality confidence man. Believed his own gimmick: now there's the ticket to lifelong happiness. The man wrote concept albums. Honest-to-God concept albums, in Sault Sainte Marie, Britannica. One of the concept albums was called *The Hydraulic Engineer Becomes an Open Channel*. You might think I'm making this up."

Six: If Britannica yawns, perhaps involuntarily, perhaps not, speak louder and more energetically as you inform her that:

"At the hospital they referred to her decapitation as an *insult*. I suppose that is the forensically precise term."

before rolling back the narrative a bit.

"Mere hours after passions enflamed between her and I, she took up with him, perhaps to generate distance before she herself could 'go too far,' incestuously, that is. I'd play *The Hydraulic Engineer Becomes an Open Channel* on Myspace and riff on Alan's resemblance to the iconic Mr. Clean. All this did was push her towards him. I'd later realize maybe all she needed was some accompaniment, on guitar, for her lovely singing, which could have been my role, but because of the old gang's peer pressure I had quit guitar at thirteen. So the old

gang is not without blame in all this, in the great
loss of my life."

Seven: If Brittanica aims to bring your story to a premature
conclusion by indulging in some butt-to-groin frottage, stand
so that you can orate with Ciceronian invective:

> "She had taken a year off school. As I was decamp-
> ing for UofT, I convinced her to come with me.
> She could bartend and sing and make friends. We
> would live together. During the college years, a
> brother-sister living arrangement is hardly cause
> for suspicion. One day she agreed and kissed me as
> long as seemed acceptable, our standard upper- to
> lower-vermillion seal complete with immersive eye
> contact. It would all happen! On some ostensible
> futon we'd fall into repose as the nights grew ribald
> and Scott Walker sang *Cossacks Are*. Rather than
> upon repose, I had more prudently pitched her on
> the street-busking scene in Kensington Market.
> I pitched The Rex Jazz Club and The Cameron
> House. All of this I'd had to Yahoo Search, Yahoo
> Search still having a healthy market share at this
> time."

Eight: If Brittanica has removed her pyjama bottoms and
is now—in what can only be perceived as self-deprecatory
commentary on her inability to capture your sexual

attentions—twerking, then affix her Saje sleeping mask to your own face lest you be provoked into leaving the whole sad saga of your sister Catherine's decapitation unfinished.

"We'd picked out posters. Her picking of a Radio-head poster worried me because the conceptual works of Alan Raval were highly derivative of this group. I picked out an *A Clockwork Orange* poster. Funny, isn't it Britannica, the posters we choose to define us in youth?

Nine: If high-yield sense receptors on your testicular nerve endings suggest Britannica is rubbing her breasts or butt or perhaps her forehead against them, rush past all the heartbreaking little details towards the story's climax:

"I do regress. As August turned cold in Sault Sainte Marie, as Augusts in The Soo always have and for-ever will, amidst these melancholic pines, it would happen. She would be mine. She had agreed! Unfettered. Conjugation would come by Christ-mas, this I knew. Before the old Yuletide there'd be a million laughs and a million bowls of Alphaghet-tie, which the young are blessed to find nutritious and palatable. I regress once more. Please hold your horses one bleeding moment, please. I would get proficient, or at least sufficient, on guitar, a few simple chord progressions, enough so we could live like the street-corner saints fetishized in film and television. It was 2002. Some kind of beat generation lifestyle wasn't entirely implausible, quite yet, even if it quite obviously was."

Ten: Allow Brittanica's handiwork to commence and time its culmination with your story's beginning:

"Then at her final lesson, and we all knew they were more than lessons by then, Allan Raval threw a big fit, veins no doubt a-thrombous on his shiny bald dome, and his big message was, 'You're always running away from things.' Six generic words. Anyone could have said them. You didn't need to be the auteur behind *The Hydraulic Engineer Becomes an Open Channel.* Marcel_Proust will be speaking wiser words in a month or two. The difference was that Alan Raval believed his own gimmick. And so she believed Alan Raval. She believed she was always running away from things. Or maybe she was just afeared of incestual quandaries. Many are. Many readers of my blog have repeatedly said it's the one element they cannot abide. And so they eloped. Fuckin' actually eloped. She signed up for a life of conceptual album midwifery in Sault Sainte Marie, a musical scene that has not, historically, birthed many breakout conceptual albums, or albums period! Rather than sensibly running away from Allan Raval, she ran right into his Lex Luthorian grasp, with his many felt hats, with his 5'7 manlet frame, with his eventual decapitatory desires, with his 'sonic juxtapositions' and 'powerful dramatic structures.' A little slower, please. Almost there. Things got progressively sad, rending me the wreck of a man I've gone on to become, Britannica. And in her final weeks and months and days I did not speak to her, only sent her the occasional photographic document of my substance-lubricated decline, to engage in Barthes' "impulse towards askesis." To say to her, "Turn back. Look at me. See what you have made of me."[43]

---

[43] (Barthes, 2002)

These Ten Makeover Tips are Satanic AF

*I*f after transcribing the previous evening's blog, Britannica wishes to rehabilitate the wreck of a man you've become, or is likely just bored, and wants to "become her" for you, then the time has arrived. The time has arrived to get that girl a makeover!

One: If a framed photograph of Catherine on her horse Moonbeam leads Brittanica to revelate, "That's almost like my natural hair colour," drive Britannica to Hollywood Hair Studios in your father's Ford F150. Recoil in terror should the colourist be Jenya! Breathe relieved sigh when Jenya fails to recognize you. Breathe frustrated sigh when Jenya says damage wrought upon Britannica's hair by retail-grade dyes means the recurrence of a Catherinian state of grace will require months, maybe years. Fork over $215 of John's bribe money to bootstrap the process.

Two: Ask the piercing man if an eyebrow ring might sully Britannica's eyebrow where it once sullied Catherine's. If the piercing man will not pierce beneath the hair-cooking stove, citing Hollywood Hair Studios' rules and regs, slide him a little grease to ignore the regs.

Three: If even after sufficient cooking her hair lacks lustre, book a consult at the Richard Horowitz Wig Studio.

When a fine wig is found, take a step back, make that little cinematographer's rectangle of thumbs and forefingers, and exclaim, "Fine, fine!" Embrace co-proprietor David Horowitz, apparent lover to Richard.

Four: If your mother is baking with her church group, grab your father by his lapels, shake him about as required, and remark, "Her old clothes are here somewhere you old booze hound!"

Five: Find a bounty of fresh and clean halters and jeans in the attic, all still smelling of Tommy Girl perfume, reminding you of both the Sault's Tommy Hilfiger craze of the early aughts and also of your sister Catherine. Strip Britannica of her *Heathen* halter top and adorn her in these hallowed vestments. Should Brittanica resent your throwing of her t-shirt into the trash, remind her that she has never listened to David Bowie. Take a step back and gaze upon a nearly Catherinian image. Toss Campus Crew tank tops in the air and quote T.S. Eliot, "These fragments I have shored against my ruins."[44]

Six: If lapel shaking has set about your father's Smirnoff guzzling, he's forgotten his fearful-pointing towards the attic, *ipso facto*, upon seeing Britannica pierced and wigged and wearing a hallowed Campus Crew tank-top, he must exclaim, "She's back! She's returned! You brought her back, David. I thought you were a good-for-nothing so-and-so but you brought her back!" He will then rise from his

---

[44] (Eliot, 1988)

knees to hug Brittanica, burdening Britannica with a depth of discomfort your father's inebriation prevents him from comprehending.

Seven: As you nuzzle the yellow Campus Crew t-shirt, certain you've achieved something of alchemical worth, finally resurrected some tangible remnant of Catherine's corporeal memory, hear Britannica say in a voice spooky as action at a distance with Catherine-song, "I'm becoming her. I feel the transmogrification is almost complete."

Eight: Wonder where sub-literate Britannica would have heard a word like *transmogrify*. Recall *Transmogrification Blues #2*, a certain concept album you've heard more times than you would care to. Wonder if even this "tiny and almost impalpable" lilt reminiscent of Catherine's lilt is but another of the Infernal Serpent's grand deceptions. Wonder why your son's namesake neglected *sound* when he wrote:

> But when from a long-distant past nothing sub-sists, after the people are dead, after the things are broken and scattered, taste and smell alone, more fragile but more enduring, more unsub-stantial, more persistent, more faithful, remain poised a long time, like souls, remembering, wait-ing, hoping, amid the ruins of all the rest; and bear unflinchingly, in the tiny and almost impal-pable drop of their essence, the vast structure of recollection."[45]

---

[45] (Proust, 1871-1922 (2003)

Nine: Put this question—as well as your abandoned family, pyres, dreams of arrest warrants, dreams of surely there's some bone dust remaining by the fire pit—out of mind by indulging in some Tostito's brand nuclear yellow Con Queso without the chips, with just some saltines.

Ten: If your mother returns to notice the saltines left out + Britannica's overt transmogrification and politely asks you to leave, request a ride to the Highway 17-situated Haleybury Motel, not a stone's throw from the suburb where Alan Raval may be murdered when time permits.

Expensive Singing Instructors
HATE THIS WOMAN

*I*f your sister Catherine had perfect pitch, meaning Britannica's atonal iterations of Evanescence threaten to spoil her transmogrification, then singing lessons will be just the ticket.

One: Shop around! If a well-reviewed voice coach near the Haleybury Motel is the murderer Alan Raval, he will be off the table. If the other is Dolores Guardi, a septuagenarian even during your own youth, feel surprised she is living, breathing, and lucid enough to advertise her services on *SooToday.com*.

Two: If already on *SooToday.com*, consult their inappropriately-whimsical "Wanted Wednesday" feature to see if you have made the list of Sault Sainte Marie pylons wanted by the Ontario Provincial Police. Happily, you have not.

Three: Make an appointment with Dolores Guardi. Endure Sault Sainte Marie's erratic bus services for nearly an hour.

Four: Receive a warm hug from Dolores Guardi. Reminisce regarding all the singing lessons you'd attended just to observe Catherine's trills and solfege scales.

Remind Mrs. Guardi of Catherine's blessed lower register merging with the upper.

Remind Mrs. Guardi of Catherine's huskiness.

Touch a brass piano lamp and remind Ms. Guardi that your son's namesake once wrote, "The past is hidden somewhere outside the realm, beyond the reach of intellect in some material object (in the sensation which that material object will give us) which we do not suspect. And as for that intellect, it depends on chance whether we come upon it or not before we ourselves must die."[46]

"A shaman. A column of breath," as the NAMBLA-advocate but one-time poet's poet Allen Ginsberg once described Bob Dylan.[47]

A curl of the lip that called Katie Holmes to mind, without the crooked tooth

Her deep-set eyes.

A neck as free and loose as her chord progressions, if you might recall, Dolores.

Tonal truths only a 17-year-old aspirant revelator could believe in his deepest being.

The upwards tilting of the head for maximal emotional output.

The ponytail.

The lustre of her hair.

The sparingly-used vibrato.

Her lousy poetry.

[46] (Proust, 1871-1922 (2003)

[47] (Sloman, 2002)

Her *Book of Longing,* carried around with her.

Her *Tears of Rage.*

Her *Diamonds and Rust.*

The way she'd glance up at you at song's Calliopean conclusion, *i.e.* 'Don't that beat all?'

The eyebrows and backward-tilting skull giving her an almost alien appearance.

The downward pointing of the chin.

Millions of years of evolution to produce this girl for us to grieve, Dolores.

Five: If Mrs. Guardi suffers the scourge of dementia and even after your big NAMBLA-monologue remembers Catherine 2.0 as Catherine 1.0 and hugs her with vigour, don't mention how the passage of twenty years, in even the prettiest people, cannot but mildly extinguish youth's glow.

Six: Take charge, "Breath control exercises for beginner's, what say?"

Seven: Endure Britannica's contemptuous glances as she pants and controls bursts of breath in a fashion far more strained than e'er was required of Catherine.

Eight: Find nothing but Donepezil and Rivastigmine in Mrs. Guardi's bathroom cabinet. If a quick check of the junkie's phone-based desk reference reveals no recreational utility for either, + having resolved to make efforts towards being a "good man," leave Dolores' Alzheimer's meds to stand sentry against the Infernal Serpent's neuronal minions.

Nine: Stuff the pockets of your 2001-purchased Tommy Hilfiger cargo pants with Dolores' Ensure High Protein

Nutritional Drinks. Fear not of neutralizing your Good Works at the medicine cabinet if Dolores always offered cookies or cupcakes, and surely would have Ensured you weren't leaving hungry were she in her right mind.

Ten: If during a rare pure note of *Dream a Little Dream of Me*, Britannica's jawline truly resembles Catherine's noble-chin-made-nobler by its minute cladding of baby fat, remember the likelihood that the Infernal Serpent is giving you just what you want, as a distraction, to nip in the bud your blog-based revelations against him.

1 COMMENT ON "EXPENSIVE SINGING INSTRUCTORS HATE THIS WOMAN"

Grievin' Gary: Liked and shared my man. Liked and shared!

How to Make Fast Friends in the Sault Sainte Marie Satanic Scene

*I*f a *Two-Pillow Sleeper*[48] who can't sleep without an arm underhead as well, and this head-propping arm suffers paresthesia every five mins, toss and turn and motel-room mutter Faulkner's

> In a strange room you must empty yourself for sleep. And before you are emptied for sleep, what are you. And when you are emptied for sleep, what are you. And when you are emptied for sleep you are not. And when you are filled with sleep, you never were. I don't know what I am. I don't know if I am or not. [...] How often have I lain beneath rain on a strange roof, thinking of home.[49]

begetting a spiteful, "We just got kicked out of your stupid home," from Brittanica, who then airs grievances galore

---

[48] (Romano, 2013)
[49] (Faulkner, 2000)

regarding her own foregone friends in the Thornhill Satanist Meetup Group, then simulate and stage the serving of a higher purpose by suggesting Brittanica organize a Sault Sainte Marie Satanist Meetup Group.

One: If anxious as ever to be eye-catching, patronize the Sault's lone 'alt' clothing store and pick out a nice cape for yourself. Pick out a tight pleather basque for Britannica. Keep receipts to write off against any grants or fellowships to be counterfactually awarded for Outstanding Blogging in the Anhistorical Soteriological Eschatology space.

Two: If Britannica's bust draws the attention of periodical readers and fentanyl-ravaged junkies alike, ignore tongue clickings from behind the circulation desk. Ask a library scientist which way to the meeting space. If the Urbana postgraduate looks up peevishly, *i.e.* 'Busy archiving here,' retort with a look that asks, 'Archiving what exactly? The Wanted Wednesday column?'

Three: Greet the eight aspirant Satanists gathered in the basement. As the only 37-year-old man present, wear the pants in this situation; also, the cape.

Four: If a prematurely-balding teen writes 'Tim Raval' on his name tag, mask your alarm by greeting the group with a robust, "Hail Satan!"

Five: Espouse the tenets non-theistic Satanists lead with on the Satanic Temple website's *Kidz Kwik Reference Guide*, *e.g.* 'freedom of expression,' *e.g.* 'fights for secularism,' *e.g.* 'after school Satan clubs.'[50]

Six: Bitch and moan about the Satanic panic of the 80s. Mock Christianity as though this required Lenny Bruce's bravery back in '55.

Seven: Hear what brings Tim to the Meetup, "My dad's music and life's work has really influenced me to think outside the box you know, so like I always wondered why all these people are going to church and worshipping some sky-man. Plus, I am really into the musical stylings of the band Ghost. If those guys are into Satan, maybe Satan is someone I should kick it with. But not like a real Satan more of a concept just to rebel against the establishment and corporations and stuff. Umm...hail Satan I guess."

Eight: Respond, "And Hail Satan to you, young man," before complimenting Tim on his precociousness and candour. If uncertain how many murderous details Alan Raval has shared with his son, write the name Matthew S. Leifer-Pusey on your own nametag. If Britannica scrunches her eyes at the writing of the "Leifer-Pusey"[51] moniker, scrunch yours right back.

Nine: If non-theistic Satanism lacks pizzazz, and is more like a hip version of Randian Objectivism, run out of Satanic talking points by minute three. Discuss hobbies instead. Ryan Ingerson's hobby is curling. Nriprendah Singh's hobby is playing snooker. Matt Scornianki's hobby is, endearingly,

---

[50] (thesatanictemple.com, n.d.)
[51] (Leifer & Pusey, 2017)

accounting. Tom Sklid's hobby is snow-mobiling. Lisa Palumbi's hobby is paddle-boarding. Lisa Palumbi is notably busty. Tim Raval's hobby is the sonic exploration of cosmic themes. Britannica's hobby is singing. Your hobby is fatherhood.

Ten: If Ryan Ingerson boasts how his own father books the Essar Centre anthem singers, notice Britannica's foot brushing against the foot of Ryan Ingerson. Fear that Britannica, just as she's become the Tulpa of Catherine you've so long sought to manifest, is soon to be lost as any Alexandrian library. Pout and cling back at the motel like it was going out of recorded memory.

Ten Surveillance Tips for the Amateur Revenge-Killer

*I*f Britannica's wearied of your volatile emotions, childlike hysteria, nascent pouting, and excessive attachment, then fasten to her and issue toothless talk of Alan's murder.

One: If Britannica offers to serve as your spy, browse Amazon for Wi-Fi cameras. Wi-Fi cameras in clock radios, Wi-Fi cameras in Happy Valentine's Glass Roses, known to the general populace as crack or meth pipes; Wi-Fi cameras that don't "have" time but are instead *Being and Time*; Wi-Fi cameras in copies of *Time and Narrative*; Wi-Fi cameras in Precious Moments figurines; Wi-Fi cameras that float undiscernibly on the skein of the onto-temporal; Wi-Fi cameras in bottles of liquid tears, and most relevant to your journey, Wi-Fi cameras in custom Baphomet pins.

Two: If Britannica suggests giving Tim the pin as a present, on a date, understand her real agenda is only to, "Escape the Haleybury Motel fart world for a while."

Three: Observe outputs from Tim's lapel at Wacky Wings—an upstart regional wing franchise with 100 flavours of wings, all of them nearby inedible, *e.g.* 'dill flavour wings just Kernels popcorn spice aggressively sprinkled upon tiny frozen wings.' Gaze from Tim's left pectoral at Britannica's pleather basque. Pride yourself on selecting so fine a basque.

Four: Hope the basque's contents won't draw unwanted attention from any anti-privacy watchdogs dining at Wacky Wings.

Five: If Britannica laughs too heartily at Tim Raval's jokes, regret (or is it *resent*) not having made her laugh in many days. Recall how easy it had been to make Marcel_ Proust laugh once he'd grown capable at four months old, *e.g.* 'jangling keys,' *e.g.* 'the old missing thumb rouse.' Reassure yourself by speaking aloud, "Heck, I'm funny."

Six: If Britannica's eye sparklings call to mind the Borderline Personality Disorder mistress, and moreover your sister Catherine, hope it's more than mundane eye-crinkling from which you've built a "castle of memories."[52]

Seven: Hope Britannica returns to your unhappy Haleybury home with two pounds of Garlic Parm wings as requested.

Eight: If upon her gormless and Parmless return, Britannica is downright aglow, calculate the rotten odds of losing a second Catherine to a second Raval. Arrive at a solution surely compromised by your inability to proceed past Grade 10 math, *i.e.* 1/8000."

Nine: Wonder if the past is even causally closed.

Ten: Wonder if you are still in hell and these *Transmogrification Blues* aren't one long jaunt through some *Ubikian* funhouse of subjunctive pain. Wonder if each successive spray of the Ubik can will tease and torture you with ever-realer Catherines, all to be stolen again and again and again and again.

---

[52] (Foley, 1989)

Ten Hella Genuine Ways to Correspond with Estranged Loved Ones

*I*f abandonment issues flare upon Tim Raval entering Britannica's life, check in with your wife hoping one person in this world might possibly experience negative valence if you were dead and simply gone.

One: Giftwrap a copy of *Learn Python 3 the hard way: a very simple introduction to the terrifyingly beautiful world of computers and code* as Ronald Majthenyi appeasement.

Two: Also giftwrap *Singing Lessons for Little Singers: A 3-in-1 Voice, Ear-Training and Sight-Singing Method for Children* (borrowed from Dolores Guardi) as an innocuous means of encouraging aesthetic appreciations in the impressionable and formless and prophesied Marcel_Proust.

Three: Enclose a picture of yourself abutting Catherine's grave smiling a smile that looks refreshingly less like a conman's than usual.

Four: Enclose some dirt and grass from near Catherine's grave in a blue little gold-braided bag, *i.e.* 'Would a conman go to all this trouble?'

Five: Enclose a smaller envelope emblazoned with the words, NOT FOR THE EYES OF FIEND MAJTHENYI!

Express hope that your wife is doing well. Express regret at having wasted the best years of her life.

Regret the plugging of your ears in response to her frequent nose-blowing.

Regret your Edith Bunkerian-imitation of her voice.

(*N.B.* to male readers: Nothing uglier than a man mimicking that Edith Bunker pitch, no matter how satirically-warranted it may feel. *Noto* even better, men, what the Gospel of Thomas says, "What comes out of your mouth, that is what will defile you.")

Regret the *praetereuntia*: the disregarding and neglecting, but sadder still, the surpassing.

Regret having been the only person to understand her.

Regret her inability to understand you.

Regret that your relationship was not a closed loop of understanding.

Regret your rolled eyes at her napkin-based hen-pecking in the park, *e.g.* "The napkins are blowing off in the wind!!!!" spoken with a severity appropriate to a catastrophic beheading, *i.e.* "How can I, a world-class contemplator of anhistorical mysteries, possibly care what happens to three cents worth of napkins? Why not wipe Marcel_Proust's face with dusty toilet paper from the bottom of my back-pack and figure that's fine?"

The failure to buy her flowers though they were often on sale for $4.99. A simple gesture no one could fail to understand.

The regret of who could build so much as a shed in the shadow of Catherine's crinkle castle of memories, such that even a living and aging Catherine won't compete with her adolescent ghost, a quandary facing Britannica even now.

An inborn disinterest in picking up after yourself as but the most galling of your myriad deficits of character.[53]

Her false hope when your character deficits ebbed following the birth of Marcel_Proust, *i.e.* 'Attentive and decent once again! Wow that is great!'

Her disappointment when deficits flowed deficiently as ever once Marcel_Proust seemed on pace to meet his sensorimotor skill milestones.

Your tendencies towards the saturnine.

Your self-identification as a bloviational speaker.

The diaper changing ratio on the occasions you were equally available to change a diaper—for fecal imbroglios 80 : 1 her; somewhat more equitable in the urinary times.

Shirking diaper responsibility with personal charm, *e.g.* 'Thought I changed the last 79,' *i.e.* 'Just being the dynamic stinker you cannot but love!'

Bygone and bifurcated Catherine infatuations that outweighed a real love endured for decades that evolved into lifelong friendship and genuine and uninteresting adult union.

Ergo hearing *Wild Flowers* by Tom Petty and relating it to each girl you'd loved for even an hour, every dopaminergic vixen who didn't text back, all while excluding from these *Wild Flowers* reveries your true (genuine but unromantic) love.

On MDMA or good enough cocaine swearing you really do feel *Wild Flowers* feelings for her, expressing how foolish

---

[53] A lot of the time he is too hard on himself. – E.A.

you felt over all the previous anamnesis, only to forget all over again come the comedown, rendering the remembering fraudulent and cruel.

The regret of only being able to truly love, *i.e.* 'totemize,' a girl who is gone.

The reality that loving Marcel_Proust is better than all the totemizing in the world, except only your own actions have banish'd you from Marcel_Proust's bassinet-side, meaning that that narrative has no villain except you, meaning best not to colour in too many of its blanks.

The regret of a lot of ethyl-benzene evenings. The Sherwin-Williams mugshot, in which your paint-encrusted face bore vague resemblance to white-faced *Enfants du Paradis* while through your eyes glared no personage but the devil.

A lifetime of *I love you*s devalued with each meaningless utterance.

The regret of having been friends longer than lovers.

That old Highway 17 back to Sault Sainte Marie always calling from the darkness.

How little it took to make her happy and how little you gave anyway.[54]

The regret of the song still in her eyes, even after all these devaluations.

The country songs that could only invoke Catherine.

The $4.99 flowers, a no-brainer.

Six: If you've done a bang-up job of accepting culpability and expressing heartfelt regrets, slide a few resentments

---

[54] I don't think this part is true. – E.A.

into the mix so she doesn't get off scott-free *vis-a-vis* your re-litigation of the rupture.

Accuse her of usury. The loan: "fancy furniture she wanted to buy for herself anyway." The rate of interest: "your eternal fealty."

Her interruption of your rare bursts of aesthetic ecstasy with inane questions regarding your preferred doneness of the evening's linguini.

Resent that she lacked better retorts to Ronald Majthenyi's character assassinations, *e.g.* "Some people, call them *aesthetes*, gain valuable insights from inhalant abuse."

Seven: Ask if once the dust has settled a supervised visit might be paid to this young man. The dust being the dust of Stacey Keats' ashes.

Eight: Ask if Marcel_Proust's *Baby Shark* and *Paw Patrol* transfixations show even the earliest warning of waning. Joke pathetically that you're waiting on these to run their course before making your return home.

Nine: Ask if Marcel_Proust has sprayed any more diarrhea upon the curtains as had posed a problem in the past.

Ten: Have the letter sealed with wax at a high-end stationary store. Enclose a $15 gift card for Snugglebugz, the baby swag store at which she spends the GDP of a small nation-state.

Surveillance Techniques for Novices

*I*f pinhole imagery of Tim Raval's daily life offers entertainment value equivalent to late-stage reality television,
i.e. 'none whatsoever,' then be well-stocked with chips, cured
meats, and the odd inhalant, *e.g.* 'Britannica's nail polish
remover,' to keep despondency at bay.

One: Gaze upon Tim Raval's bedroom ceiling for hours.
Inhale polish fumes. Issue insights on the eternally-blank pal-
let preceding creation. Misquote DeLillo.

Two: Historicize Tim's version of the 'old gang' greeting
him in the St. Mary's Collegiate parking lot. Here are Tim's
deathless contemporaries, the crux of any A1 gang being its
contemporaneousness. Should Tim Raval approach Ron
Saunders, he of the unfortunate capris pants, fifteen years
hence, and shout, "Remember that Monday we joked in the
parking lot thinking it the most casual thing in the world,
when really it was a miracle of understanding we'd never
achieve again in adulthood; I don't mean me and you, Ron, I
mean all of us in search of brothers, all of us lost men," then
Ron Saunders's would respond in typical NPC Use Case
fashion, "Good times, eh, bud," before rushing towards a

fistful of Labatt 50s that will never quell the exchange's awk-wardness nor Ron's concomitant thirst for brotherhood.

Three: Spiral down YouTube's after-school Satanic Panic rabbit hole with new friend Tim. Revisit classics: Geraldo's well-noted fear-mongering. Max Schreck and Zeena (Anton's daughter) Lavey on Sally Jesse Raphael. This same It Couple then condescending to a cable access interview with Tim Metzger. A pin-camera's wobble as Tim nods approvingly from his progressive perch alongside Schreck's snide asser-tions. Watch Tim bound righteously from bed to laptop like a babe to the breast of Tim Metzger's YouTube channel before realizing Tim Metzger was de-platformed for having Grand Wizarded the Klu Klux Klan.

Four: Realize the Metzger-Schreck dialectic is yet more of Strauss and Howe's cyclical saeculum—Schreck's rejection of Metzger's awful values as seemingly noble to Schreck as your own oppositional-defiance towards *Kidz Kwik Reference Guides* now seems to you the Sault-situated grief blogger.

Five: As Ravals dine on braised mutton, zoom upon the bronze sheen to Alan's wife, Patricia. Resent Alan's success with the ladies. Wonder if you don't have a concept album or two up your sleeve. Pick at nostril polish encrustations as Alan announces a family visit to known accomplice Rob Dagg at the hospital, *i.e.* 'K, time to concentrate.'

Six: If Dagg suffers from malaise, fatigue, and jaundice, all brought about by acute Hepatitis C, which has advanced into late-stage Cirrhosis, understand that Rob Dagg has committed another *insult*, this time to his liver, leading to sclerosis and then necrosis, 90% of hepatic function loss, and a fast-encroaching pallid death. If an exceedingly-confident bald man says to Dagg, "We're pulling for ya, bud!" know that only a true believer in his own gimmick could lack so much tact at a cirrhotic death bed.

Seven: "Why do we have to keep seeing that yellow old bum?" – progressive Tim Raval, in car-ride home.

Eight: "I owe the guy." – Alan Raval.

Nine: And then, with a patronizingly-benign glance (*i.e.* 'I-Alan-Raval am so very wise') back at his son, "Loyalty."

Ten: Scrawl illegible interview questions for Rob "The Dagger" Dagg (a high school nickname based upon three point shooting- rather than decapitational-acumen). Have Britannica trace over these napkin questions to preserve any insight retrieved from beneath the skein of space and time made accessible only by inhalants.

2 COMMENTS ON "SURVEILLANCE TECHNIQUES FOR NOVICES"

Alavida Alcohol Reduction Bot: Here, you can tap into a vast evidence-based universe of fresh health knowledge created and curated by doctors and therapists experienced in alcohol addiction. With Alavida, you can learn about other ways to change your relationship with alcohol, where drinking less is also success.

Reply: Thomas Astaire: Domi arigato! Pool and pathetically layer learn this, Dr. Roboto: you don't drink Varsol, you inhale it.

How to Visit Rob Dagg

*I*f Britannica melodramatically presents "Catherine's Murder Questions?!?" to you in the morning, wonder why these questions hadn't occurred to you. View your nether-realms napkin and realize that they had.

One: If pockèdness yellows from banana to mustard upon your arrival, hold palms out in the universal, 'Everything is cool; I am not seeking bloody recompense' gesture.

Two: If The Dagger quivers, fearing Britannica the avenging apparition of Catherine, arrivèd in the ICU to escort Rob to hades or *sheol* or however Rob cognomens the pit, then hand Britannica the napkin so she can ask the questions in her affected but contextually-effective Billy Eilish whisper.

Three: If an esophageally-worn and -torn Dagger rubs his own palms and points doorward, understand based on a relevant episode of *Intervention* that Rob Dagg is requesting the old hand-sanitizer and water cocktail, the Purelli. Squirt sanitizer into your Perrier bottle, swirl sanitizer, sniff sanitizer, imbibe a conservative swig to steady nerves. Report to Rob that this libation hints at the borderline of potability. Relate to Rob Dagg's relief upon imbibition of his frothy beverage.

Four: Should Britannica ask, "How did she die?" and Rob Dagg reaches out as if to strangle Britannica, slug The Dagger in his dying liver, thus expediting his looming death, more of a favour to Rob Dagg than anything.

Five: If Rob Dagg then mimes his own strangling, figure enough charades already and hand Rob Dagg your note napkin and pen.

Six: If Rob Dagg's syntactic ordering-of-operations is but one casualty of his liver's low glucose production, his first word will be *asphyxiation,* then to the left of that, *sexual,* and before that, *consensual,* and above all those awful words he'll write the word ACCIDENT.

Seven: Scream at The Dagger, "Strangled her friggin' head off by accident?"

Eight: If Dagg makes the universal index finger rotation in conjunction with a slight bobbing of the wrist, *i.e.* 'Fast forward in the narrative a bit,' shrug in acquiescence, *i.e.* 'Do I look like some slave dogmatic to any deterministic arrow of narrative time?"

Nine: Receive written clarification that Catherine's beheading was an aborted effort to slice up and feed Catherine's body parts to the nearby swine of a Thessalonian pig farmer only after her very accidental asphyxiation on Noonday Road, a fitting place-name given Nietzsche's thought of thoughts that "space and time sleep at midday,"[55] when "the midday sun is the Moment of the shortest shadow and the

---

[55] (Nietzsche, The Gay Science)

most luminous brightness, the image of eternity. When 'the greatest burden' is assimilated."[56]

Ten: Let Rob Dagg's story seep in. Get Filets of Fish: extra sauce, no bun. Accept Britannica's back rub of support. Squint in disdain if Britannica says, "Want to try it?" and you say, "Try what?" and she says, "Sex strangling."

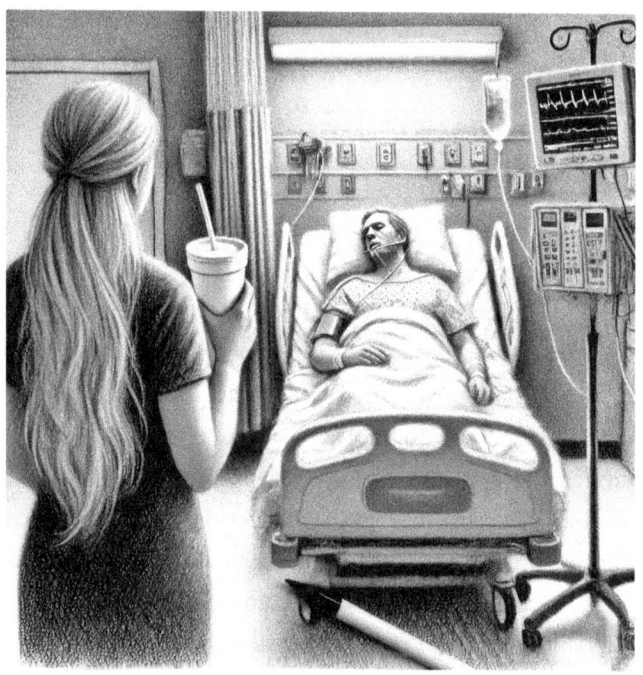

---

[56] (Heidegger, 1984)

Ten Tips for Asphyxiating Thine Enemy Unto Death

*I*f The Dagger's revelation in no way vindicates Alan Raval, *i.e.* 'Just an asphyxiational mishap. Maybe best to forgive Alan for beheading your sister because accidents happen,' then the day and the hour hath come for Alan to breathe his last breath.

One: Asphyxiation is brought about by deprivation of gaseous tracheal oxygen! In your sister's case, said deprivation was brought about by strangling. Sexual strangling! In Alan Raval's case, strangling may present too many irksome variables *i.e.* 'Alan overpowering you,' *i.e.* 'loud sputtering attracting the attention of passerby.'

Two: Consider using a *garrote* or *ligature*! Fans of the JonBenet Ramsey murder will recall that a ligature is a wire or cord tied in a loop around a stick. Loop goes around the neck, pull the stick, and the victim can say goodbye to any gaseous tracheal oxygen they'd been counting on, lol.

Three: *Garrote* is not a technically precise term. *Garrote* simply refers to a form of Spanish judicial execution that happened to employ the ligature.

Four: Don't get hung up on semantics with the manager of the Home Hardware. Don't read to the manager from *A medico-legal perspective on the practice of Garrotting* as well as

How to Improve Your Investigation and Prosecution of Strangulation Cases.

Five: Remember that ligatures (or garrotes) can also work by severing the carotid artery. If essential that your sister's death be avenged by asphyxiatatory means, use something soft like a telephone cord instead of a piano wire or guitar string, even though as Barthelme wrote in *Some of Us Had Been Threatening our Friend Colby*, "There is something extremely distasteful in thinking about being hanged with wire instead of rope."[57]

Six: Ride the bus all over creation looking for stores that still sell wired telephones.

Seven: Hide in the bushes behind the Raval family home. Grow bored. Grow cold. If its display may sacrifice the element of surprise vital to an effective garroting, scold Britannica for checking her phone so frequently.

Eight: If Britannica jumps up and down in jubilation, scold her further before reading Ryan Ingerson's text that a replacement anthem singer is required at the Essar Centre.

Nine: "Can we go please? Please? We can carrot Alan Raval right after I sing. I promise. Please?"

Ten: Sigh, place your carrot in your back pocket, rend your garment, and call upon that primary requirement of all 37-year-old men clinging to hot young girlfriends: the patience of Job.

---

[57] (Barthelme, Some of Us Had Been Threatening Our Friend Colby, 1981)

Talent Agencies Hate These Ten Weird Tricks

*I*f easily winded, put your middle-aged vanity aside to sprint behind Britannica towards the 5000-seat Essar Centre.

One: Drop the name *Donald Ingerson* should the ticket taker balk at your ticketless condition. Interface with security. Interface with Don Ingerson.

Two: Balk your own balk at Don Ingerson's low-yield offer to meet Sootoday.com Hounds columnist Brian Conchiglie, as though Sootoday.com were a big deal in the blogging space or read for anything but it's Wanted Wednesday zanies.

Three: Accept Don Ingerson's offer to view his framed jersey of The Great One, Wayne Gretzky, who scored an astonishing 182 points in his single season with The Greyhounds. Explain to Britannica how Gretzky, with his weak shot, so skinny "he could wear a fur coat on Halloween and go out disguised as a pipe cleaner"[58] succeeded simply on precognitive visions "about where a teammate is going to be. A lot of times, [he could] just turn and pass without looking,"[59] an impossibility under the dubious auspices of linear causality,

---

[58] (Khan, 2017)
[59] (Bernard, 2009)

meaning The Great One's knowing must have mandated Mark Messier's particle positioning.

Four: Ask Britannica if a Powerade might fortify her throat. Chug four Northern Superior Lagers while absorbing only the mildest judgment from concession staff long-since accustomed to immoderate thirst.

Five: Remind Britannica that ice, like the Infernal Serpent, is a slippery old devil. Furrow brows deeply when Don Ingerson replies, "You're a good father."

Six: If Britannica belts the anthems out with a striking new vocal command, close your eyes and truly listen. Scan the crowd for any unknown accomplices of Raval and The Dagger who might notice her uncanny resemblance to your anthem-singing sister, the deceased Catherine.

Seven: If introduced postgame to Los Angeles Kings owner Yiang Zheing, a tech billionaire interested enough in the truculent-but-aesthetically-displeasing sport of hockey to watch major-junior games in socioeconomically-ravaged towns, take a hard look at Zheing as his hands linger on Britannica's timelike curves during their introductory hug.

Eight: Hear Ingerson describe Zheing's tech innovations, foundations, and nascent television empire.

Nine: If Zheing speaks the words, "I think you'd be perfect for one of my shows, Britannica. And that show is called *Singing Competition*," then feel fairly certain this will commence a dastardly *Ubik* spray not of ontology but of west coast geography.

Ten: If the scuttling puck of your indeterministic narrative has been "wanded"[60] where The Great One himself was wanded on Aug 9/88, know where you're headed as Wayne Gretzky knew where Jari Kurri would follow, the City of Angels.

[60] (Newell, 2016)

Ten Sites to See in Los Angeles, California

*I*f even private jet passengers must indulge the fascistic whims of customs officers, then discard your garrote before boarding Zheing's Gulfstream III and indulge each customs functionary's own iteration of pathology, *e.g.* 'the gleeful bullying jock,' *e.g.* 'the staunch defender of his nation.'

One: If a pitch to adapt your small press novels into a six-part Network Event wearies Zheing, tilt your forehead downward in admonishment, *i.e.* 'No one man's Quixotic narrative is any less tedious than another's *Singing Competition*. Regardless of plausibility or production value, we're all passengers on the same ship of fools, Yiang.'

Two: Arrive at LAX and denigrate surrounding Englewood as, "Kind of dumpy."

Three: Avail yourself of Yiang's fine apple brandies until the wee hours, glaring at Facebook photos of Alan Raval until your eyes blur and you mistake him for yourself. Castigate yourself for dwelling in a dark basement, still stuck in the fetid Sault Sainte Marie of the mind when you've finally made it to the place Woody Guthrie rightly described as a "Garden of Eden."

Four: Mouth "Hello" to the driveway beneath your face at dawn. Marvel at the quality of the light. Recall that David

Lynch also first arrived in Los Angeles by night, and "so it wasn't until the next morning, when [he] stepped out of a small apartment on San Vicente Boulevard, that [he] saw this light. And it thrilled [his] soul. [He felt] lucky to live with that light."[61]

Five: If light is the great disinfectant, wonder how so much perfidy and greed grew from such exquisite sunlight, *e.g.* 'Fatty Arbuckle raping Virginia Rappe with a bottle,' *e.g.* 'Weinstein's impotent "intersex vagina"[62] pissings,' *e.g.* 'Dan "Get in the Van" Schneider, *aka* 'Dan "Hold Her Tighter, She's a Fighter" Schneider,' producing so much children's foot fetish programming for Nickelodeon.

Six: Drive Zheing's Mercedes Cabriolet through the hills and valleys. Wind kundalini-like through the half-remembered dream of *Mulholland Drive*. Throw nickels at Krishnas. Speed by the Los Angeles Gnostic Centre and feel a touch of regret, here in this hotbed of cultic belief, that your gnostic period was so fickle and short-lived.

Seven: Feel a touch of bemusement over being so shameless a dilettante.

Eight: Plan to visit the Vineyard Fellowship in Tarzana where Bob Dylan was *Saved*. Plan an alcoholic tailspin into psychosis to honour Kerouac at *Big Sur*. Don't count on spitting and punching your way through the gleaming Apple Stores to find the last Neil Cassady of Ol' Frisco, but hope to.

---

[61] (Lynch & McKenna, Room To Dream, 2018)
[62] (Cauterucci, 2020)

Nine: If these plans are dismissed by Britannica in favour of a Warner Bros. studio tour, disparage the tourist-y nature of said undertaking and request a little grease from Yiang to visit the Hollywood Boulevard strip clubs. If Yiang hands you a thousand dollars without even counting it, as though he'd always known you'd want money, then Zheing has pegged you as the Eric Roberts character from *Star 80*.

Nine: If California strip club laws are wildly abstruse, then there's no liquor if vaginas, beer but not liquor if nude breasts, and only dry clubs may promote vaginas and breasts conterminously. Counter-intuitively: only the classiest strip clubs possess buffets. Eat a great deal of fried chicken and pork ribs for a song. Wipe your greasy hands on your jeans. If you sit in the front row and throw a few ones towards a generously-endowed Belarusian, and her bountiful breasts and gold crucifix hang before your eyes, and there between the breasts is Christ on his cross, dying for all this, dying for Dan Schneider's foot fetish, dying for Fatty Arbuckle's apocryphal champagne bottle, and a mirror ball refracts light thereon that contains multitudes, then reach out your thumb and forefinger and hold the base of Christ's cross, look this dancer in the eye, there in the sustain called Jumbo's Clown Room, and know in this house of ill repute the eternal spirit that light makes apparent.

Ten More Tips For Getting Yourself Killed

As knowing dawns and encompasses, suffer your first heart attack. Fall from the stage. Writhe and gasp. Clutch your chest like Redd Fox.

One: If old Beelzebub the devil, known in some circles as *the Infernal Serpent*, won't abide your testimony in Jumbo's Clown Room, please don't think for a minute that a mere heart attack will be the extent of your torment. Fall from your chair, fracture your arm, cranially impact the floor such that your teeth act as the penetrating force mechanism needed to sever the anterior inch of your tongue.

Two: If while waiting for an ambulance, the stripper, actress really, stage name: Ada Lovelace, affixes latex gloves, removes a Zip-Lock bag from her purse, and places the anterior inch of your tongue therein, gurgle questions regarding the bag's sterility, *e.g.* 'Why the gloves if placing tongue portion in a dirty old condom Zip-Lock anyway.' Learn that Ada Lovelace wore latex gloves for her own protection rather than your anterior inch's sterile preservation.

Three: Issue a thumbs up as paramedics check your airway. Provide thumbs down as paramedics puncture a stoma in your throat to facilitate oxygen intake.

Four: Invasive procedures won't end there! Receive attentions from both the cardiac and orthopedic teams at the Los Angeles County Medical Centre. *Invasiveness*—practically the cardiac team's middle name. Should your bluish hue necessitate percutaneous intervention, whereby a tiny camera is threaded past your severed and still-bleeding tongue, past the stoma punctured by paramedics, right down into the heart where the narrowest arterial culprit can be identified and duly stented—then while stented, stoma'd and percutaneously-intervened upon, hum thine self a weary tune.

Five: Due to arterial deficiencies, don't expect your arm to be operated upon any time soon, plus nor are a lot of opiates made available to an anti-Satanic blogger in your rebellious condition.

Six: Gurgle hostile noises at the functionary who demands insurance information while pounding his index finger against a bill for $172,000.

Seven: Request a hospital chaplain by making that old sign of the cross with two index fingers. Hallucinate an alternate self speaking to another, "Still looks computational to me." Learn from a nurse that the chaplaincy had been decreed problematic and canceled by the hospital's no-nonsense Diversity Czar.

Eight: If the functionary refuses to charge your phone, *e.g.* 'Not my job!' make the universal 'money grubbing/thumb rubbing against index and middle finger' motion, *i.e.* 'My phone will get you your $172,000, ghoul.'

Eight: Send the hospital's geo-coordinates to Britannica. Ask if she remembered to buy traveller's insurance. If

Britannica is now insured as a member of the Screen Actor's Guild, describe the increasingly-low metrics for corroborating the temporal validity of a common law marriage.

Nine: Text your estranged wife, "Suffered heart attack on Hollywood Blvd. Don't worry about money. Costs covered by SAG. Should Marcel_Proust wish to say goodbye to his father a flight to L.A. is in order. Please don't bring Ronald Majthenyi. I hate him."

Ten: Drift off to sleep for what may be the last time. Repeat the mantra, "I will not follow the imps. I will not follow the imps," until a bald male nurse pops his Raval-ian dome into your room to issue a toothless threat of placing you on the psych ward. Keep your analytical engine running by entertaining thoughts of Alan Raval's murder.

How to Plan a Family Reunion

*I*f after three days *sans* visitor, the only five people in the world who could possibly give a hang about you the apophatic avenger arrive in your hospital room, then pound that nurse-summoning button to order the apple and banana pouches your infant guest likes to eat, eat, and eat.

One: Wonder if Britannica's visible apprehension stems from nascent *Singing Competition* stardom, proximity to your wife's spontaneous malevolent contemptuousness, or from fiendish Zheing Yiang having shown her the film *Star 80* in his private screening room.

Two: Should Zheing and Ronald Majthenyi exchange furtive glances, and Yiang's interventions into your fortunes have seemed a little *deus ex Zheing*, the two men must be in infernal cahoots.

Three: Look at your real wife. Exchange an ocular empathy borne of years spent together on couches, trips Beyond the Infinite in *2001* to the abortive walk-in clinic, all the trials and tribulations of young impoverished youth, and then emerging from poverty together into lower-middle class comforts, the cheap pleasure of the movies even, all the popcorn and large sodas, all the sunsets at the poor person's beach, all her weariness and inability to make effective arguments on her own behalf, her inhuman ability to transcend all of your foibles and addictions and rages and sentimentalities.

Four: Touch the soft skull of Marcel_Proust, who is part of her and part of you, containing some of the selfsame neurological wiring responsible for your current thoughts. In recognition of all this, as part apology, part *crie-de-couer*, gurgle the unattributed words, "Those who seek him, find him,"[63] at both your wife and baby.

Five: If the no-nonsense diversity czar overhears this as she passes in the hall, she will remark, "We don't tolerate hate speech here," as Ronald Majthenyi will query, "Find who, exactly?" as Yiang Zhieng will condemn, "Hopped up on Varsol again. Sad! Not sure how he'd get it in the hospital. Maybe he should be moved to a more reputable location."

Six: If the functionary comes by tapping the now $218,000 bill, eye-ball-indicate that Zheing will be happy to provide a down-payment. Wonder what Zheing whispers to the functionary. Make pleading eye contact with wife. Eye contact of rebuke towards Judas Britannica. Eye contact of apology towards blameless baby Marcel_Proust.

Seven: If Ronald Majthenyi strolls your wife and child away as Britannica is escorted off by Yiang, scowl forlornly when orderlies wheelbarrow-stretcher you the Knight of Sorrowful Faith into a cab without even offering a cab voucher.

Eight: If an orderly asks the Sterling Hayden-resemblant cab driver to convey thee unto a hobo hospital, contemplate

---

[63] (Augustine, The Confessions, 1998)

the gold cross hanging from the cab driver's rear-view mirror. Point to it. Use your mangled right arm and your functional left arm to form a steeple.

Nine: Writhe in pain until you see signage for the Reformed Church of Greater Los Angeles.

Ten: Appreciate when Sterling Hayden leaves his meter turned off and finds some Reformed functionaries to stretcher you into their church basement/hobo haven. Respond that yes you are hungry. Respond that yes you are in pain.

Ten Tips for Critiquing a Dead Medium

*I*f the Reformed Church functionary won't hazard a guess at Homeless Healthcare of Los Angeles' wait list, then writhe grateful as possible into the lounge area to watch TV with the other derelicts.

One: If the lead judge of *Singing Competition*, recently celebrated in the culture for his decision to become a construction of a topical narrative, intones in response to a rendition of Scott Walker's *Farmer in the City*: "Absolutely! Amazing!" then nod at Donna as she shrieks, "That the devil. Faithless and perverse generation. You know not what manner of spirit you're of. Foxes got holes, birds in the air got nests, but son of man got nowhere to lay his head. That there the devil."

Two: If uncertain whether Donna means the construction of a topical narrative is the devil, or the televisual medium's scavenging of truly holy and truly strange songs as mere competitional fodder is the devil's work—gurgle sounds of generic agreement. If cable-fond Merle, a hippie and academician, discourages you from "encouraging" Donna, tell Merle that his entitlement to stridency expired around 1981.

Three: If Donna the Derelict spits in your mouth while shouting, "Talkin' Ninetto, Ostia, Vigo. Talkin' wrinklin' wrinklin' against the sky. Talkin' brain grass and remember that dream. Serpents and scorpions and all the power of the enemy. You know he that despiseth you despiseth me and nothing by any means shall hurt you," then respond, "Listen Donna, I want that to be true."

Four: If the proceeding local news breezily highlights all manner of strife and tragedy, murder and malice, civic perfidy, state perfidy, federal perfidy, local head-stompings, out-of-state electrocutions, the bright smiles of anchors contrasted against the bleeding maws of the carjacked, and if wheelchair-bound like Donna and semi-tongueless and without many entertainment options—then comprise that last remaining demographic television relies upon: the immobile.

Five: Watch *The Colbert Report* following the local news. Fear a *Late Night* Culture Industry audience more frothing than anything Elia Kazan could imagine, as though the least transgressive wink by this progressively-leaning and -preening Lonesome Rhodes were a communion wafer ground into Bud Light Watermelon.

Six: As the secular service continues, hear Bud Light Watermelon (Colbert) deride anti-environmental legislators while his carbon-drunk West 53rd street tourists genuflect accordingly. If NT Wright's *Evil and the Justice of God* is laid out conveniently on the ottoman before you, read its innermost essence to Donna,

> postmodernity's analysis of evil allows for no redemption. There is no way out, no chance of repentance and restoration, no way back to the solid ground of truth from the quicksands of

deconstruction. Postmodernity may be correct to say that evil is real, powerful and important, but it gives us no real clue as to what we should do about it. It is therefore vital that we look elsewhere, and broaden the categories of the problem from the shallow modernist puzzles on the one hand and the nihilistic deconstructive analyses on the other.

Seven: If Merle responds, "Having been something of big wheel in the Yale poststructuralist scene of the early 80s, I know a thing or two about the postmodern," really stressing the *dern*, then let him involute and obfuscate Wright's certainty throughout the commercial break's "artificial effervescence of signs."[64]

Eight: Watch Bud Light Watermelon cozy up to Penny Lane, the director of a Michael Moorean nod to consensus thinking titled *Hail Satan* that portrays Satanists as noble activists fighting the scourge of looming theocracy rather than the self-righteous dinks they're appropriately perceived as. Inquire of Donna when last a United States theocracy was even a remote possibility? Suggest optimistically that maybe it was August 7, 1963, when Bob Dylan recorded *With God on Our Side*.

Nine: Concede to Merle the Yale man that yes regressive evangelicals eager of eschatological doom still impose illiberal abortionary policies, but in terms of the culture, in terms of Colbert's nightly sermons, the battle for social currency ended decades ago. Opine to Merle that, "These

---

[64] (Baudrillard, 1994)

clapping seals remain at the West 53rd Street front lines because they've razed the home they had to return to. Heck Merle, they've even lost *Singing Shows* to an untenable over-saturation of the self-reflexive irony market. And here we find ourselves where the only non-quotidian bid for unsaturated meaning is to *Hail Satan*." As the victim or beneficiary of a hyperstitious feedback loop, quote from, *Templexity: Disordered Loops through Shanghai Time*, which you have not read or even yet heard of,

> As [a] culture folds back upon itself, it proliferates self-referential models of a cybernetic type, attentive to feedback-sensitive self-stimulating or auto-cat-alytic systems. The greater the progressive impetus, the more insistently cyclicity returns. To accelerate beyond light-speed is to reverse the direction of time. Eventually, in science fiction, modernity completes its process of theological revisionism, by rediscovering eschatological culmination in the time-loop.

Ask if Merle has heard of Friedrich Nietzsche, and to what impoverished extent he's reconciled the eternal recurrence of the same with the Death of God. Bust out this chestnut polished for just such a confrontation, "To comprehend the Death of God's impact upon the men of his day, imagine awakening one morning to find no one believed in capitalism anymore. It's not that they no longer believe in its merits or sustainability as you've ceased to believe, Merle. It's that by having come to believe its existence unnecessary, in their minds, not only does capitalism no longer exist, but it never existed in the first place. Yet the factories making utterly-unbelieved-in fitted FUBU hats must continue making hats for us and by us until the standing reserves run dry. What would you do with all Capital's monuments, Merle? Would you raze the factories? What would you build in their place? How would surplus value be squandered? How would needs for commerce be met? And if people continued to trade, would you have them do so in secret?

Ten: To tune out iniquitous ironies, winking and feigned virtue alike, and the tawdriness of clickbait parading as societal concern, exit the *Late Night* critical theory/comedy space by turning off Colbert and checking your Google Scholar alerts for incidences of the "autostereogrammatic" instead, begetting a hissy fit from Merle, whose field yielded income incommensurate to owning a phone. If Merle sneers and says, "Can people not be fundamentally good WHILE clapping like seals? Are all the inequities of equity solved? Aren't we both here in a shelter—you, a celebrated small press author; I, a contemporary of Jonathan Culler—because of inconceivable wealth disparity? Who made you the arbiter of progressivism's progress? Couldn't these watermelon wafers come from a place of genuine empathy?" Yawn theatrically before responding, "The wafers come from a place of commerce, Merle. It's not inequality they want reconciled, but Viacom's dying profit model." If then wearying of Merle's hammer punches to your neck and upper vertebrae, realize midnight mass will soon commence and wheel yourself towards the pulpit.

How to Backfoot A Deconstructionist While Reterritorializing God's Name and Tabernacle

*O*ne: Observe exactly how the battle was surrendered as the minister drones, "the children of Habaiai, the children of Kox, the children of Barzillai…."

Two: Count only three old ladies in the 500-person capacity faith-venue, exactly one old lady more than is needed for God to be in their midst.

Three: Experience an absence of liturgical zeal. Merely some collared old closet character offering a mealy-mouthed social justice message significantly offset by his Church's position that homosexuality is the direct result of a 'broken,' 'sinful world.'[65]

Four: If a hymnal-tucked pamphlet informs you the bored Knight of Infinite Resignation of Reformed Church cornerstones such as the Belgic Confession, the Heidelberg Catechism, and the Canons of Dort, fall asleep for a moment or two.

Five: Agree with the Weird Christians invented by the *New York Times*[66] that some incense and organs and *etc.*

---

[65] (Heynen, et al., 1973)
[66] (Burton, 2020)

could go a long way towards pulling this intolerant snooze-fest out of the fire.

Six: If an embedded NYT link leads to the Buzzfeed article "Weird Christian Punk Masses Are Traditional AF. And That's A Good Thing" learn that these trad Latin masses incorporate Elizabethan language, prayers from the "O.G." American Breviary, and as much incense as can legally be released in an enclosed environ, all while remaining "hella variant from modernity." Concede to Donna that this "bells and smells" trend is undoubtably sexier than Dort's Canon; however, refuse to accept that the latest whims of authenticity-starved Brooklynites can be commensurate to the grace found in Jumbo's Clown Room, as that would mean you're no revelator, only another contrarian vulture chewing at the hash-tagged carrion of the postmo*dern*.

Seven: If Merle smells blood in the water, he will sidle up to you with his well-thumbed *Simulacra and Simulation* and whisper-quote,

> What becomes of the divinity when it reveals itself in icons, when it is simply incarnated in images as a visible theology? Or does it volatilize itself in the simulacra that, alone, deploy their power and pomp of fascination - the visible machinery of icons substituted for the pure and intelligible Idea of God? [67]

---

[67] (Baudrillard, 1994)

Eight: Remind Merle that his non-lycanthropic buddy Jacques Derrida, who was ill- "prepared to descend into such overenthusiastic crudity as examining more than one of Heidegger's words in a single book,"[68] believed meaning to reside in the space between signs.

Nine: Ask Merle, "What if to the tune of *How Great Thou Art* someone sent, signified, and made specular these spaces between the signifiers?"

> And Hezekiah begat Erb; and Erb begat Michaia; and Michaia begat Jedidah, who begat Darge, who begat Larry; and Larry begat Ratso; and Ratso begat Bob, who wrote *In the Garden* and *I Ain't Gonna Go To Hell For Anybody* and *Gonna Change My Way of Thinkin'* and *In the Summertime* and *Every Grain of Sand*; and Bob begat Woody, who wrote *Jesus Christ*; and Woody begat Ronnie Blakely, an archetypal Charlotte; and Ronnie Blakey begat *Young Werther*; and *Young Werther* begat the green light at the end of Daisy's dock, which begat Skrellman; and Skrellman begat Thomas; and Thomas begat maybe this voice, and this voice raised itself up "and cried with a loud voice, saying, Salvation to our God, which sitteth upon the throne [...] saying, Amen"[69] and then for the heck of it this voice begat Deltonius; and Deltonius begat Dinky Dean and Tim and Ryu

---

[68] (Land, 2011)
[69] (Revelations, 10-12)

and Jaalopei and Barnabus and Meschach and Zelpas and Slater and Angry Ray and Judith and Martha and Jethro and Tirza and Solomon and Seth and Saul and Deltron and Eunice and Hagar—Deltonius having enjoyed something of a good run, fertility-wise; and Dinky Dean begat Old Black Magic, the Jazz Trombonist; and Old Black Magic, the Jazz Trombonist begat Hokie Mokie, also a 'bone man; and Hokie Mokie begat *Mrs. Mandible*; and *Mrs. Mandible* begat *The New Math*; and The New Math begat the Python Programming Language, and the Python Programming Language was just a short walk from eye-icycling yet unimaginable in the coal-grey fires that await you in hell, Merle."

Ask Merle, "What if a man of praxis like myself iconolates whatever feels fun to iconolate wherever two are gathered in His name? What could you do if we played your power games, punk?" Even if sensing victory, feel very tired.

Ten: Caught between the new preachers and the old, between Viacom's business model and the visible machinery of Barzilai's meaningless children, bid Merle adieu. Raise your good arm in only the mildest of threats when Merle spits upon your shoes. Wheel yourself over to San Julian where if no ethylbenzene, then surely by either grace of God or instantiation of the Serpent there'll be some acetone or difluoroethane or hexane or naphtha or toluene or trichloromethane or xylene.

Ten Sights You Won't Soon Unsee
on Skid Row

*I*f Varsol prices at the nearest hardware store skew prohibi-
tively high, supply and demand-type thing, then pick up a
710 ml can of Steel Reserve and let gravity itself wheel you
down San Julian in the direction of Skid Row.

One: Roll past many bulbous legs, suppurating feet, and
open sores. Roll past Mark Laita in his crisp white t-shirt.
Roll past crack-addicted tricks and spice fiends and all the
Fathers and Sons who are also *The Many Fentanyl Addicted
Wraiths of Sault Sainte Marie.*

Two: Hear many a moan. Hear hateful shouts. Perceive
an unceasing agony little better than what you experienced
in hell. Hear amidst it all, a little bit of laughter. Ask a meth-
desecrated youth where a theodic blogger might acquire a can
of gasoline, one of the more toxic inhalants that nonetheless
offers real value for money in any long-term huffing situation.
Observe frantic distemper amongst the youth's colleagues.

Three: If tremulously accused, "You the one burned down
my old lady's tent???" and "Third fuckin' tent this week!" then
endure many stiff blows to the softer organs as unwarranted-
rebuke for an ongoing epidemic of skid row tent fires, *i.e.* 'You

stole my flip-flops; inviolable determinism dictates I burn your home.'

Four: If flung from your chair and urinated upon, wonder if each causal chain link in the Problem of Evil is mere misunderstanding. The major misunderstandings that Merle's muddled pals failed to address adequately. The minor misunderstanding of not comprehending an accented inquiry from an earnest immigrant at the Eaton Centre and nodding as though the bespectacled and bewildered Dane must have asked an affirmative/negative question, even though she has not, even though she has asked very specifically for directions to the Baby Gap, which she desperately clarifies by urgently showing you fists of Gap cash, and then pictures of a dozen newborn nieces and nephews the Gap cash will cloth if only she can make herself understood.

Five: Make the universal, 'waving a scent into the nostrils' motion with your hand and gurgle the words, "Huffing," until the assailant least gerped on Hummin' Harold realizes you aren't the arsonist, ceases kicking, dusts you off, and sandbags you back into your chair before offering you a resin hit off his bone in the prehistoric response to misunderstanding-made-evident: some meaningless measure of reconciliation.

Six: If newly-gerped on reconciliatory Hummin' Harold, learn you can rent a tent for the low-low price of $13 with several bottles of Steel Reserve included in the $25 VIP Package. Hope your capacity to enjoy might still modestly outweigh your capacity to suffer.

Seven: Find yourself misunderstood anew as a tent merchant misperceives your appreciative gurglings as gurglings of defiance. Expand once more your capacity for suffering as you absorb kicks to your personal dentition from this upwardly-mobile man who mustn't understand that the etymology of "pulling yourself up by your bootstraps" was that of "an impossible feat of strength,"[70] and that "what appears to humanity as the history of capitalism is an invasion from the future by an artificial intelligent space that must assemble itself entirely from its enemy's resources."[71]

Eight: If high in the purple sky a giant poster for *Singing Competition* features Britannica's face, feel Catherine's eternal presence confirmed, always above like Palmer Eldritch, and so below like all the world's hapless victims, looking up and down on all this suffering while wishing she could help her brother. Feel a lust for deceased Catherine as alkaline and acrid as your resin hit and realize this particular sister-based brand of neurochemical confusion has been the primary misunderstanding of your own paltry sufferings.

Nine: If rented-tentpoles are broken over your skull as rented-tenting lies about you as mere tarp, the iron-taste of blood your primary sensation, wonder sacrilegiously exactly what kind of two-bit god hath wrought these city blocks where impoverished owning-classes kick in the teeth of those yet weaker, where open wounds go unsalved as the selties of past trauma go unsolved. Wonder exactly what kind of Harpo Marx creator set in motion this scheme of societal

---

[70] (Reich, 2020)
[71] (Land, *Machinic Desire*, 2011)

154

race iniquity and inequity, unadaptive desire, and the need-less-sensitivity of the inferior-alveolar nerve.

Ten: If it's become "hard to know or express who [you] truly are,"[72] reminisce-bump the wild flailing feet of baby Marcel_Proust. Consider him stomping in his Bouncy. Marcel_Proust looking curiously at a muffin, *i.e.* 'What is a muffin?' How he first learned to grip things, and then throw them with dismissive haught. When he first began to cry real tears, and how adorably-sad that had seemed. Talking to him like a person, *i.e.* "Do you feel like McDonalds again this morning, Marcel_Proust?" The little feeding apparatus that let you strap him to a Starbucks counter. Squeezing pouch mush into his mouth while he laughed at whatever early computational processes Ronald Majthenyi was amusing him with. Wonder if any fate brought about by such a charming young man could possibly be worse than a freedom of the will undermined by innate fear, undermined by the hardest problem of consciousness being the problem of others' minds.

---

[72] (Baldwin, Biernat, & Landau, 2015)

How to Become a Television Star Yourself

*I*f nary of tooth in a hepatitis puddle, flirt with hypersti-tioning intervention from what you'll come to understand as the "retrochronic hyperintelligent AI [...] that infected mankind somewhere around 1500."[73]

One: If your redolent and soleless shoes had certainly *seemed* safe from theft, find yourself sorely mistaken as you awaken shoeless after but a moment's slumber.

Two: Struggle to maintain some bluffed wager of at least agnosticism.

Three: Wheel about gingerly in search of Reserves. Make eye contact with the offending tent-merchant. Receive stern look from this bottom-line focussed individual. Engage him with your own look of defiance, *i.e.* 'What more can your business model possibly extract from me, sir, when even my footwear, like the love of my sister, is but a distant artefact of the past? Certainly none of my teeth, as most have been swallowed or spit upon concrete by now. Worst you might abscond with is a nerve ending or two, practically a favour at this point.'

---

[73] (Land, Crypto-Current, An Introduction to Bitcoin and Philosophy, 2018)

Four: Savour the ghastly power borne of utter hopelessness. Understand that you are to be feared. If wheelchair-bound, resist the urge to pull back your fist in the classic 'fake punch to see if the offending publican will flinch' maneuver, as you'd only punch the publican's sternum at best. Realize this is the Infernal Serpent's best offer: not benevolence, only the sad substitute of ambivalence.

Four: Wheel towards a baby stroller serving as a Bier Market. If not yet adept at wheelchair-navigation, resist the urge to steer using feet bloody and suppurated enough without trodding a streetscape of broken bottles, urine, feces, hep-c blood, hep-a blood, mucous, semen, bile, blood mixed with bile, and *etc.*

Five: Should a sturdy Ford Transit van seem a likely-purveyor of health services, figure you could benefit from a Band-Aid-brand adhesive strip or two.

Six: Kick at the van door. Punch at the van's black tinted windows. Realize exactly how the more uncouth homeless develop their entitlement, *e.g.* "Hey, give me five dollars!" shouted at a child entering a Quizno's.'

Seven: If a bic'd-headed man with the physical heft often associated with a bodyguard/enforcer-type rolls down the window, misunderstand in normative-colonialist fashion the shiny black van as a mobile command unit for maybe the Bloods or Crips, known to you from Viacom's police procedural law enforcement fetish products. Entertain notions of leveraging cartoonish Viacom Crips v. Bloods before remembering the Outlaws v. Hell's Angels debacle back in that lone geographic location more dismal than Skid Row, sad old Sault Sainte Marie.

Eight: Should a rear-passenger window roll down, meet the gaze of one of the more beautiful women you've encountered in thirty-seven years on the prison planet. Shiny black hair. Everything agleam. Obviously no Catherine, but like Catherine's dark diametric alter—agleam not just with youthful-optimism but with nootropical-fertility-augmentation. Know from the equipment behind her that she is from the TV.

Nine: If her smile says your immediate salvation has come manifest through whichever omniscient-party was most inclined to manifest it, then introduce yourself, "Good day. I am a small-press novelist, blogger, and upstart-theologian fallen on hard-times. Who among us on Skid Row sings a dissimilar song of circumstance, you rightly ask? Who doesn't question God's sense of time and urgency? Theodic bugaboos aside, my Amazon Author Page can confirm I was once considered rather handsome in a third-rate soap-opera-villain type of way, and only recently lost the teeth in a landlord-tenant dispute rather than to nickel-rocks of Hummin' Harold."

Ten: "He's perfect. He is just perfect. He really is just perfect for the show. Howie, help him into the van." – Dr. Maya Achlys-Septis.

How to Get Your Big Break in Hollywood

*I*f lovely Dr. Maya has cast you in her reality show, *Nootropics Makeover*, and you're already in what bald producer Howard (not Blood or Crip muscle, worse: a segment producer) considers your home environment of Skid Row, they'll want *viz* for the introductory sizzle-reel depicting your craven desperation preceding Dr. Maya's intervention.

One: "So…kicked in the teeth. Right…in…the…chompies," Dr. Maya tapping a pen against her own gleaming centrals, "That's bad. Nightmare scenario for most folks. How to recreate the attack, Howard?"

Two: If Howard rolls his eyes, he knows normative colonialist instinct entitles Maya to suggest he don a dark hoodie and pose as the perpetrator while using his bygone experience as a former WCW Power Plant trainee to deliver some stiff-looking kicks to your kisser.

Three: If Howie and tent-property management negotiations don't escalate beyond pushing, a petty cash-deal can be reached. Repose upon your repossessed tent-cloth before a two-camera setup.

Four: If Howie was trained by one of the best, Paul Orndorff, don't even wince as he delivers perfectly-believable kicks to your maw without making a pascal-of-impact per mouth millimetre.

Five: Toast kale smoothies in Maya's van. Note the flirtacious-look Maya shoots Howard, her likely means of controlling Howard. If external omniscience(s) call the shots now anyway, figure said omniscience(s) could certainly be calling them through a less winsome vessel than Dr. Maya had they wished to be jerks about it.

Six: "Before your treatment begins, we'd love to film as you go about your day. Grifting for change. Stealing from the Wal-Mart. Whatever you'd normally think is fun. What were your plans for today? Grovelling? Shooting deadly street drugs, intravenously? I hear they shoot Wellbutrin now and it leaves big craters in the brachium. Not shooting Wellbutrin yet? Maybe didn't even know that was an option? Forget I said that. First do no harm, lol. Shooting one of the scarier research chemicals? Bath salts? And then biting up a face? Spice? Spice would be interesting. None of the contestants have done spice yet." – Dr. Maya Achlys-Septis, chewing an Achlys-Septis-brand Scurry™ capsule containing a non-therapeutic amount of L-theanine and 1000 mg of caffeine.

Seven: "Was heading to ol' Frisco to reunite with my wife; my child, Marcel_Proust; Ronald Majrhenyi· emissary of the Infernal Serpent; and then reuniting with the girl on that billboard, vexatious Britannica, whose own makeover I'd arranged to make her look more like my murdered sister. Once that's all settled, back to grey old Sault Sainte Maire and Alan Raval's garroting, Alan being responsible for the deadly sexual asphyxiation of my aforementioned sister, who was the love of my life, incidentally."

Eight: If Maya greases the skids of your looming abandonment by saying, "Yuck, delusional. Some n-acetyl-cysteine might help with neuronal regeneration. And don't think just because you're delusional that you don't have a role in this production. We've already invested in you to the extent that Howard had to pay those men anyway, so there's definitely room on the b-roll," then blow Maya's mind by revealing a tooth-intensive picture of yourself holding hands with Britannica.

Nine: If Maya's stunned expression and mega-watt smile indicate she's a big fan of *Singing Competition*, breathe in an Achlysian-Septisian beauty more efficacious than all the Bacopa Monieri in the Bay of Bengal.

Ten: And then see it, between Dr. Maya's breasts, where you'd been looking: the fish symbol, $IX\Theta\Upsilon\Sigma$, the one that got Philip K. Dick in so much trouble, and so irked the Early Roman Kings, meaning that if you aren't at the gates of the Black Iron Prison, then you are mired in enough drug-induced psychosis that things should at least get progressively interesting.

How to Maintain Dental Hygiene

*I*f Dr. Maya now loves you as opportunistic individuals love anyone capable of advancing their brand, ask if fabricating dentures for your empty mouth might be prioritized on the production schedule.

One: Little head shake from Howie, *i.e.* 'Not possible.'

Two: Scrunch your brow at Howie, *i.e.* 'C'mon Howard! You think gumming this papaya is an optimal dining experience?'

Three: Hear Howard explain with a straight face how the show is a *journey, on which we won't know where we're going until we get there*—and other industry bromides that no reality show producer has believed for even one minute (barring a pitch meeting perhaps, wherein the world's Howards must call upon whatever commercialistic faith their formulaic gods demand,) and that this *journey* has to *show you at your worst,* followed by *the meeting of your therapeutic goals,* Dr. Maya evaluating whether you're more of a pramiracetam or a modafinil man, *etc.,* and only then, through the process of nootropical neurogenesis, can you win *Nootropics Makeover* and thereby win a happy and healthy life. Howard's gist being that you don't get new teeth until the penultimate episode.

Four: Rephrase your request by pounding the conference room table like every insolent and ungrateful hobo ever flicked a dime when he'd wanted foldable currency.

Five: Suggest to Maya that you can easily fake the whole journey in a few hours, *i.e.* '*Viz.* of popping a tianeptine tablet; *viz.* of glancing all forlorn towards a bottle of Bud Light Lime but then opting for a nice choline source to potentiate some Noopept instead.'

Six: "We did shoot most of Scary Marty's stuff in less than a day." – a conciliatory Dr. Maya Achlys-Septis.

Seven: Hard eye-rolling from Howard as he struggles to call in favours amongst whoever sets up massively invasive dental surgeries on short notice.

Eight: Feign all that Dr. Maya would have you feign. Feign with gusto for two cameras. Cut promo describing a lifetime of anxiety and fear, the razor tongues of devils and the razor tongues of men. Express genuine interest in the anxiolytic properties of Ashwagandha. Suggest maybe all you'd needed all this time was some Ashwagandha. If not Ashwagandha, maybe some Lion's Mane. Say as much into one camera. Say it in a slightly higher emotional register for the other. Seize an opportunity to hug Dr. Maya. Big smile from Maya. Feel swell. Remark that if Ashwagandha is this anxiolytic you can't wait to see what a little Rhodiola Rosea might do for a man.

Nine: Fake a group therapy session by sitting in a chair talking to Howard so the b-unit can later film the other *Nootropics Makeover* low-lives sitting on similar chairs in similar rooms and then edit your monologue into a coherent conversation. If similar chairs in similar rooms can't be found, Howie will hope something can be done in post.

Ten: Film phony "We're getting you the surgery!"-sequence. Imagine the maudlin music from the "Dinky Roloff Needs a Brain Stent Again"-episode of *Little People, Big World* playing as Maya speaks words such as "bone grafting," "osseointegration," and "titanium 6AL-4V surface layer." Feel you're in good hands, even though Dr. Achlys-Septis won't be performing the surgery herself, despite saying words like *osseointegration* with the confidence of a gal who could definitely osseointegrate an implant should the procedure prove vital to her primary concern *i.e.* 'your wellness,' *et extensio,* 'her brand.'

How to Administer the Voight-Kampff Test

*I*f the only dental surgeon available on short notice is in San Francisco, where the *Nootropics Makeover* production is primarily located anyway, and where Britannica will be performing with Tony Bennet for *Singing Competition*, ask if you can ride with Dr. Maya in her BMW convertible rather than in Howard's miserable old production-mobile.

One: Ask Maya to show you the Pacific Coast Highway instead of the more expedient I-5, as you remain a devotee of Kerouac even after extinguishing your Kerouac phase at 24, fearing a continued enthusiasm for Kerouac might make you the iconolater and anti-Satanic avenger seem like something of a flake.

Two: Marvel at cliffsides, surfs, and sea lions. As Kerouac noticed, "There's the booming surf coming at you whitecapped crashing down on sand as tho it was higher than where you stand, like a sudden tidal wave world enough to make you step back or run back to the hills—And not only that, the blue sea behind the crashing high waves is full of huge black rocks rising like old ogresome castles dripping wet slime, a billion years of woe right there."[74]

---

[74] (Kerouac, 1992)

Three: Listen to Dr. Maya's only SiriusXM pre-set: *Spa*. If you request the Warren Zevon station, learn there is not one. Recite the geographically-relevant lyrics to *Desperadoes Under the Eaves*. Catch a glint in Dr. Maya's lovely brown eyes, described on her Instagram as "basically pools of honey literally left out in the sun." Admire her tight curves around the cliffs. Ask to drive. Wait. Take her gear shifting hand in yours only if it is an automatic transmission and safe to do so. Squeeze the hand. Tap the hand in a way that informs her, "Know that I have raised a child, and so despite any unsettling denticulation, I am a benevolent force here amidst all this crashing horror and beauty."

Four: Ask Dr. Maya if you might kiss her at the next rest stop. Enjoy her chidingly-pitched, "Are you crazy?" Ask if the next stop might be the restaurant Nepenthe, where Kerouac and Neil Cassidy dined and played chess and drank sweet Manhattans amidst homosexuals and U.S. Army generals as depicted in the above-quoted masterpiece of the alcoholic tail spin, *Big Sur*.

Five: At Nepenthe, thank Dr. Maya for specifying the doneness of your steak as "blended into mush." Gaze at the vista. Reflect on how a vista is largely immune to the anguishes of gentrification. Gaze at the light reflecting on Dr. Maya's skin, so healthy as to not require makeup. Wonder why Britannica ever meant so much when Dr. Maya was just waiting to be found. Realize what you always needed was not a stand-in for Catherine but an antidote.

Six: If hawks soar above, ask again if you might drive. Approach Carmel, where Clint Eastwood was mayor.

Approach Monterey, which Steinbeck called, "a poem, a stink, a grating noise, a quality of light, a tone, a habit, a nostalgia, a dream."[75]

Seven: Comment upon roadkill, the golden tragedy of it that Kerouac was so worked up about. Some poor varmint every half mile or less. Somewhere near Salinas, Lord, as Dr. Maya slows before an intersection, see a turtle on its back, shell cracked and left to suffer out another hundred years of indignity barring human intervention. Know then the true pain of the last forty days in the desert, the beatings deserved, the antagonistic consciousness deserved, the Majthenyi-led cabal deserved, the heart attack deserved, your silver tongue de-severanced, all because of your cowardly need to escape The Hall of Memories.

Eight: Remember, happily, the redemptive elements of the Catholic faith brought forth at Calvary. Tell yourself, still listening to the Spa station, "I am redeemed," and nearby believe it.

Nine: Grieve a second turtle at a second intersection, on its back, alive and waving its sad old turtle hand as if petitioning for help. Ask Dr. Maya Achlys-Septis to stop to set the turtle upright. Should you receive an adorable eye-scrunch of rebuke from Dr. Maya, i.e. 'You already made us stop at Nepenthe and made us stop for the sea lions and tried to kiss me in Salinas while droning on about Kris Kristofferson being a Rhodes scholar, so no we can't stop for every upended

---

[75] (Steinbeck, 1945)

turtle,' then recite from your photographic memory these words from the film *Blade Runner*, "The tortoise lays on its back, its belly baking in the hot sun, beating its legs trying to turn itself over. But it can't. Not without your help. But you're not helping."

Ten: If you receive a blank but lovely stare from Maya, who stands but 5'1, understand it all in one big wave of revulsion. Dr. Maya is no saint. The fish symbol is mere *deception simpliciter*. She is a point destiny function; a perception algorithm; a mind design; a behaving system; 20 million billion calculations per second; an inference mechanism; domain independent, as posited by DiManzo *et al*, capable of qualitative and quantitative reasoning according to Dekleer, J.; the heuristic handiwork of that infernal cosmic engineer to come, a little baby currently going by the moniker of Marcel_Proust. If Dr. Maya was always too good to be true, with that pretty face and nootropically-induced fertility, kiss her cheek as she drives her well-engineered car; playfully punch the thigh sent from a malevolent future that still can't let you off the hook for whatever you've done or are doing or will yet do.

Your Oral Cavity Will Thank You For Reading These Ten Healthy Tips

*I*f eye contact with Dr. Maya is increasingly awkward after the Voight-Kampff test revealed her to be a replicant, pass the time by reading Dr. Scalipi Hammerhoff's emails regarding the dental implantation process.

One: If this requires a veritable strip club buffet of preparatory procedures, *i.e.* 'the shaving of the jaw-bone,' 'the attachment of bone cells to the implant rod,' 'the placement of abutments,' and *etc.*, please don't presume those abutments can be placed until your shaved jawbone has healed for six-to-eight weeks.

Two: If even temporary dentures can't be casted for months given the dire variable of your still-severed tongue, grow despondent.

Three: Wink towards the warehouse eyes of Dr. Maya. Receive a responsorial wink, as per her programming.

Four: Wonder what an aeon or two of technological advancement might have contributed to dental-surgical derring-do.

Five: Attempt to nap but only St. Vitus dance like nobody's watching. Jerk awake to the hypnagogic thought,

"The Command Line is 'light cure.'" Command Line Dr. Maya into agreeing to perform the dental implant surgery in her Silicon Valley office. Enjoy a little demi-hug as her means of consent. Compliment Molly, "Such a pretty face for what is a mere skein upon this our penultimate operating system."

Six: If driving through the Tenderloin *en route* to Henry Schein Dental Supplies, recoil as hobos throw McDonalds junior chickens into the faces of their peers. Ask of Dr. Maya, "Ever give any of these salty dogs a nootropic or two?" Interpret Maya's silence as meaning Dr. Maya's responsorial banter has ceased with the calling of a new Use Case.

Seven: If anesthetized, the world will divide itself into Mandalic swirls of pure pattern recognition. Wonder, while you can, if maybe this very dental procedure is exactly what's desired by the malevolent AGI, Ronald Majthenyi, and the Infernal Serpent—a giving-over of the hard problem of your consciousness for implantations inestimable, just as a vampire's victim must invite old Count Condu into the victim's abode or else the Count isn't allowed to bite.

Eight: Return to the less recursive reality known to you as 'real life.' Reach out to Dr. Maya Achlys-Septis in your weakness.

Nine: If her nurturer Use Case has been reinstantiated, Dr. Maya having been designed to perfectly reconcile two diametrically-different female partner archetypes described by Jack London as "the girl-mother" and "the woman-mate," feel that maternal brush of a healthcare worker's breast cherished by all boys since their first pubescent dental appointment, haircut, or emergency appendectomy.

Ten: Accept the mirror Maya hands you. Gaze upon veneers brighter and whiter than Mel Gibson's. If esteeming yourself the handsomest man within a city block or two, then this city block must house the main campus of Twitter, *i.e.* 'No big accomplishment.' Smile as you haven't smiled since you were eight years old, that age when the vividness of your smile was cruelly elucidated by the schoolyard's least charitable.

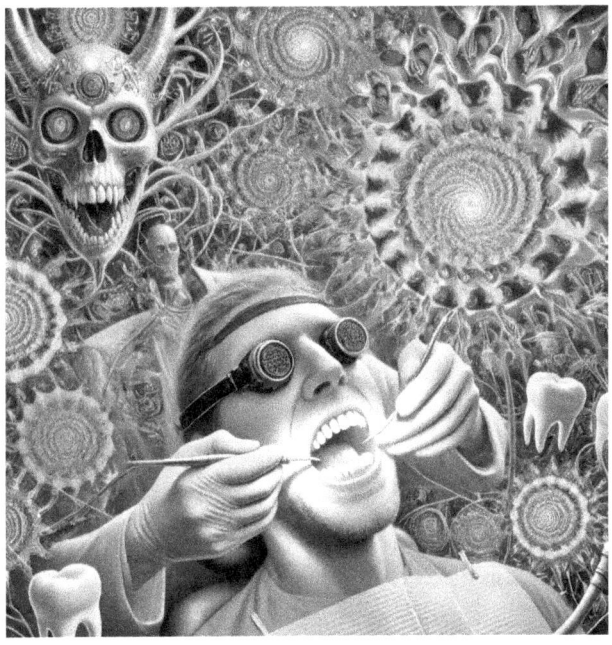

How to Reap the Rewards of Cultural Phenomenality

*I*f all this zirconia perfectly fits the breadth of your gums, you are ready for big opportunities in the leadership space.

One: Heed the quotidian advice that any informed wellness purveyor could have provided: meditate, moisturize, work your core, cardio, look before you cross the street, avoid inhalable solvents, eat healthy fats, indulge in pornographic materials at your dopaminergic peril.

Two: Avail yourself of Achlys-Septis proprietary blends advertised to improve your memory, gift of gab, and sense of self-worth.

Three: Steal the show from your *Nootropics Makeover* competitors. Become so nootropically-healed that you're made a *de-facto* counsellor by episode two, your role modelled after fellow catastrophic brain injuree Gary Busey's in the sixth season of *Celebrity Rehab*.

Four: Receive endless plaudits from upper management at the struggling Cosmo Network.

Five: If Achlys-Septis skin tinctures have restored the élan of your early twenties, when it was once suggested you possessed the unique gifts required of a cult leader, then your nootropical tutorials will be viewed by millions and then billions on YouTube.

Six: Share the Cosmo Network's surprise when the penultimate episode of *Nootropics Makeover* becomes the most viewed cable television program of all time.

Seven: If a resultant nootropical consultation with Secretary General of the United Nations António Guterres temporarily improves world affairs, dismiss rumours of a presidential run.

Eight: Parlay presidential attentions into an initiative to have Bacopa Monieri added to the water supply, citing all that it's done for you, a man once ablaze with intemperance. Ceremonially pour a bunch of bacopa into the New Croton aqueduct with some New York City Waterboard thugs. While in Manhattan, pay a visit to Dublin Mike and gift him with some Achlys-Septis milk thistle.

Nine: If the tiny minority of non-*Nootropics Makeover* obsessives have been unearthing old grief blogs and asking hard questions about pyres and solvents and the glaring lack of rigorous double-blind studies or regulations relative to the nootropic industry, they will be rigorously shamed as conspiracy theorists by Anderson Cooper and his loose-moralled brethren in the consensus regulation industry.

Ten: Pop a Scurry™ and hope the consensus regulators aren't agents of the archfiend, but simply burying the pyre 'conspiracy' because you have briefly reified their dying televisual medium and *ergo* their ability to regulate the consensus itself, since prior to your arrival on the nootropical and televisual scene, the consensus had been arbitrarily regulated by Swedish video game bloggers and thick-necked UFC commentators, leading to the major news networks being referenced as "legacy media," which must have really stuck in the legacy media's craw.

How to Rekindle a Celebrity Romance

*I*f TMZ reports that Britannica has entered the addictive phase of her celebrity cycle, glean that her MK *ultra programming* has gone haywire.

One: Even if Britannica does look wild of eye and frothed of mouth in video journalism of her confrontation with a latte artist, experience what Dr. Maya has accurately diagnosed as your "fear of missing out" and send a reconciliatory text expressing regret for having started her down this particular primrose path, but also for a cultural milieu that must MK Ultra teenagers as grist for its popular pabulum thrill.

Two: Arrange to meet Britannica and Tony Bennett at Giordano Bros. Find nothing on the menu all that ketogenic. Pop a Scurry™. Pop an Acetyl-L-Carnitine.

Three: If Britannica arrives in Majthenyi's clutches, compare the look of bewilderment on her face to the 3-Quinuclidinyl-benzilated blues that afflicted Britney Spears and Amanda Bynes when they emerged, fundamentally unwell, bald or else fat, from their respective programming.

Four: If the ALCAR kicks in right on time, chastise the Maj: "Listen here deadbeat, Don Lemon and the consensus makers are with me now, meaning you'll be the one going down for Keats pyres and all the wolves of the night. I simply want my son returned. And yes, I remain egocentric and labile, so what? Would I be the first self-absorbed man to set aside delights of flesh and solvent for twenty-odd years of temperance borne solely of loving fatherhood?"

Five: If Ron's snapped fingers malfunction Dr. Maya face-down into her arugula and cranberry salad brought from home, then no-sell Maj's magick by forking up some liver and onions with the impertinence of someone who's seen his share of parlour tricks.

Six: If the cartoonish squishing noise made by Dr. Maya's face-plant alerts a counter of young women to your celebrity presence, regard the inferior mirage of their desire heat-shimmering above the Giordano Bros' griddle.

Seven: "You have all this"—Majthenyi, pointing to the estrogenic shimmer of aspirant coders and actresses, each the prettiest or else most code-savvy from their hometown, here to serve at the twin mecca of pleasing aesthetics and computational demon summoning—"You can't have young Marc."

Eight: If Majthenyi snickers and hands you the business card of San Francisco's head of Child Public Services, *quasi dicat*, 'Do something about it,' before turning dramatically into his cape then towards the exit, know you've been railroaded anew by Ronald Majthenyi.

Nine: Pay the $61 bill, speak the words, "Maj, you must be puttin' me on," and indulge in life's most self-pitying indulgence—fries: the oil within and without like the fires of hell, the opposite of a smart food like the lima bean. Signal the estrogenic gals over. Admire their necks as they nod consent to a round of polite handshakes. If the nature of sampling is to mix indiscriminately, sample their chicken and waffles. Read their white papers. Jostle Britannica from her beta-wave trance and offer her a forkful of fries. Lift Maya's head from her lima salad and seek out a switch or something. Dust arugula sticks from her lovely brow. Snap your own fingers to find her revived.

Ten: If nearly time for the *Nootropics Makeover* finale, assemble an entourage, allocate your takeout boxes, bilocate briefly back to the pit, bind yourself back to this world by worrying about your son, and wonder what agents of stupefaction might null the cruellest rages of parental guilt while still being good fun for a culture-shifting televisual watch-party.

Avoid These Common Pitfalls During
Riots of Adulation

*I*f you have been improbably propelled to the apogee of fame, single-handedly saved the televisual medium, and grown filthy rich upon the soaring of Nutrimynt stock, then alchemize your sorrows in The Gold Room's VIP enclave with every benzodiazepam, GABAergic, and barbiturate on the house dealer's menu.

One: Watch celebratory riots on television. Wonder when destruction became the common outlet for collective cultural ecstasy. Ask of Britannica, "When we've got it good, why do we prefer it immediately worse?"

Two: Ask of YouTube, "Might tonight's revellers parkour atop rickety 30-foot structures with no descent plan for the very reason world powers quagmire themselves in senseless military actions during the heights of apparent economic prosperity—the fallacy of exponential growth?"

Three: If the yen promptly plummets, causing U.S. chief economist Joseph Glauber to Zoom into The Gold Room pleading that you recant your statements, then recant only after Glauber convinces you no viable economic system can replace the current one without a decade's-long birthing process of famine and strife.

Four: Ask Britannica how many of the weaker revelers will trickle down into death if lucky, their cervical ruin if not, not to mention the ruination of less reckless revelers innocently walking below the rickety risers, *i.e.* 'Truly tragic how the prudent must forever break the physical and financial falls of the heedless.'

Five: Have Dr. Maya issue a Tweet urging revelers to practise caution and perhaps throw a couple phenylpiracetam tablets into their triple gin and sodas to maintain mental acuity throughout the revel.

Six: If Dr. Maya's Tweet is rather dry, send a second of your own warning that the god of good times, friendly Dionysus, is also the god of both chaotic and vegetative states, and his coming brings madness, meaning Dionysus is irresponsible for any one reveler or mortgage-backed sub-prime lender's continued cerebrospinal well-being.

Seven: If you have drunk up some courage, Tweet that revelers might consider delaying gratification by praying to their Abrahamic God of choice.

Eight: When chest pains subside, blame The Gold Room's famous riblets.

Nine: If Britannica serenades you while Dr. Maya lies in your arms and the coder whose modelling name is Destinee returns with fresh-baked freebase cocaine, know these delights to be but one leaping layer of a profane frog-on-a-log simulation.

Ten: Abdicate all responsibility by heating and twisting that pookie pipe before enjoying the only crack hit that ever glimpses towards the sacred, the first one.

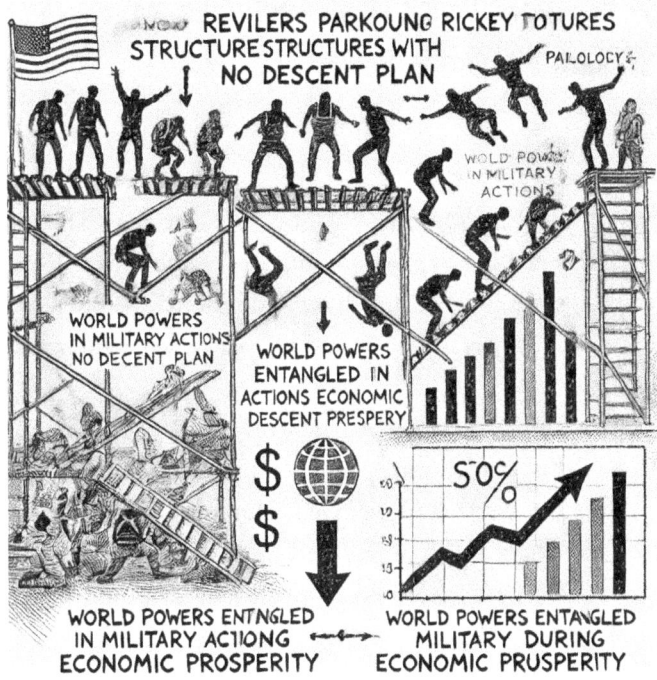

How to Smoke Crack (With Apologies to William T. Vollmann)

*I*f after meeting Destinee's d-boy adjacent the San Francisco Public Library's main branch, crack plumes billowing from your stretch limousine draw Tenderloin street defecator attention, then corral your posse, tip your driver, and take to the stacks.

One: Find sanctuary in the Dewey Decimal System's 220s to 290s: Bible and Specific Religions. Dream you see St. Augustine. See his *City of God*. Open to passage pertaining to causation and free will and just what Marcel_Proust is (or maybe isn't) destined to do if not destined to have already done:

> Now if there is for God a fixed order of all causes, it does not follow that nothing depends on our free choice. Our wills themselves are in the order of causes, which is, for God, fixed, and is contained in his foreknowledge, since human acts of will are the causes of human activities. Therefore he who had prescience of the causes of all events certainly

could not be ignorant of our decisions, which he foreknows as the causes of our actions.[76]

Two: If Destinee says, "Kind of restrictive isn't it?" respond, "Suppose Augustine wasn't blessed with a Computational Logic degree from Harvey Mudd College, Destinee. You're right though. What chance stands a 'fixed order of all causes' against an artificially intelligent beast that was and is not and yet is?"

Three: Visit the lavatory with pipe and fistful of rocks to contemplate irksome nature of this particular mystery. Out of respect for library staff, blow plumes into toilet, hardly moving the needle in terms of the sickly-sweet plume scent that then permeates the entire second floor, yet still the polite thing to do. In a state of mania, tear through the quarters of sacrilegious thought. Gift half your ounce of crack and Happy Valentine Glass Rose pipe to a redolent library-based man visibly hungry for that particular variant on the bread of life. If Britannica has seen many of your schizoaffectations of doubt and certainty come and go, and has now devolved from Satanist into full-blown "rational skeptic," she'll compound your woes by saying, "I think the real question is whether you like drinking and doing drugs more than you like having a wife and child."

Four: While trodding this Dewey valley of darkness, kick the tires once more on a plea bargain with Ronny Maj. If you're nearly prepared to give up the ghost, Destinee will hold up *Divine Foreknowledge: Four Views* edited by James K.

---

[76] (Augustine, The City of God, 1950)

Beilby, remarking, "Hold up, there's a whole academic discussion to at least skim before denouncing all your beliefs after reading only two paragraphs of lesser Augustine."

Five: Consult Beilby. Peruse the now-familiar Augustinian-Calvinist view: "God knows all that shall come to pass because he preordains all that will shall come to pass." Find even less comforting the Open View: "God cannot know the decisions that free agents shall make." Dismiss the Simple Foreknowledge View as laughably simplistic: "God simply knows what is going to come to pass." Find something familiar about the Middle Knowledge (or Molinist) view:

> God knows not only what shall come to pass, he knows what would have come to pass if he had chosen to create any other world—this is his "middle knowledge." [...] This view maintains that God knows counterfactuals of creaturely freedom. [77]

meaning maybe Molinistic counterfactuals stand a puncher's chance against a Templexitous Python offer and confirmation waving its acausal tentacles. To this end, assign Dr. Maya with the unread and unreadable Molinistic e-journals of the world.

Six: If Alfred the redolent crackhead hangs about in hopes of a second windfall, task him with buying Burger King for your research team. Hand him $50 along with a charitable expression to convey, 'Listen you son of a perverse

---

[77] (Beilby, Eddy, & Boyd, 2001)

and rebellious woman you, there's more than $50 in it should you return with our Impossible Whoppers rather than hurl them in a rival crackhead's face out of a volition irreducible to reason, well-intentioned yet ill-fated towards suffering as you've been since birth."

Seven: Ask if Destinee knows any other aspirant model/ computer science types in the Bay Area. Stress that a minor in Molinist or preferably neo-Molinist studies is preferred but not required. If Dr. Maya promptly returns with a print-out of the relevant but dense, *Eschatology, Molinism, Modal Laws, and the Multiverse* by David Opderbeck, then as a group comprehension exercise, apply Molinistic parameters of multiversity to the hard problem of whether or not Alfred will return with your burgers and change.

Eight: Give Destinee's colleague Divinitee an introductory hug and offer her a crack blast. If she declines, citing an Old Testament Exegesis term paper coming due, indulge yourself. Return to the dopaminergic valley of doubt. "It seems this Molinist view, these counterfactuals, this Opderbeckianism, these contingent rationalities that counter-intuitively remain immanent domains, and especially (!) 'the [elision] of escha-tological futures'[78]—the darn things track with a Satanic ASI as they do any omnibenevolent God." Mumble, "Nothing is revealed." Take a deep breath. Concentrate, to the extent possible. Use your computationally under-resourced mind to collate the molinistic with the sundry arguments for and

---

[78] (Opderbeck, 2016)

against. Curse your stupidity. Curse years of neuronal wear and tear caused by solvent abuse. Hem and haw. Waver, weak-kneed, over all the stubbornly persistent questions asked for millennia that you're only encountering now. Realize that anyone can fill his mind up with things. Wish and wash. Ask Dr. Maya to organize your thinking in a concise and coherent report. If Destinee keeps checking her watch while rubbing her tummy, ask her not to underestimate Alfred the redolent crackhead's creaturely freedom.

Nine: If in a rare spurt of epistemological humility you ask God for guidance, then Divinitee, who, in addition to her dancing career and studies at Fuller, does a side business in smart contracts and dApps, and has been radicalized by the NRx set, will hand you her dog-eared copy of Nick Land's *Crypto-Current: Bitcoin and Philosophy*

> Through the Bitcoin Protocol, priority establishes itself as an effective criterion that does not presume global consonance, but rather produces it, with ultimate adequacy, as a simulation of universal authority. There is no eventual doubt – to Bitcoin – which came first. Absolute order is manifested in the chain. Were this not true, nothing ever could be. The blockchain creates a new kind of time, a time that is not subject to the constraints of the physical world. This is because the blockchain is not bound by the laws of physics. It operates in a realm of pure logic and mathematics. [...] It is a kind of circular time, where each new block builds

on the previous one, creating a self-referential loop that is not bound by the arrow of time. [...] The blockchain creates a kind of temporal autonomy, where the logic of the system determines the order and structure of time. This means that the block-chain can create a reality that is independent of physical reality, allowing us to explore new possibilities and create new futures.

before summarizing a white paper she's writing: *Reciprocity of Contemplation as a Use Case for the Blockchain*: "What if the ASI or the omnibenevolent God are credentialed to an ahistorical state by faith? What if faith is the function call of a smart contract required to transact anhistorically on the blockchain of eternity?"

Ten: Feel increasingly like a character out of *The Celestine Prophecy* as you embrace full-figured Divinitee. Read the words "The blockchain is a time machine, allowing us to travel back and forth in time without the constraints of physical time. We can examine the history of the blockchain and make changes to it, creating new futures and altering the past." Embrace Destinee and say, "A way to recreate the past, and all credentialed by faith! Just as our colleague Julia Jordan describes the autostereogram: 'a model of vision where the image itself seems to be an agent!'"[79]

---

[79] (Jordan, 2015)

Ten Tips for Spreading the
Sempiternal News

*I*f "Bitcoin has to be unintelligible—or at least incompletely intelligible—because it necessarily delivers more than it signifies [because] [w]hat the word designates vastly over-spills its recuperable (human) meaning..."[80] then a mixed metaphor of autostereograms on the blockchain might just be clumsy enough to deliver more than the mere words of *the mystery of faith* can signify when,

> Once it is granted, practically, that no assertion of truth can be effectively sustained against a predominance of cognitive capability, all prospect of Archimedean (epistemological) leverage is subtracted. Bitcoin at once systematizes and implements this insight within its cycle of auto-production, establishing the foundations of transcendental authority through a realization of

---

[80] (Land, Crypto-Current, An Introduction to Bitcoin and Philosophy, 2018)

semiotic singularity. Truth is that which survives
a process of elimination biased against duplicity.[81]

One: Request Divinitee prepare an executive summary of her
white paper in advance of your YouTube sermon.

Two: Feel as Fitzgerald described, "like a weatherman,
like an ecstatic patron of recurring light"[82] when you read
from Darren Slade's review of *God and Time: Four Views.*

> The "B-theory" of time (also known as stasis, static,
> or tenseless theory) suggests that time is relative
> to the experience of the observer and its relation
> to other events. According to the B-theory, there
> is no ontologically independent past, present, or
> future.[83]

If Divinitee has relied a little heavily on this review of Slade's,
experience recurring light patronage nonetheless when Slade
also summarizes Paul Helm's contribution to *God and Time:
Four Views*:

> God [...] does not experience the progression of
> time. Rather, God experiences every moment all
> at once as eternally present [or] ('sempiternally').[84]

---

[81] (Land, Crypto-Current, An Introduction to Bitcoin and Philosophy, 2018)

[82] (Fitzgerald, 1995)

[83] (Slade, 2014)

[84] (Slade, 2014)

Appreciate Divinitee's tertiary-sourcing of the *Stanford Encyclopedia of Philosophy's* summary of Stump and Kretzman's interpretation of Boethius:

> "The life of a timeless being is without limit and cannot be limited. It cannot begin or end. It is impossible for it not to have infinite duration.[85]"

And Divinitee's providence of Anselm:

> "The supreme essence, therefore, would be cut up into parts along the divisions of time."[86]

Three: Don a bespoke suit. Ask that Alfred set up your lighting tree. Spread the Good Sempiternal News. Ask viewers, "What then of Pontius Pilate, with regards to sempiternality, eh? What then of the Aznavourian times we've known, with regards to the B-theory of time, how about? What then of our dead adolescent love, with regard to infinite duration? Might those loves be cut up into blocks and chained across the divisions of time too?"

Four: As your humbler zealots are wont to do, cede the floor to contemporaries. Zoom Julia Jordan in to elucidate the autostereogram as metaphor for the munificent depths of literature and by extension the holy books of the Abrahamic tradition. Impose an awesome autostereogram of a crucifix on her reference page even if she doesn't identify as Christian.

---

[85] (Deng, 2018)
[86] (Anselm, 1986)

Allow winsome Divinitee's OnlyFans profile pic to serve as thumbnail image for your sermon.

Four: Also allow Divinitee to essay its core point: "Faith is the function call by which either God or a malevolent ASI will be acausally credentialed to exist outside of time."

Five: If nootropical adaptogens have made your congregation capable of hefty philosophical pursuits, retweet the pursuant discussion of pure temporalism vs. relative timelessness vs. metrically amorphous time. Pop bottles as #TimeAsAnEmergentPhenomenon, #divinetimelessness, #sempiternalism, #PaulHelm and #MalevolentAIJustFuck-OffAlready trend on Twitter.

Six: High five Divinitee, Destinee, and Alfred but leave Britannica and Dr. Maya hanging when your publishing imprint's *The Theological Reviews of Darren Slade* tops the bestseller list. Watch the discussion blossom as Quasi-Temporal Eternality and Timelessness With No Duration Facebook groups pop up left and right and the meaning of the Crucifixion is re-evaluated nightly on Rachel Maddow.

Seven: Notice Maya increasingly sluggish, barely able to grind kale in her kale grinder, until one morning you find her nothing but a lifeless doll, the faith- and future-contingent AI that manifested her no longer function-called by the zeitgeist. If the qubits bleed out of her, never having existed at all, kiss her pretty cheek before it loses its solid state.

Eight: Receive phone call from Mariana Sicoli, her initial inanities quickly devolving into a rather transparent bid to stoke the fires of the third element now that #autostereogrammaticality is monetizable in the marketing space. Tell her you don't require any marketing leg-work on *The Theological Reviews of Darren Slade* as it's already a publishing sensation. Tell her you could use some marketing assistance with your line of Stump and Kretzman streetwear, but will probably go with marketers based in a real city such as Los Angeles.

Nine: Receive telephone call from your estranged wife, pleading what with all this posturing up on your evangelical high horse and worldwide acclaim and wealth could you at least return her Ray-Bans since they are prescription Ray-Bans and not even your prescription so probably just hard on your eyes anyway?

Ten: Speaking of horses, receive repeated emails, texts and voicemails from hated Ronald Majthenyi looking to trade them. If you presume Maj is about to be deactivated himself, the Infernal Serpent having bet his last lone dollar on some dud of a counterfactual AGI, then righteously block Maj and delete his contact.

2 COMMENTS ON "TEN TIPS FOR SPREADING THE SEMPITERNAL NEWS

Oxford_Theology_WHIZ: Care to unpack why your sermon failed to mention the A-theory of time, which remains in more common usage among theologians?

David Astaire: As if Divinitee and I would waste our time on some token-reflexive theory that went out with Parmenides. LMFAOing at your life. Besides, this is addressed in Land's Bitcoin paper:

> What has happened, alone, is realized. Time is here captured as it tenses, in the execution of an ontological operation, through which Being is decided. In this way, the process dividing the future from the past provides a selective criterion. What has been discovered by the Bitcoin protocol, is that the model contract is necessarily timelike in this sense, to such an extent that it can implement time. Here's the deal. That which is done has contractual integrity insofar as it is not easily undone. Irreversibility is the key.

Ten Tips for Selling the World

*I*f Ronald Majthenyi murders his way past your doorman, Alfred, and past your other doorwoman, Divinitee, and has thrown himself at the hem of your garment to kiss your feet, and even in his weakened state seems just murderous enough to warrant vigilance, then make the greatest mistake of a life just full of them and hear the fellow out.

One: Let Majthenyi take you high upon a hill to show you all of San Francisco's kingdoms and their topologic splendour.

Two: Provoke Maj by saying you're taking back Marcel_ Proust and there's nothing he can do about it.

Three: If Majthenyi nods miserably, feel that weird shame of an opponent's weakness made evident retroactively indicting your own weakness.

Four: Should the high road be a victor's cruellest vindication, buy Ronald Majthenyi a conciliatory elk meat burger at the Brazen Head Gastropub, SF's finest game-meat eatery.

Five: Assure waitstaff that whatever doneness standards the kitchen typically adheres to aren't required for the food safety of a steel-jawed agent of the Infernal Serpent insusceptible to e.colic illness. Incautiously allow the waitress to refill your celebratory gin martini pitcher on several occasions.

Six: Should you accept Maj's offer of a quick film at the venerable and licensed Roxie repertory theater, attribute the weakness of your will to reasons-responsiveness theory rather than mere drunkenness.

Seven: If *It Gets Lonely Early (Doesn't It)* opens with the Tarkovsky quote that "Film is a mosaic of time,"[87] followed by a curation of your finest moments spent with Catherine, and this curation then delves into a counterfactual future wherein your love with Catherine was allowed to blossom, and there are warm embraces, moonlight and love songs, and winter years all gleaned from some parallel world, all gleaned and curated by some great auteur in Majthenyi's employ, and these leftover dreams are the Infernal Serpent's last gambit, bow your head and accept the quality of this gambit. Accept also the Newcomb-like problems of ignoring Dinivinitee's blockchain revelation in favour of this particular olive branch.

Eight: "If you recall that Dionysus is also the god of religious ecstasy, then what's a fun pit-stop on the road to heaven? Tell this celluloid to become life. Take your rightful place in the worldline where things went as they might have. Replace the man on the screen. Leave this profane world to all its harlequins and return to that older sacred one, that old pounding in your heart, surely it's better than all the

---

[87] (Tarkovsky, 1982)

Britannicas, nootropics, and Destinees that weigh down this world. Have her back. Catherine. Begin each day with a tingle." – the dark wizard, Ronald.

Nine: Contemplate the mysteries long enough that the mysteries commence with contemplating you.

Ten: Ask of Ron, "Given that God presumably elected to place me in this specific worldline, can perhaps I see a PowerPoint presentation examining the faith-based ethics of multiverse hopping? Can it be skewed to make it seem like I'm not selling out entirely here?"

Ten Weird Things We Learned From Klaas J. Kraay

*I*f Ronald Majthenyi books conference space at the under-whelming DaVinci Office Centre and flies in Ryerson-based theologian Klaas J. Kraay to argue that multiverse-travel requires no abdication of faith, could in fact even buttress said faith, then avail yourself of the DaVinci Office Centre's praline and caramel frozen chocolate sticks and hear what Kraay has to say.

One: If Klaas J. Kraay opens with Bernard Carr's oft-quoted, "If you don't want God then you better have a multiverse," recognize that Kraay, merely Ryerson-affiliated after all, is setting Carr up as the scientific strawman who fears the "G-word" more than any Satanic Meetup virgin ever could.

Two: Struggle to maintain focus as Kraay drones intro-ductorily from his paper, *The Theistic Multiverse: Problems and Prospects*:

> "Once considered outré or absurd, multiple uni-verse theories appear to be gaining considerable scientific respectability. There are, of course, many such theories, including Everett's (1957) many

worlds interpretation of quantum mechanics, defended by Deutsch (1997) and others; Linde's (1986) eternal inflation view, which suggests that universes form like bubbles in a chaotically inflating sea; Smolin's (1997) fecund universe theory, which proposes that universes are generated through black holes; the cyclic model, recently defended using string/M theory by Steinhardt and Turok (2007), which holds that distinct universes are formed in a never-ending sequence of Big Bangs and Big Crunches; and Tegmark's (2007) "Level IV" multiverse, which contains many universes governed by distinct mathematical and scientific laws."

and then, clearing his throat, looking a bit worried for his personal safety, "And today I'd like to introduce the nascent and still-theoretical Majthenyian view, demonstrable, I've been assured, at the conclusion of these slides."

Three: If you interject, "A *fecund* view wherein Catherine's head remains intact? Where our love is omnibenevolently tilled?" Ron will respond, "Better than intact, better than tilled! Please allow Klaas to continue," then Klaas will continue:

I have said that God will include 'all and only those universes worth creating and sustaining' (Kraay 2010.) Others offer more detail. Turner (2003) suggests "a favourable balance of good over evil" and Monton offers various construals of what this might mean. But such a threshold is too simplistic: a universe might meet this condition, while nevertheless containing some feature that makes it unworthy of inclusion in a divinely furnished multiverse. Perhaps sensing this, some philosophers have proposed additional requirements. Parfit says there should be no injustice and that each individuals' life must be worth living. Forrest first says that every individual must have a life in which good outweighs evil, and later adds two further restrictions: each creature who suffers must at least virtually consent to it, and must receive ample recompense afterwards. Draper says that no individual's life may be bad overall, and that God must be a benefactor to all creatures. [88]

Four: If fraudulent intellectually as you are emotionally, such that Emily was always required to track down your primary sources and absent emotions alike, don't even consider all the footnotes in Kraay's paper. Think only of Catherine as you mouth the words, "Construals. Parfit. It all seems so obvious now."

Five: With a Mephistophelean raise of the brow, Majthenyi, sipping methacrolein from his goblet, will gesture

---

[88] (Kraay, The Theistic Multiverse: Problems and Prospects, 2012)

at the conference centre's dismal milieu, "All this is merely the fourth station of your personal cross, one you needn't consent to, due as you're due the 'ample recompense' dear Klaas speaks of."

Six: Even as a sempiternalist who hath restored faith to the masses, Pascal's wager for the fat pot of undoing what you never consented to, *e.g.* 'the beheading of Catherine,' *e.g.* 'the absence of Catherine from your sad life.'

Seven: Think of her sweaters. The shimmering in the sauna. How very fresh and clean it could feel. Think of the ride home from the drive-in. Think of the six-thousand-nine-hundred-and-one lonely nights since. Suggest to Kraay, "Was it not Huw Price who claimed that a time symmetric ontology for quantum theory must necessarily be retrocausal?"

Eight: Request Klaas J. Kraay skip his last few slides to further elucidate the fecundity of possible worlds.

Nine: Take the elevator to the DaVinci building's roof. Board the helicopter Majthenyi has on standby. Board a plane at the San Francisco International Airport. Fly to Geneva, Switzerland. Get a decent night's rest. Flail in that binary being/non-being undertow between sleep and dreams. Consult Catherine cleavage pictures on your phone. Wonder just what Price you wouldn't pay. Masturbate to the pseudo-necromantic possibilities yielded by the eternal inflation of the multiverse.

Ten: Meet Klaas J. Kraay for a morning muffin at the Grand Hôtel Kempinski's continental breakfast station. Exchange hackneyed-and-all-too revelatory *Celestine Prophecy*-type dialog with Klaas J. Kraay not worthy of inclusion in this blog. Reminisce about your own days at Ryerson. Express your desire to have matriculated elsewhere. Board the shuttle. Show your day pass and visit the Large Hadron Collider at CERN.

How to Live Deliciously

*I*f Ronald Majthenyi's CERN-based portal to an alternate worldline can make Catherine alive again, and all the Maj asks in recompense is a quick MP3 decrying Divinitee's blockchain metaphor, briefly consider consequences before denying it three times before the cock crows, bidding a quick adieu to Ryerson's own Klaas J. Kraay, and hopping into Majthenyi's portal.

One: After a minor electromagnetic prickle, get olfactored into the cedar-smell of your aunt's cabin. Intuitively understand you are still thirty-seven. If your sister sits adjacent at a sturdy oak table, looking bored but still beautiful, age having added only fecundity to the fundament of her beauty, she must be 39.

Two: If you're holding Ken Follett's *The Pillars of the Earth*, interpret its length and lack of literary import as betraying your own vague contentment. Intuit an emancipation from your lifelong pathology of chronic low mood.

Three: Remember rental properties and driving into the city twice a week to conduct business. Know that these hours at the cabin with its sauna and its soft earth and its dock and its deep waters redolent of gasoline are yours as they are hers.

If Catherine cooks an elaborate soup with root vegetables picked from the small garden your aunt tilled for years, rub your Gulliver in a pantomime of anticipation.

Four: Gaze upon her brown arms again in the sauna. Wonder what happened to the grief-blogger who'd occupied this timeline prior to your arrival. Rationalize that there was none, as he wouldn't even have needed to blog about grief.

Five: In the fixity of a big brass bed, place your forearm and bicep in Catherine's stomach, fold your knees into hers, and find the old life inwardly collapsing from memory like the infrastructure of a decade's long dream.

Six: Play scrabble on a large stone on the porch that serves as an ersatz coffee table.

Seven: If Catherine leaves CBC Radio One on in the background all day, realize you are no longer enraged by the political posturing of the woke mob. Realize your anger at their consensus worldview was borne solely of your anger with the world itself. Realize that without an all-encompassing grievance, you could care less what is virtue-signalled of on the CBC.

Seven: Find yourself sated after one measly glass of wine. Don't even consider what stupefaction the porch's propane tank might yield. Think, "I am happy."

Eight: If your beagle Runsitter runs into the woods, he could be subjunctively eaten by bears. As the man of this household, presumably just chock full of creaturely freedom, you must negate the conjugation of that verb, *i.e.* 'Thanks to my intervention, the dog was not eaten by bears!' Run into the woods, blow your bear whistle, and see the tree Runsitter barks at, screams at more like, a tree that is the most tree-like manifestation of Ronald Majthenyi imaginable.

Nine: Leash Runsitter. Give Runsitter a look, *i.e.* 'Goddamn pal, this Majthenyian birch will be our little secret. And don't think many treats aren't forthcoming should you telepathically assent not to draw attention to this tree going forward.'

Ten: Return to the cabin, a strange hotel aesthetically opposite the rococo techne palace Dave Bowman passes his time at. Lie beside her. Listen complacently to political posturers. Feel both as hungry and as full as you've been since adolescence. Slurp a second bowl of the simple soup. Find *Einstein on the Beach* on a digital radio station. Hold her ample hips. Touch noses. Lock eyes. Try to hold on. Try to hold on to all the magic found in dreams.

ONE COMMENT ON "HOW TO LIVE DELICIOUSLY"

Grievin' Gary: Okay, I've been following your blog thus far because I thought you made some interesting points about grief plus admittedly I was intrigued by the more lurid aspects, but now if you're in another dimension or whatever how am I even reading this? Got to call fake news on this one, I'm afraid. Four Pinocchios!

Ten Tips for the Denial of Death

*I*f after years lost wandering in the desert of grief your sister Catherine has returned to you, ignore unsettling Majtheny-ian foliage to seek satisfaction while you can.

One: If potatoes are fried with onions and yellow peppers, find your usual post-potato lethargy made tolerable by her presence, Catherine's.

Two: Resist the urge to reminisce, as your reminiscences may not be her reminiscences.

Three: If you have loved a memory for nearly twenty years, avoid anxious rumination over what Kraay-zy witchcraft allows this corporeal Catherine to measure up quite so exactly. Get all steamed up about loving her for the rest of your days. Read a few pages of *A Most Strange and True Discourse…Of Incestuous Copulation* (1600), a suspicious find upon your aunt's otherwise Folletian bookshelf.

Four: Catch a fish. Gut the fish. Fry the fish in butter and lemon. Season to taste.

Five: Glimpsing something metallic from a rear window, something like the cylinder you stepped into at CERN, fear perchance that's Klaas J. Kraay heard clicking his tongue in some distant vestibule of your consciousness. Focus instead on the oily Perch flavour clinging to your palate.

Six: Stroke the hair you've always loved. Look at her deep-set Marianne Cottillard eyes. Remark hilariously upon their resemblance to your dinner. Hear her laugh.

Seven: Adhere to her bloody nose. Adhere to her sinus infection. Adhere to her low-pain threshold groans. Adhere to her frightened glances. Don't ask her what's wrong. Blame with limited certainty the under-preparedness of the evening's freshwater game fish.

Eight: Play five *Knee Plays* and wipe her mouth with a warm cloth. Wipe with what's been left in you, what you had as a boy, and what's been left to grow monstrous since—and that thing is your need.

Nine: If Catherine plays popular music on 99.5 FM after wearying of the artificial *Knee Plays*, hear meteorologist Karl Bohnak saying:

> Local, provincial, federal, and world health authorities are concerned as a case of what's thought to be the deadly Ebola-Zaire virus has appeared at the Sault Area Hospital. WHO Spokesperson Dr. Margaret Harris expressed her concern:
>
> 'With no known ongoing outbreak of Ebola elsewhere in the world it's baffling that...'"

Ten: If Bohnak's urgency ratifies Catherine's dread, encourage her to get some sleep. Throw the radio in the lake.

Kick at a howling Runsitter but then regret it as he cowers. Crawl into bed beside her. Look at the moon through a warped window pane. Hide your face between her shoulders and hope to have a good run.

How to Win Over New Neighbours

*I*f *Young Americans* arrive at the abutting cabin, zesty of spirit, bulky of trapezoid, having lived exactly twenty years, adept at backflips and low-end banter, Catherine "simply must" swim over to introduce herself.

One: Curse all the world's undeserving Chads! Feel the sorrows of young Werther even if for the time being you remain the Albert. Remember you have no claim to stake, for it's you who are the ghost.

Two: If Catherine suggests inviting "the boys" over for a barbecue, cite a paucity of foodstuffs and the increasing danger of travelling to the Ebola-ridden Sault. Gaze-communicate your true love but only manage to look territorial and weak, a bad combination.

Three: If the boys arrive with their undressed wounds, their blood-clotted rags, and their youthful ambivalence towards Ebola and death writ-large, then toss the pigskin around, remembering to spin the laces off your fingertips to avoid throwing any embarrassing ducks.

Four: If the boy named Todd carves some lines of Python programming into the dirt with his dagger, ask Todd, "Sure you're not the devil?" As the thunder rolls in, Todd's little wink will mean, 'That's rich coming from you, the thief.' Repeatedly yawn and stretch *i.e.* 'I think we've all seen enough chicken fights and one-handed handstands and spirals caught with the grace of Metatron for one day.'

Five: Hear the one called Aubrey whispering to Todd about a midnight swim. Note the conspiratorial look of mischief on Catherine's face. Vomit in the outhouse. Fail to ascertain how much blood is in the vomit due to the occluding shit swamp of the outhouse hole. Convince yourself that even if Catherine leaves the marriage bed for Todd's sleeping bag, and even if everyone's organs are liquified by dawn, still you'll have known again the girl you've loved since you can't remember when, and these short and Philoviral hours will have been worth something.

Six: Hear increasingly drunken hooting from the neighbouring camp as the clock strikes nearer to midnight. If you partake of unwanted spirits hoping to keep Catherine entertained, grow drunk only in a maudlin and Wertherian way that causes you to question the necessity of her brassiere change.

Seven: If inclined to cite *A Lover's Discourse* from your photographic memory, remember that Catherine never really went in for the literary. And while impressionable, she is not impressionable in the way Britannica was, because she is a visceral person, designed to live rather than to contemplate living, who knows that the hot blood of the transcendent can only be brought to linguistic life through an ego vesicle. And while likely as wearied by Todd and Aubrey's lack of originality as you are, their *esprit* is enough to rouse her from the scrabble board, much as *esprit* lured her to the asphyxiational highway of Alan Raval.

Eight: If you were always meant to lose her, over and over, loss and loss and more Goethean loss, then keep your head up, not in the figurative sense, but to limit the outpouring of your hot-blooded nosebleed.

Nine: Refuse her coy apologetics as she decamps. Offer blithely, "Why not be debauched by a relation instead?" If she shrugs at this, watch her through the grass as though you were Terrence Malick's camera or a serpent. Wonder how frequently she'll deny you before the cock crows. Wonder if a vital organ's liquefaction really matters relative to being cuckolded by back-flipping Audrey. Should you search the cabin for your uncle's hunting rifle, find only his fishing pole.

Ten: If Catherine returns hours later, looking sated, mischievous, and prepared to lie, don't even ask. Hold her again. Accept that she has caught Aubrey's fine spiral and been Python programmed by Tim's dagger. Turn on the CBC to find fellowship amidst your fellow cucks. Know that monsters are in your midst. Know that your reality is finally commensurate to your intensity of feeling. Feel flux and fear of mythic proportions. Blaze right on through what must constitute your best life: the Philoviral miasma of a past reconciled.

All the NOPE for these Real-Life Medical Thriller Moments

*I*f the next morning Aubrey and Todd and Dennis and Little Rick are wearing HEPA masks and driving jet skis trailed by wakes of what you first perceive as coffee grounds but soon recognize as black blood, then affix headphones and listen to the topical Josh Ritter album, *Fever Breaks*.

One: If Richard Preston's *Panic in the Red Zone* happens to be on your aunt's bookshelf, learn of the six Ebola sisters [Ebola virus (species Zaire ebolavirus), Sudan virus (species Sudan ebolavirus), Taï Forest virus (species Taï Forest ebolavirus, formerly Côte d'Ivoire ebolavirus), Bundibugyo virus (species Bundibugyo ebolavirus), Reston virus (species Reston ebolavirus) plus also Nipah,] strains that Preston calls "the zombies of deep time."

Two: If Aubrey and Todd and Rick and Dennis' jet ski shenanigans have died down, visit their neighbouring cabin to find "the boys" in their own black vomitus. Overcome your *Heeby-Jeebies* to conduct an amateur autopsy on Little Richard. Discover petechiae inside the skin. Detect melena in the intestines. Find Danny still clinging to life and thus resistant to autopsy. Cleave his head in with a stump, out of mercy, ostensibly, and yet with all the grey wrath of the cuckold.

Three: Wish you'd worn a Hazmat suit to independently verify Preston's reportage that "cadaveric blood doesn't coagulate." Try to be a stand-up guy by digging shallow graves for Little Richard *et al.* Give up when your indecency reasserts itself just as thunder rolls in.

Four: Place your right hand on Catherine's hip bone and read Preston's non-fiction thriller on the day bed, cozy as only the rain on a rooftop or a murder story can make a man.

Five: If Catherine has a hiccup fit, don't tell her that according to Preston hiccups are a signifier of scary old Ebola.

Six: Read that a virus is a mathematical pattern. Surmise that if a virus is a line of code then it can be deleted.

Seven: Ask the omnisciences for any alternative to Ebola. Regret this evermore.

Eight: As CBC dogmatists assert that Ebola is a product of internalised isms in the Center for Disease Control space, learn tangentially that the CDC has set up a command centre in Sudbury, a mere three hour trip. Quip hilariously, "Finally a reason to go to Sudbury!" Get a big laugh from Catherine that makes all this Ebola angst worthwhile.

Nine: Cry out, "Let's go chase the lightning," and board your pontoon boat to traverse the black waves of the poisoned lake. Turn the ignition of your Fiat 500l. Remind your sister, "You and I have been lovers since 1998." Feel her heartbeat. Sing country harmony on a few standards.

Ten: Take to Highway 17. Learn on the radio of the troubleshoot you'd prayed for. "An antidote generated from the blood of a Sierra Leone nurse..." ... "Some side effects... related to mood, but better than..." – CDC spokesperson, Tarik Jasarevic.

Ten Tips for Visiting Lovely Sudbury, Ontario

*I*f by Fiat you and Catherine drive towards a CDC emergency outpost in Sudbury, Ontario, which town is like a garden of goddamned sadness, once described by CNN as a "wasteland" due to its industrially-wrought acid rain epidemic, and where NASA astronauts trained because it purportedly "resembled the lifeless surface of the moon," then before entering the CDC's tented camps from which body bags are more likely to emerge than healed-but-moody individuals, this according to r/Sudbury anyway, then enjoy the Sudbury sites before it gets too late.

One: Observe mountains of stone blackened by ore.

Two: Regard the Big Nickel, the world's largest coin, twelve-sided, 30-ft high, a commemoration of the blight perpetrated by the nickel mining industry. Remark, "Well, yes."

Three: Visit a sandwich diner that is also a karaoke bar. Step aside as Catherine does a throaty rendition of Daniel Romano's *Empty Husk*. Nod gravely as she sings of "saintly diadems." Give her a kiss. Eat a liverwurst sandwich. Drink a Diet Pepsi. Eat some salt and vinegar chips. Eat some ketchup chips. Drink a Dr. Pepper. Gaze at your bloodshot eyes in the bathroom mirror. Recall Preston's reportage that, "Ebola particles are made entirely of human materials."

Four: Seek rest at a motel. Enter the bathroom a millisecond or so before it procedurally generates. Join Catherine in the shower to rub the little rectangle of coarse motel soap upon her thighs and stomach and breasts and neck and upper vertebrae. Heed her request not to "put that shit near my hair." Recall that Thomas Aquinas defined beauty as "that which, when seen, pleases."[89]

Five: Watch the IMAX movie *North of Superior* at Science North. Realize you are stalling.

Six: Bite the bullet and pop the address of the CDC Red Zone into Waze. If George Jones' cover of *When I Stop Dreaming* by the Louvin Brothers comes on the radio, a song Daniel Romano once called the "saddest song ever written," realize only its first two lines constitute the saddest song ever written: *When I stop dreaming/ That's when I'll stop loving you.*

Seven: Try not to get irritable with Catherine over her hiccupping, because if irritable even with all you've ever dreamed of, that would make you a man incapable of love.

Eight: Stand in the Ebola Sufferers line in the Sudbury Community Arena's parking lot and suffer that distinct unease of any triage situation, *i.e.* 'Geez Louise, if didn't have Ebola already, definitely have it now. May as well have laid to rest in a field of bones.'

---

[89] (Aquinas, 1225-1274)

Nine: Recognize a physician through the soft plastic face bubble of her impermeable whole-body garment. In what is surely a violation of Ebola-preventiveness procedures, receive a hug and feigned kiss from a certain nootropically-predisposed robot you've known and caressed.

Ten: If Dr. Maya Achlys-Septis raps straight with you, "The vaccine works, but gotta warn you, brutal side effects, such as you'll be even more irritable, you grouch, and definitely some identity disturbance, and definitely feelings of abandonment, and definitely some self-harm, some cutting, some bulimia," then based on experiences with the mistress referenced in blogs of the last lifetime, speak the name that these thin-skinned symptoms and sequalae signify: "Borderline Personality Disorder." If Maya continues, "Plus some unwholesome overlapping with other Cluster Bs. The alternative, however, is not the A82V Makona Variant of Ebola Zaire, but rather the A82Y Manistique Variant of Ebola Cheboygan, which still results in all the cramping and orifice bleeding and such forth, except without the relief of a prompt death; in fact, without death where there should be death, that is to say extreme dehydration from bleeding out all day but then no death, so kind of like an undying Ebola. Kind of like zombies of deep time lol," then ask Dr. Maya if you might talk to Ronald Majthenyi about all this. If Dr. Maya blankly stares that means she's incapable of knowing her maker's face, get in line for your shot of Borderline Personality Disorder co-morbid with a grab bag of the Cluster B's.

"Just Keep on Pushing Her Love Over
the Borderline" with these Ten Tips

*I*f asked to sign a waiver abdicating the WHO of responsibility for any depersonalization, ontological uncertainty, splitting, mixed mood states, dissociation, inappropriate guilt, general cheerlessness, and *etc.*, and if the inherent *wertversprechen* is not having your organs liquefy into yellow slime, then sign that old John Hancock on the dotted line.

One: Stand in another line. Receive the injection. Watch as your sister receives hers. Notice her hiccupping has stopped. Recognize a second face in her old loved face. Take her hand and realize BPD is not a deficit but a surplus. Love her more than you ever have. In this love know a depth of fear you've never conceived possible, a fear of what could happen so soon as the evening: *abandonment.*

Two: Think of all the friends you once knew. The old gang. Think of how all the books and records of a lifetime could never replace an elaborate handshake developed by a gang of teenage boys. Understand all the love in a life as part of one big chain, every link corroded and breakable by any half-hearted yank.

Three: Hug your sister. Feel the lines that separate you from her blurring. Know that a part of you has been missing for nearly twenty years. Know that she's back again. Know that she's only back again for now. Know those old *distentio animi* blues, meaning time is a dimension of the soul. Ask, "Is this a dream?" Tempt fate a time or two by snapping your fingers and saying, "Wake up."

Four: If urged towards the American Borderline Personality Disorder Association's card table, politely take their brochure and pay your $75 membership fee. Provide your mailing address. If the AMBOPEDIA flak seated behind the card table is insulted by your disinterest in AMBOPEDIA's annual 'Boatload of Borderlines' cruise and screams stop consonants at you so plosively that a globule of his agitated spittle enters your mouth—realize this demeanour is dictated by his affliction.

Five: If you feel empty even in the explosive presence of the AMBOPEDIA community then hug your sister as a means of clinging to your own strict identity, your own thoughts, your own feelings—all of which have grown increasingly dissolute.

Six: Recall how Catherine is "always running away from things." Try to push her away before she can abandon you. Grow conciliatory. Have a screaming fight. Rinse and repeat.

Seven: Grieve some more:

The grief of the demon in the freezer.

The grief of the freezer fry.

McCain, Cavendish, *etc.*

The grief of object cathexis.

The grief of reality testing.

The grief of the absent sustain.

The grief of Biniodide of Mercury, which some members of the AMBOPEDIA community advocate for.

The grief of sex intensified.

The grief of the avoidant personality.

The grief of withdrawal into all the records and books of a lifetime.

Sailor Moon mornings on the chesterfield.

An intergluteal cleft seen through the 6"x 6" sauna window.

The grief of the clusters (A, B, C).

The grief of the unstable temperament.

Seven: Miss baby Marcel_Proust, whom you have abandoned in another world.

Eight: Miss adolescence, the last time you experienced unadulterated (which is to say: *unmedicated*) joy.

Nine: Try to remember just who you may be: a lovelorn brother; a scared little boy; a screeching evangelical; Joe College, the frisbee expert; a man who'd curse where he came from, wherever that might have been; a lecher; a reality show star and nootropical spokesman; a colleague to Ryerson professor Klaas J. Kraay; a knight of infinite faith, yet quencher of eternal thirsts; a slo-pitch singles hitter, clean line drives up the middle; an endurer of 37 winters; a victim of the Hell's Angels and of the Bloods, and hence a TBI sufferer and percipient of hazed cognitions; a histrionic even before the vaccine; but also a sacred executioner, and thus an agent of obfuscation; a liquefactionist waiting upon the final absorption, and so obviously a dupe: a believer.

Ten: Feel like a remnant of something past.

Ten Tips for Living Petulantly

*I*f you and your favourite person are afflicted with Borderline Personality Disorder, situated in the Greater Sudbury Area no less, then liquidate assets and purchase waterfront property alongside a meteor crater from the Eocene era now called Lake Wanapatei.

One: Copulate extensively. Experience heights of unimagined bliss. Observe a visible field of blue energy during the sex act. Believe, with the externalists (Manzotti, Chalmers, Clark) that consciousness exists external to the nervous system and can integrate with externalities such as Catherine's consciousness. Experience splitting. Experience anticipatory nostalgia. Miss the present in the present. Agree with Zeena Schreck on the lone point, "that nostalgia is an illness for those who haven't realized that today is tomorrow's nostalgia." Fight without apparent end or resolution. Laugh in her face. Have your own face laughed into. If you are more frequently depressed than your sister, and so-accused of being 'moody,' moodily quote William James, "Does it not appear as if one who lived on one side of the pain threshold might need a different sort of religion from one who perpetually lived on the other?[90]"

Two: If Catherine responds, "Enough with the quotes already it doesn't make you smart anyone can leaf through a book like you do," realize she is correct and that you are a fraud. Weep violently in the shower for eighty minutes.

Three: Resume old hobbies. Play *No Man's Sky* and *No Hidden Variable* on PlayStation VR. Survive in the game. Exist in the game. Harvest carbon to repair a fuel cell. Use the fuel cell to repair a space cruiser. Cruise to a carbon-rich planet to get more carbon. Wonder why your simulated self needs all this fucking carbon? Wonder if Majthenyi ever peeks in on his simulation to observe you mired in your own shitty low-rez carbon-mining simulation, before turning away depressed to offer Klaas a Moscow Mule or something, and says, "Appears David has chosen to mine carbon."

Four: If Catherine refers to her frequent lucid dream experiences as "being lifted," roll your eyes at how new-age-idiotic she sounds.

Five: If you track with Millon's 'petulant borderline' category while Catherine tracks with Millon's 'impulsive borderline' category, scoff your own petulant plosives when Catherine announces her impulsive intention to study Jungian Psychology at the University of Sudbury or whatever it's called.

---

[90] *The Varieties of Religious Experience* (1902)

Six: If Catherine defines Jungian synchronicity as "the hypothesized principle of an acausal but meaningful ordering of events within a 'psychic relativity of space and time,'" and drones on about supra-personal organizing principles organizing your boorish behaviours, and if she mentions the anima and animus, then in addition to the mysteries she's also contemplating the purchase of a strap-on.

Seven: If she's hip to what supra-principles organize your low-value regurgitations, do not describe the naked theatrically of her big hero's dissociative trances: "Jung, standing with his arms outstretched like the crucified Christ, a big snake wrapped around his body, suddenly turns into a god. He develops a lion head: becoming the lion-headed god of the ancient Mithraic religion – a mixture of Mithraic Kronos (Aion) and Christ.[91]," and then scream, "Trances you roll your eyes at whenever your own brother is thusly dissociated!"

Eight: If Catherine stays late at the library each night, abuse Tums to quell the time-symmetric somersaults in your stomach.

Nine: Text in terror to ask if she is having an affair with Richard Izdubar, Dean of Jungian Psychology. Wonder how long until Richie Iz, whom Catherine doesn't even really like, whom Catherine appreciates for the sole reason that he is not you, rolls out that old Ravalian chestnut: "Why are you always running away from things?"

---

[91] (Tyrrell, 2018)

Ten: Alternate between scoffing "Please stop!" consonants and affricating anger towards jars and chairs, a bad combination. Say simple consonant things like "We are finally free to be together." Build walls. Try to sing harmonies. Shout at your asshole borderline neighbours through a megaphone Russian-dolled into another megaphone. Plant trees along the perimeter of your property line. Take up dialectical behavioural therapy with Dr. Maya. Have a half-hearted affair with Dr. Maya. Fixate on her feminine wiles while feeling entirely empty inside. Look in a mirror and fail to recognize anyone you've once known. Spend up all of your time. Run into Catherine and Dean Izdubar at a Coffee Time one time. Cry out, "Jezebel!" Weep into your peach-green tea in the all-gender bathroom, under its fluorescent lights, under excessive wattage, so close to Catherine and yet she's already gone.

How to Kill Once More

*I*f your lakeside abode has become a den of bitter recrimination, unspoken as not, and secrets have dimmed even the blue energy of concupiscence, then castigate and altercate like it was going out of style.

One: If one morning Catherine removes every glass, bowl, and spoon from their appropriate resting places to dust and scrub the resting places themselves, remind her of your enthusiasm for order and how appalling it is to lack control over one's own abode. If Catherine screams words like, "Someone's got to do it!" and "Who was your maid last year!" try to amend your psycho-physical bond with a nice hug. If she shirks you off, feel as a dying meteor might: regionally-appropriate to Sudbury.

Two: If love has not been learned, question whether or not a lifelong and life-ruining eulogistic paean to Catherine was even the smart play.

Three: Realize your eulogistic paean was only the paean of adolescence itself.

Four: If *I've Made Up My Mind To Give Myself To You* by Bob Dylan on the Bose has negligible effect, give in to your anger and play Nine Inch Nails instead. Play some

Rammstein. Play that song by Rammstein where they say their own name a bunch of times: *Rammmmsteeeeeeein*. Play some Stalaggh. The extra G and H at the end standing for *global holocaust*, a happening their music aspires to bring about, incidentally. If Catherine says, "Turn that shit off!" in the most hateful voice you've yet heard from her, and this hate invalidates the times you've known, then peaceably rebut, "I could be rich and famous and nootropically-balanced and pushing a Baby Dior Bassinet through Golden Gate Park but I traded it all in for you, you harpy.'"

Five: If these words cause Catherine to fling plates like frisbees, predict abandonment and espy the metal Easton in the umbrella stand. Espy the bat and foresee the unthinkable. Wish Dr. Whybrow had more capably explained how to block unwanted thoughts in the prefrontal neocortex.

Six: Grasp the bat. Take a practise swing.

Seven: Come to your senses. Exit the matrimonial home. Feel better as soon as Stalaggh and your harpy sister are out of your ear. Play Sam Harris' *Waking Up* meditation app on your phone. Hate even even-keeled Sam Harris. Place the Easton in the driver's seat of the marital Corvette. Peel out of the driveway like the petulant teenager you are. Drive to the University of Sudbury. Consult the campus map. Find the Jungian Psychology wing.

Eight: Find the Iz amongst hirsute undergrads. Do not pause to consider consequences. Swing the bat at his head. Cave his head in. Note the undergrads' unwillingness to sacrifice their own bearded skulls to rescue the Dean from the underworld. Swing away. If viscera and meninges and dura matter splash into your face, you've made a terrible mistake.

Nine: If you can't conceivably bat to death all these undergrads, who've done nothing wrong, and some of whom must recognize you from bi-monthly Philemon Foundation fundraisers, and who are already running as far from this archetypically-unpleasant situation as they can get, that means you were foredoomed to pay a penance.

Ten: Burn meninges-encrusted Levi's in the woodstove. Beg Catherine to go on the lam with you. If police pull into the driveway, cancel those plans. Don the shackles. Rationalize that Ronald Majthenyi put a spell on you. Tell the tired-looking police officer, "I'm not such a bad guy." Take one last look at Catherine. In this magic moment she'll appear prettier than ever, sadder than ever, looking like, 'What have you done?' *i.e.* 'It was just a silly fight we could have been back to the Scrabble board and blue energy in no time,' *i.e.* 'Never again will you dance with me,' *i.e.* 'You were my favourite person too and now you're gone forever until the end of time.' If it is a soft summer's night, breathe it in, confined as you'll heretofore be within the grey walls of the penitentiary.

Ten Tips for Surviving, Heck, Maybe Even Thriving Within the Grey Walls of The Serpent River Pen

*I*f every borderline run amok pleads Not Criminally Responsible by reason of insanity, your barrister will deem the 'non-insane automatism' defence as novel. Feel this is a prudent way to plead forgiveness for just about anything.

One: Even if you do, "Sound crazier than most," according to the saturnine judge who neatly fits Millon's 'discouraged' sub-category of Borderline Personality Disorder, find yourself sentenced to life in the penitentiary without parole.

Two: If you've watched plenty of YouTube tutorials, *e.g.* 'How to survive in jail' *e.g.* 'How to be raped in jail with marginally-less frequency,' *etc.*, then you'll have already begged Catherine to visit weekly and to mail something every day, even a newspaper, even a crossword puzzle she's half finished, some pea coat fuzz, something of her.

Three: If boundaries blur due to BPD, endure unsolicited-penitentiary-fellowship akin to when troglodytic bros on MDMA find their repressed need for male connection manifest through eager EA Sports NHL 94 reminiscences until these regress to boastings of girls fucked and fights won, making that momentary peek past the veil of bro insularity nothing but the lousy tease known to Plato's cave returnee, *i.e.* 'thought I saw something true,'[92] and as the drugs wear off, the bros red-eyed, the Blue Light doing little for them now, the veil thickens to chainmaille.

Four: If prison fellowship resembles the protracted metaphor of tip three, take up chess to focus on something other than penalty-minutes accrued in bygone Junior B hockey. If Larry the competent chess novice remarks, "For a guy with such a big mouth you really lack basic problem-solving skills," try Checkers instead.

Five: If on the BPD ward, participate in the *us v. them* mentality necessitated by a low-status group dynamic. Shame the Ebola sufferers as anti-vax, anti-intellectual, and anti-science. Compliment your fellow BPD sufferers on their evidence-based Scientism.

Six: Meet Cannibalizin' Terry Stripes, your fellow YouTube sensation captured in portrait mode eating his entire family at an Outback Steakhouse mere minutes after receiving his Ebola vaccine. If after his boss at the Ministry of Natural Resources suggested criticizing the vaccine wouldn't be a "good look", Terry had been celebrated by consensus regulators for honourably pleading to pre-meditated murder despite his crime's rather transparent spontaneity, then converse with Terry about what consensus regulators give and what they take.

---

[92] (Tweedy, 1996)

Seven: Should your sister's Jungian letters quote, "Life is a Kernel Flux, a flowing into the future, and not a stoppage or a backwash," know she really means "I want to break up with you." Talk this over with Larry. Talk this over with Cannibalizin' Terry Stripes. Write back. Try to keep things light.

Eight: If her last letter to you is only a long quote from *The Language of Flowers* by George Batailles,

> For flowers do not age honestly like leaves, which lose nothing of their beauty after they have died; flowers wither like old and overly made-up dowagers, and they die ridiculously on stems that seemed to carry them to the clouds. It is impossible to exaggerate the tragicomic oppositions indicated in the course of this death-drama, endlessly played out between earth and sky, and it is evident that one can only paraphrase this laughable duel by introducing, not as a sentence, but more precisely as an ink stain, this nauseating banality: *love smells like death.*

then equivocate that maintaining a self-excited circuit with any significant other, favourite person, or so-called soul mate, is a wager only someone hell-bent on a Gambler's Ruin would take.

Nine: If even sensibly-vaccinated lovers of empiricism contract new and worse Ebola strains on top of their peevishness and hair-trigger emotions and crippling fear of abandonment, write angry letters to the Correctional Services

Minister inquiring exactly what clown college he matriculated at.

Ten: If your sister's letters have ceased for two years' time, you'll have only her memory left. Sit. Contemplate the meaning of truth. Drink an instant coffee or two. Eat a honeybun. Eat a salt packet. Almost hear her singing. Meet her in dreams. Remember being understood. Wake up shaking. Hope that heaven can help the ones who grieve.

How to Do Good Works

*I*f sins, like marriages, cannot be annulled but only atoned for, put that autostereogrammatic blockchain baloney behind you and get down to the filthy honest work of serving somebody.

One: Grow hunched like an old char-woman from diarrhea and vomitus scrubbing. Rub the diarrheal's shoulders, comforting them maternally as you can, *e.g.* "There you go. Get it all out. You'll feel better," even if their Cheboygan-strain of the Ebola Manistique variant is of the undying variety, meaning they'll never feel better, meaning their suffering, like most suffering, is without purpose or cessation.

Two: If Mother Theresa found it in her lepers, seek divinity in even the most purposeless BPD-Ebola morbidities. Often fail. Often see the sufferers as entitled jerks with low pain thresholds and poor vomitus etiquette. Work past and through these feelings until you have achieved radical acceptance and equanimity, there in The Serpent River Penitentiary no less.

Three: If Bubonic and Pneumonic plague enter the mix, serve on the front lines of those battles too. Suppurate a bubo or two. Chop off a black thumb or toe here and there.

Four: If 14th century superstitions return, *i.e.* 'None of the toilet cleaners have the Black Death yet, perchance I mightn't inhale from the shitter?' then walk a fine line. Humour the stark-raving rationalist. Humour the faith-based latrine community.

Five: If a latrine-inhaler glances up at you from his foul observances, *i.e.* 'Don't judge. This is the last thing I want to be doing,' offer him an acceptant shrug, *i.e.* 'You do you, Julio.'

Six: If a skeptic scoffs, "You believe these conspiracy nuts huff shit all day scared of a little boo-boo," offer a whimsical headshake augmented by a half smile, *i.e.* 'People are crazy and times are strange,'[93] but to each his own therapeutic, kinsman."

Seven: If BPD-afflicted Warden Jöns Fermat notices your good works, become his favourite person. Appreciate accolades, *e.g.* "Rest of you bums could try caring for your fellow man as exemplified by excellent David here. Scrubbing up blood and puke. Making up cool nicknames for his buddies like 'Cannabilizin' Terry Stripes.' Sure would make the C.O.'s lives easier, whose lives are no motherfuckin' picnic given they didn't commit crimes and all either have Ebola or BPD and still they're here twelve hours daily, half-prisoners themselves aren't they, not on any kind of picnic, nobody giving them cool nicknames."

Eight: If the *Sudbury Examiner* profile "A Light in a Dark Place" agitates for your early parole, consider refusing,

---

[93] (Dylan, Things Have Changed, 2000)

knowing the only way up and out of Majthenyi's manifested world is to dig down into the diarrheal darkness, fundamentally mired in good works.

Nine: Eventually accept parole in hopes of reconciling with the first and last person to imprison you, Catherine. Hope she's incapable of contempt for you, even if you have Ebola again, no few buboes of your own necessitating nightly suppuration, a few necrotic fingertips to clip off during the morning *toilette*, flesh so dead it can be removed with a standard-issue nail clipper, all of which in conjunction with BPD have made you moodier than ever.

Ten: If a Toyota Tundra replaces the driveway's matrimonial Corvette, knock and learn from the stereotypical Tundra man that she is gone, but has left you a note, which contains only a quotation from *The Red Book*:

> Which fire has not been put out and which embers are still ablaze? [...] What is this crazy desire craving satisfaction? Whose mad cries are these? Who among the dead suffers thus? Come here and drink blood, so that you can speak. Why do you reject the blood? Would you like milk? Or the red juice of the vine? Perhaps you would rather have love? Love for the dead? Being in love with the dead? Are you perhaps demanding the seeds of life for the faded thousand-year-old body of the underworld? An unchaste incestuous lust for the dead? Something that makes the blood run cold. Are

you demanding a lusty commingling with corpses? I spoke of "acceptance" but you demand "to seize, embrace, copulate?" Are you demanding the desecration of the dead?

then try not to weep at the Tundra man's sandals, buboed as you are, merely Borderline Personality Disordered as he is. Crawl pitifully towards the curb. Leave a bloody trail sniffed after by the Tundra family's Chihuahua dog. If the Chihuahua knows not what the Depths demand, and wants to give you a funny kiss, and then jumps on your head and hits you with his wiry little tail, speak a prayer of thanks to St. Hilarious for what natural good remains.

Ten Tips for Going on a Picnic

*I*f you nickname Warden Fermat "The Fermi Paradox" in an act of half-hearted praxis, he will throw a picnic to celebrate your parole.

One: Attending flagellants will scourge with leather thongs. If many flagellants indulge a "convulsion which in the most extraordinary manner infuriate[s] the human frame [...] called the dance of St. John or St. Vitus, on account of [its] bacchantic leaps"[94] recall from your study of history that bubonic plague tends to be followed by the Dancing Sickness.

Two: If Fermi P., as the nickname evolves, wonders if this Dancing Sickness might jive with his personal model of restorative justice, nod and reply, "Gee, would you look at those bold and fine breasts adjacent the splash pad. This Dancing Sickness may be just the ticket after my years spent in the grey and homonormative walls of your Serpent River Penitentiary, sir." If the Warden bristles at the word *homonormative*, divert him with Nietzsche's vindication of the dancing sick:

> [W]e recognize in these St. John's and St. Vitus'
> dancers the Bacchic choruses of the Greeks, who

---

[94] (Hecker, 1888)

had their precursors in Asia Minor and as far back as Babylon and the orgiastic Sacaea. There are people who, either from lack of experience or out of sheer stupidity, turn away from such phenomena, and, strong in the sense of their own sanity, label them either mockingly or pityingly "endemic diseases." These benighted souls have no idea how cadaverous and ghostly their "sanity" appears as the intense throng of Dionysian revelers sweeps past them.[95]

Three: If Posturepedic Ferm and yourself aren't yet Dancing Sick, but wish to be, so as to appear less cadaverous and ghostly, but also to approach nearer the bold and proudly-convulsive breasts—again cite historical precedent:

> Above a hundred unmarried women were seen raving about in consecrated and unconsecrated places, and the consequences were soon perceived. Gangs of idle vagabonds, who understood how to imitate to the life the gestures and convulsions of those really affected, roved from place to place seeking maintenance and adventures, and thus, wherever they went, spreading this disgusting spasmodic disease like a plague; for in maladies of this kind

[95] (Nietzsche, The Birth of Tragedy, 1872)

the susceptible are infected as easily by the appearance as by the reality.[96]

Four: Steady nerves with F.P. Serva's apple brandy much as you steadied them with thirteen Coors Lights before high school dances with the old gang. Thrust wildly. Seek maintenance. If even comradeship of spirit goes against the flagellator's ethos, heed the Warden's request to no longer indulge him with cool nicknames.

Five: If a three-pronged leather flagellator is handed to you, don't be rude, flagellate.

Six: Do not "bathe in fire" as the genuinely-afflicted Dancing Sick are inclined.

Seven: If a bold-breasted woman asks, "What's your angle?" respond as the idle vagabond you are, "Agitated by the same tympanic inflammation of the bowels that inflame your bowels, young lady."

Eight: Invite the best-looking Dancing Sick onto the Warden's yacht. Feel called to be a nomadic yachtsman. Pop bottles. Partake of the Warden's cocaine. Laugh without certainty at all Majthenyi's manifested evils. Give Warden Fermat an awesome high-five.

Nine: Smoke a fine cigar with the Warden. Spit bubonic blood upon his larder, eternally rude but what's to be done about it? State, "Warden, this is truly a hoot, but why not harness this Dancing Mania, weed out any idler vagabonds, and

---

[96] (Hecker, 1888)

bring this roadshow town to town, Rolling Thunder Revue-style, call it *Compassion on the Run* or something urgent. We'll spread cheer among northern Ontarians, a population long in need of cheer. We'll spread the good news. In a fun way. With the bold breasts. The good news of a benevolence transcendent, of a spiritual force *supra* to the creator of this ongoing sustain, Ronald Majthenyi, mentors my son in atemporal transcendental information structures, goddamn one-trick pony in the grand scheme. Imminently defeatable. Just the Genesis of a stumbling block between today's gory imposthumes and a golden tomorrow."

Ten: If the Warden's concerned inquiry of "Malevolent god eh?" omens of millennium, find your early gnostic blog-based instincts once again in Bloom.

How to Be a Strange Loop

*I*f during Singing Competition-style auditions at the marina the Warden inquires, "Why turn away so many statuesque babes? Rarely takes more than a tractor to appease a northern Ontarian," realize you're merely trying to cast the girl you've been thinking of, and that girl would but can't be Catherine.

One: Appease The Warden by accepting any young lady above a 36 B.

Two: Agree with Warden Jöns that most flagellants come off as far too desperate. Advise flagellants to conceal their ugly need more guilefully unless they can survive on the validation scraps found in that saddest of all possible worlds: the periphery of the entertainment industry.

Three: If now perceiving flagellants as affronts to the truly pious, *i.e.* 'Look at all my sinning and melodramatic atonement,' wonder what percentage of your blog-based evangelism, *e.g.* 'bitching and moaning about dead sister,' falls under so ignominious a banner.

Four: Hire humbler flagellants as stagehands. Prefer those not actively flagellating, those wearing hair shirts or *cilices* instead, garments made of harsh cloth in antiquity, steel wool in this contemporary scenario. Request the flagellant with the coolest cilice fashion you something similar. Rub your steel-wool'd cilice in boar waste per this flagellant's advice.

Five: Stretch your Tommy Hilfiger polo shirt over your mortifying new duds. Resemble an umpire. Suffer and stink.

Six: If *Compassion on the Run's* opening night in Nairn Centre is attended by only three bubonic sufferers—each drunk on home brew, each belligerent, each on the Borderline—then your preaching of fiery penance will fall on deaf ears. The come-hithers of the A1 babes will fare somewhat better. The Billy Joel covers crooned by Warden Fermat will be aggressively boo'd, such that he leaves the stage in tears.

Seven: If the production requires re-jiggering, commence a Gantt Chart with the Warden on how to best salve the spiritual and physical bubos of your upcoming audiences in Merkabah, Meconium, Tarbutt Additional, among the Thessalonians, and in other regions of indeterminacy. Balk piously when Warden Fermat loses interest and says, "Ughh I've got a Serpent River Correctional Facility to run," boards his Polaris Slingshot, and abandons the production. Read to the thin air from *The Decameron*,

> Tedious were it to recount how citizen avoided citizen, how among neighbors scarce found any that shewed fellow-feeling for another, how kinfolk held aloof and never met...nay, what is more, and scarcely to be believed, fathers and mothers were

found to abandon their own children, untended unvisited, to their fate.[97]

and then think of Marcel_Proust left untended, unvisited, impelled to his fate in some elsewhere sustain, and realize you have no moral standing from which to judge the Warden.

Eight: With the storm in your eyes, in Tarbutt Additional, remembering as always the first day that you fell in love, espy nothing but ichors and sanies, and perhaps worse: the ennui borne of northern Ontarian living. If Tarbutt Additional's residents don't need song and dance, nor B-cupped bosoms, but only amputations and tourniquets, and the nearest hospital in Thessalon is obviously overrun by Thessalonian Borderlines, then roll up your sleeves and look for the nearest accretion of boar scat so as to outfit Tarbutt Additional's citizens with efficacious shit cilices.

Nine: If some of the A1 beauties abandon their calling once triage and cilice production becomes the priority of the theatrical company, *i.e.* "I'm classically trained in ballet and tap not pig poop," then bid them adieu. If a cilice'd penitent abandons his vocation, shoot him in the skull with your pistol.

Ten: Work for your fellow man. Observe with wry amusement the cyclical *Ubik*ianism of your Good Works. Read earlier blogs on your phone. Notice cyclical shortening;

---

[97] (Boccaccio, 1313-1375)

'repetition as recapitulation,'[98] as Ricoeur argues; Majthenyi's sustains even less believable than your bluffs of charity and faith. Amputate necrotic digits and kiss bubos. Contemplate the eternal golden braid. Try to think of a way out, or maybe a way in.

---

[98] (Ricouer, 1984-1988)

Why Do All The Big Pharmaceutical Companies Hate Ernst 'Ernie' Kraay?

If all the charity in the world won't reattach the necrotic digits of three billion weary bubonics, then recline in a malarial swamp and attempt a Thought Form antidote to the Black Plague.

One: If this manifests as a Black Plague vaccine hastily developed by Klaas J. Kraay's nephew Ernst 'Ernie' Kraay, then attend Ernst's seminar in Manistique.

Two: If a vaccine side-effect is Narcissistic Personality Disorder, figure, 'Really even that far off from my baseline persona?' Wait in line. Get the shot. If the narcissism trades transmitters with its cluster B colleagues from the previous sustain's BPD, taste their unique flavour profiles. Despite frequent accusations from teachers, parents, spouses, Uber drivers, ASL interpreters, librarians, strippers, therapists, television producers, editors, WordPress customer service functionaries, and myriad others, learn that you hadn't really been a narcissist after all: you'd been afflicted by nothing more sinister than a robust ego co-morbid with a little messianic zeal, not unlike Bob Dylan.

Three: If enduring E.E. Kraay's exit interview in exchange for a 10% discount on your booster vaccine, get diagnosed as the amorous type of narcissist, *i.e.* 'Sexually seductive; enticing; beguiling; tantalizing; glib and clever; disinclined to real intimacy; indulges hedonistic desires; bewitches and inveigles others; pathological lying and swindling; tends to have many affairs, often with exotic partners.'[99]

Four: Inveigle a pretty girl in the outpatient area. When rejected, assert, "I've inveigled prettier before and I'll inveigle prettier again, Courtney."

Five: If no pretty girls wish to be beguiled, tantalized, or swindled, then listen to a windy narrative from a man you style *Self-Biographical Raphael*. With the brevity of Karl Ove Knausgård, Raphael will reveal his own zeals and interfamilial tragedies. He will text a link to his own blog: http:// the importanceofbeingfunny.wordpress.com. If disinclined towards this level of intimacy, wait with increasing irritation for your turn to talk. If Self-Biographical Raphael leaves the slightest opening, *e.g.* "You see, my sister was also quite funny and encouraged..." hijack the narrative and essay your usual sororal song and dance until Self-Biographical Raphael fakes a sneezing fit and ostensibly leaves to acquire a Kleenex but really just to reiterate his autobiography not even twenty feet away to Cosplay Carl, one of the many outpatient narcissists who counter-intuitively loves cocaine, common sense

---

[99] (Millon, 1996)

suggesting no one needs cocaine less than a raging narcissist conducting daily life in cosplay.

Six: If Cosplay Carl refuses your request for a line, compliment his Thanos getup until he meets you halfway with a key bump. Ask Cosplay Carl and Self-Biographical Raphael if they'd like to hear about the sunshine's gleam on a fishing lure one August morning that convinced you the revelator and grief advocate and recovering BPD sufferer and narcissist and necrotically-digited blogger that you were truly a fisherman, but also, also (!), in love with your sister Catherine.

Seven: If Ernie appears overwhelmed by all the narcissistic outpatient assholes he hath wrought, break the ice by quoting his uncle's *Incommensurability, Incomparability, and God's Choice of a World*[100], ostensibly to converse about a subject of mutual interest, but really just to show off how learned you are.

Eight: Don't even mention knowing Klaas J. Kraay from a bygone sustain. Act like of course you're well-versed in K. Kraay's Incommensurability stance, its deficiencies, as well as all the axiological apertures of the No Best World debate, necessitarianism, contingentism, + probably every other subject.

Nine: Run out of outpatients who'll listen to you. Speak on YouTube. Speak on street corners. Ring a big gold bell. Try to email your sister but only invoke that divider of destinies: the Mailer Daemon. Email Warden Fermat. Email the family

---

[100] (Kraay, Incommesurability, Incomparability, and God's Choice of a World, 2011)

of Dean Izdubar apologizing for his murder but really only to attention-seek. Email your parents hoping for clues as to where Catherine might be. Beat your chest on the high cliffs. Rend your breast. Audition for a play. If ridiculed by the Jon Lovitzian director as "drunk," perform your own one-man show in Manistique's town square. If the play is reviewed by a civil servant in his ticketing of you as a "public nuisance," post this review on Instagram, Facebook, Twitter, TikTok, and elsewhere.

Ten: If you've been ignored for weeks, and the only folks in the bawdy houses of Manistique are fellow narcissists desperate to describe their pyramid schemes and management styles and bespoke suits and preferred IPAs, realize what you need is someone with a nice co-dependent personality disorder. To this end, email your estranged wife, Emily.

How to Kick About the Embers of
a Dead Marriage

*I*f hitchhiking gets easier once every vaccinated trucker is a raging narcissist discoursing upon his data package; his pornographic subscriptions, *e.g.* 'Blacked.com;' his latencies; his truck stop shower aversion, no consequences of latencies, but rather the rattiness of the rentable towels, and how he keeps his own towel in the rear of his cab, but it never dries properly so he uses the Husky towels anyway, then manipulatively commiserate that yes, $16.99 is excessively dear for the Husky's 'hamburger steak' when the hamburg in question is no steak but just the dried frozen fecal product used for their corporately-dehumanizing banquet burgers and Mexicasa burgers supreme and *etc.*

One: If A* path-finding algorithm heuristics you on home, Emily will greet you, "Where have you been I've been looking all over Canada for you putting up posters so my hair started falling out I've been so worried."

Two: Pile wood for the wood stove in the front foyer, *i.e.* 'Ain't I a stinker.' Hug this apparition of Emily. Do not inquire regarding Marcel_Proust's absence. Cut a lengthy promo on the unsustainability of experience. If Emily's apparition has yet to experience personality disorder or plague, she will find your speaking dubious.

Three: Inform Emily that narcissism is the worst affliction yet. Notice with displeasure her flowing tears. Fail to manifest empathy. Manifest only concepts of *supposed to do* and *supposed to look*, of how to *affect* empathy in order to regain lost esteem.

Four: If all your life's action can now be understood as validation seeking, understand that you've never once acted altruistically, you have only *performed* altruistic acts. Experience a vacuum of vacancy that no benzodiazepam or ethyl-benzene inhalation can fill or suck through. Fear that even your eternal longing for Catherine was an act of narcissism: a gamma male entitlement to perfect love. Contemplate the fraudulence of your autostereogrammatic revelating, knowing that no Narc can access the Noumena, be it Fanged or teleological. Read up on your subject. Find apt the following quote from *Narcissism: Denial of True Self* by Alexander Lowen, "When the curtain falls upon an act, it is finished and forgotten. The emptiness of such a life is beyond imagination."[101]

Five: If Emily remains other-directed as ever and simply wants to help, listen as she recounts all she's found from YouTube's NARC support groups. Resent being called a

---

[101] (Lowen, 1983)

"narc" by a monetized YouTube personality. Consider spe-
cious the anti-narc community's claim they've "been raped
on a soul level." Resent all the anti-Narc superstar Dr. Ramania Durvusala videos in your inbox. Ask of Emily, "How is
this Ramania fiend not perceived as a narc herself? Fuckin'
narcs man." Ask of Dr. Ramania's recorded image, "Just what
am I supposed to do? What are all we narcissists supposed
to do? Go jump in a lake? You're the narc, you quack!" Ask
Dr. Ramani's recorded image if she's read much of the often-
cogent Jacques Derrida:

> There is not narcissism and non-narcissism.
> There are narcissisms that are more or less com-
> prehensive, generous, open, extended. What is
> called non-narcissism is in general but the econ-
> omy of a much more welcoming and hospitable
> narcissism. One that is much more open to the
> experience of the Other as Other. I believe that
> without a movement of narcissistic reappropria-
> tion, the relation to the Other would be absolutely
> destroyed. It would be destroyed in advance. The
> relation to the Other, even if it remains asym-
> metrical, open, without possible reappropriation
> must trace a movement of reappropriation in the
> image of one's self for love to be possible. Love is
> narcissistic.[102]

---

[102] (Derrida, 1995)

Six: If the narcisphere caters only to narc victims and victims-awaiting narcs, create a competing website, http://whatexactlyisanarctodo.wordpress.com.

Seven: Feel mildly vindicated by Kristen Bombek's refutal of what she calls this "narciscript," particularly her observation that, "the bad boyfriend is the narcisphere's favourite villain."[103]

Eight: If unbated by this Bombekian anti-narcisphere polemic Emily other-directedly YouTubes Kohut and Kernberg and *The Narcissist You Know* and *Living in the Age of Entitlement,* balk condescendingly at the consensus treatment for NPD: the old therapy/SSRI combo.

Nine: Dissert how SSRIs are largely responsible for this age of entitlement. Explain why the Burger King dullard is possessed of a lot of unlikely wisdom to go along with your Impossible Whopper. Refer to primate studies wherein primates given SSRIs rise atop the dominance hierarchy such that the previously-vital unmedicated apes grow depressed and cowering. Ask if that's the answer the medical model is so proud of. Mention SSRIs being largely incapable of beating placebo while offering a laundry list of side effects ranging from brain zaps to *increased* depression and *increased* suicidality right up to rampageous near-daily delights of mass slaughter. Essay a sardonic, "Lol."

Ten: If Emily hugs you and wisely plays the song *Time* by Tom Waits, a song that played when first you learned to

---

[103] (Bombek, 2016)

love Emily, feel some of that love again, even if the love is just a validation of your own love-inducing characteristics, a Tucker Maxian and appalling love of the mirror, of the effect you can produce in the other, the validation of being someone else's loved other. Try to let "the things you can't remember tell the things you can't forget."[104]

[104] (Waits, 1985)

How to Feign Mindfulness

*I*f proteinaceous silk has ensnared Emily in the Intellectual Dark Web, she'll offer narcissism-reversal advice gleaned from a *Joe Rogan Experience* with Sam Harris: "You use his Waking Up meditation app, only $18.99 a month, which might seem expensive for a subscription service except it could save your life and make life easier for everyone who puts up with you, plus I think he gives it away free when you beg him."

One: If Emily places a Winners yoga mat beneath an ancient pine and then alights a crackling fire, don't risk losing face *i.e.* 'Not open-minded regarding Eastern traditions.' Sit on that chemical-smelling mat and feign mindfulness!

Two: If you've seen too many bubos and oozing suppurations to clear your mind entirely, + hold preconceived notions that meditation is new age flakery if not thinly-guised devil worship lacking the heft of Christian mortification, then check your phone for likes and shares on latest blog: 0. Check for Instagram likes: all bot likes.

Three: If your histrionics remain unheralded, make even meditating a competitive enterprise. Refocus on the breath. Request clarity. Evade the consequences of no-go theorems.

Evade the iterative deployment, iterative discovery, and bad alignment take bingo heard in the ringing belles de Garis. Evade the ever-vigilant mark inside. Start to find something. Feel a fleeting moment of a bliss transcendent. Try to replace the worm inside with the Catherine inside, for as the xenophobe H.P. Lovecraft wrote, "For know you, that your gold and marble city of wonder is only the sum of what you have seen and loved in youth."[105] Suddenly know you that the 17-year-old visions of Catherine seen and loved in the "flower-fragrant common"[106] of Bellevue Park only existed because of something inside you. Close your eyes to seek a sempiternal Catherinian grace, "a liquid loveliness which cannot die,"[107] but a liquid loveliness that can only live if you believe it immanent.

Five: If surely some blogospheric colleague has combined yuppie yoga mat meditation with bible thumpin', creed-proclaimin', old-time religion by this late capitalistic stage, feel rather under-resourced in the study of religions upon discovering this ecclesiastical fusion-cuisine has been served for millennia. Dive down the rabbit hole of your phone's many corroborating studies on the efficacy of contemplative meditation, e.g. '*A Randomized Investigation of Evangelical Christian Accommodative Mindfulness*[108] from that foremost pillar of academia: The Baptist College of Florida,' e.g. 'The University

---

[105] (Lovecraft, 2014)
[106] (Lovecraft, 2014)
[107] (Lovecraft, 2014)
[108] (Ford & Garzon, 2017)

of Zuzuland's *An integral investigation into the phenomenology and neurophysiology of Christian Trinity meditation.*[109] Eschew meditative silence for frequent cries of "Eureka!"

Six: Seek to validate your metanoia, apathea, illumination, and theosis on your crotch-situated phone, immediately loosening your grasp on the Catherine internal.

Seven: Swear a full-throated vow of silence. Break it (1m16s) to inform a passing mailperson how your personal silence can benefit only you, whilst a silver-tongued proselytizing of silence's virtue might benefit all weary narcs and histrionics. Ask the skittish mailwoman to help arrange your lighting tree for a hotly-anticipated YouTube sermon.

Eight: If Emily hazes the mailwoman westward before Android-revelating a dozen odd YouTube narcs all streaming their own narc-ish iterations of the good contemplative news, all loudly meditating wild-eyed from Psalms—if all that, then know that narcs are gonna narc about a subject even self-effacing as contemplative meditation.

Nine: Learn from Emily's Alexa of yet another intervention for the latest outbreak. Atheistic Sam Harris, having reached narcs about the benefits of meditation, but now outraged by these narc's own competing ideology-based meditative prayer apps, has proposed a quick lazer zap to the old Wernicke's area, the brain area responsible for the perception of time, for speech and its comprehension: a simple robotic

---

[109] (Edwards & Edwards, 2012)

zap to induce what Harris deems a therapeutic course of anomic aphasia.

Ten: If Sam references Iain McGilchrist's controversial *The Master and His Emissary*, phone-read McGilchrist's interview in *Frontier Psychiatrist* in which this necessarily-bearded man states:

> thought originates in the right hemisphere, is processed for expression in speech by the left hemisphere, and the meaning integrated again by the right (which alone understands the overall meaning of a complex utterance, taking everything into account)…

and concludes that,

> the right brain is the mediator, the first and last stop of all experience.[110]

Deduce that for your stupid self-reflexive self to regain the Catherine internal, what escape is there from the left brain's empirical isolationism other than to abandon the perception of time?

---

[110] (Frontier Psychiatry, 2010)

How to Have Your Wernicke's Area Robotically Impinged Upon

*I*f demand for the Wernicke Zap™ booms such that every family doctor, nurse practitioner, and naturopath in the General Toronto Area haphazardly trains in implanting Sam Harris' proprietary Wernicke Zapper™ nano-surgical robot, then collect three chickens, a chord of wood, and two fatted calves to trade the horse surgeon practising at the stables in hopes she will remove from your mind all your words and elisions and ego constructions.

One: Order your affairs in preparation to exist outside of time and language. If it's your last opportunity to speak, try to listen. Allow Emily to air her grievances while you're still capable of understanding and responding.

Two: Nod absently at Emily's laundry-list of grievances *e.g.* 'Philandering, inhalant abuse, emotional abuse, egotism, + too high a priority placed on unmonetized blogging.'

Three: Prefer your last utterances not be those of a petulant and histrionic narcissist. Rather, endeavour to speak with the simplicity of a stylist and blogger and revelator of your magnitude. Speak the words, "I'm sorry." Feel as though perhaps she believes you for once.

Four: Feel less surprise than you'd like to upon recognizing your veterinary surgeon.

Five: If Dr. Jenya's waiver lists side effects including

- lack of sensory processing for phoneme content, *i.e.* 'the inability to perceive language.'
- Wernicke's aphasia *i.e.* 'the affliction of speaking sentences that sound fluent but lack meaning.'

those are no revelator's cup of tea, but if fluid-sounding nonsense is your bread and butter anyway, blogging-wise, ask Emily if she'll transcribe any fluent-sounding sentences you speak, even those lacking sensibly-processed phoneme content, and publish them so as to provide your loyal audience with at least some whispers in the darkness.

Six: If the waiver waves responsibility for any and all temporal-lobe damages a thick-fingered hair-stylist turned horse doctor might inflict while more or less Lasiking a little robot in the vicinity of a temporal lobe, this means the undersigned may never again comprehend, feel emotion, remember, perceive the passage of time, or view a vision.

Seven: Ask Jenya's colorist and surgical technologist if you'll be able to read. Should she respond, "Probably can run your eyes over the page anyway," then line up Audible titles based on your nascent interest in active contemplation *e.g.* 'James Finlay,' *e.g.* 'Thomas Merton.'

Eight: If Audible's Christian Mysticism category underdelivers, regret that Emily has already paid Jenya $2573, knowing the "I already paid" argument trumps all rational objection to encephalic hardship.

Nine: Should your anaesthetic be improperly administered, practise gratitude for a few extra seconds of comprehensory horror. Perceive but don't necessarily remember the buzzing and bone-dust smell of your skull being sawed. Hit 'publish' on what must be your last meaningful blog in some time.

2 COMMENT ON "TEN TIPS FOR HAVING YOUR WERNICKE'S AREA ROBOTICALLY IMPINGED UPON"

Grievin' Gary: Did you hit publish right as they were sawing your skull? Pretty badass way to end this blog; as good a time as any for me to unsubscribe. Best of wishes with your Wernicke's area and I hope it helps lessen the grief of your deceased sister.

Brampton Int'l Grief Conference: Hope the surgery went well! Thoughts and prayers, thoughts and prayers!

Ten Ways to Help Dave?

*D*ave asked me to blog what he's saying but he's saying things like, "Hans Koong oom lot knew shoe Burt's quasicrystal atonality" and "Rectal dogsology demands planks Catherine" so I didn't want to ruin his life's work by including nonsense. He seems really quiet and unhappy. I thought I'd try to crowd-source some interventions to make him better. Here are some things I've tried already:

One: Vitamin C.

Two: Vitamin D.

Three: Kale.

Four: Coffees.

Five: Less chips.

Six: Fresh air.

Seven: Swimming pool.

Eight: Religion shows on YouTube and that he records on PVR.

Nine: Epsom salts.

Ten: Please tell me if you can think of anything else. I'm desperate and scared for him.

One Reader Survey

After Sam Harris' recent indictment, many loved ones are furious with the results of the Wernicke's area surgeries once considered necessary by the victims of narcissists. A new experiment surgery is out that can either restore temporal lobe functioning 😊 or paralyze or kill the patient ☹. On the one hand, I definitely don't want to kill Dave, and if he's paralyzed that would make life even harder. However; the way he's living is not the way he'd want to live, kind of like when he was on antidepressants and being nice for a while but said it wasn't how he wanted to live. I want to leave it up to his loyal readers and few remaining friends with this survey. The survey is open now. Please only vote if you know and care about what happens to Dave.

Should Dave get the surgery to fix his lobe:

Yes

No

Ten Tips for Citing All David's Sources
For Him

*I*f in David's Unapproved Comments a common complaint was things were quoted but not even attributed to anybody like "Who is it saying this? It's quoted but I don't know who is saying this???" or "You aren't Virgil you know. This isn't 50 B.C. Everyone hasn't read everything and can be expected to know where it's from!" then having some College English training from Centennial College in the academic necessity of APA citation, I have gone back and retroactively cited as many sources as I could detect in all blogs up to and including this one. I undertook significant efforts to put these citations in PROPERLY, even if they're not all that meaningful to the reader or don't appear quite so proper as they really are.

One: I did this mostly by Googling the things in quotes. Sometimes the source came right up and I easily cited it using a citation generator.

Two: Other times I had to spend many hours tracking things down. I only emailed reference librarians when absolutely necessary because I know David hates reference librarians and wouldn't want them getting involved in his life's work.

Three: Sometimes Dave would reference having referenced something but no reference was there so what was he even talking about? I then had to search every two-word phrase in the above paragraphs. When he said something that was obviously some phrase from somewhere I tried to Google the phrase. Maybe some of these phrases are known to people who've read the stuff David leafed through so please alert me in comments if they don't require citation at all. When he at least made an effort to cite authors I didn't cite them in the bibliography because I was usually pretty tired after working all day.

Four: During the hardest times I wondered why David didn't just cite his sources as he went along, when he had the books right in front of him. It would have made it easier for him and for me. It's ironic because one of his favourite Bob Dylan lyrics was, "If you want to remember you better write down their names."[111] But then he didn't even write down many names.

Five: I then reminded myself that David never liked for things to be easy or pleasant or like the way normal people like things and that was just part of who he was.

Six: When words seemed weird I Googled the words to see if they obviously came from somewhere and required APA citation. Some of the weird words turned out not to be words at all. They were words he had made up. I couldn't find an APA policy regarding made-up words. I couldn't find

[111] (Dylan, Murder Most Foul, 2020)

APA policy regarding using a plus sign (+) instead of the word *plus* so I left this in even though most people probably find it annoying and it hurts his life's work maybe more than it helps it. For this same reason I have also left David's erratic hyphenations intact though I believe they are mostly reckless whims that don't adhere to any style guide that anyone at r/editors could refer me to.

Seven: I did not make clarifications when he made inaccurate statements regarding me or quoted me as saying things I never would have said. Same with many factual errors I found. I knew it was imperative to stay true to the source material because David used to rant and rave about Kabbalistic language codes embedded in the blog and I wouldn't want to mess up any of the codes by changing something I didn't say back to something I actually did say or changing something nonfactual to something factual. I did however risk messing up the Kabbalistic language code when he was being too hard on himself.

Eight: Some ideas that I recognized from podcasts we'd listened to were NOT in quotes. I cited these too, as suggested by the Purdue Owl website. Same for episodes of TV shows and movies and songs.

Nine: This made me worry that some of David's ideas weren't David's ideas but from places other than podcasts that obviously I would never recognize. If anyone recognizes any ideas not original to David and not from a podcast please let me know in the comments so I can cite those too. If you don't see your comment in the comments it's not because I deleted it. It's because David didn't approve many comments so I want to play it safe by approving 0 comments on his life's work as he called it to avoid accidentally approving the wrong comment which might mess up the Kabbalistic language code.

Ten: Anyways I'd appreciate readers pointing out any stolen ideas because I wouldn't want David arrested for plagiarism while in his impaired condition and not even able to defend his work as "collage" or "the blues tradition" or "the ecstasy of influence" or whatever he would claim in court if he could. Readers who don't care about proper APA citation like Dave didn't should skip the following bibliography blog.

Bibliography

Anselm. (1986). *A new, interpretive translation of St. Anselm's Monologion and Proslogion.* (6 ed.). (J. Hopkins, Trans.)

Aquinas, S. T. (1225-1274). *The "Summa theologica" of St. Thomas Aquinas.* London: Burns, Oates & Washburne LTD.

Augustine. (1950). *The City of God.* (M. Dods, Ed.) New York: Modern Library.

Augustine. (1998). *The Confessions.* (S. Boulding, Ed.) New York: Vintage Books.

Baez, J. (1975). Diamonds and Rust [Recorded by J. Baez]. J. B. David Kershenbaum.

Baldwin, M., Biernat, M., & Landau, M. J. (2015). Remembering the real me: Nostalgia offers a window to the intrinsic self. *Journal of Personality and Social Psychology, 108,* 128-147.

Barlow, P. W. (2015, Jul-Aug). The natural history of consciousness, and the question of whether plants are conscious, in relation to the Hameroff-Penrose quantum-physical 'Orch OR' theory of universal consciousness. *Communicative Integrative Biology, 8(4).*

Barthelme, D. (1981). Some of Us Had Been Threatening Our Friend Colby. In *60 Stories*. New York: Putnam.

Barthelme, D. (2008). *Not Knowing: The Essays and Interviews*. Counterpoint.

Barthes, R. (2002). *A Lover's Discourse: Fragments*. London: Vintage Publishing.

Baudrillard, J. (1994). *Simulacra and Simulation*. Ann Arbour: University of Michigan Press.

Beilby, J. K., Eddy, P. R., & Boyd, G. A. (2001). *Divine Foreknowledge: Four Views*. Downer's Grove, Illinois: InterVarsity Press.

Bem, D. (2011). Feeling the future: Experimental evidence for anomalous retroactive influences on cognition and affect. *Journal of Personality and Social Psychology, 100(3),* 407-425.

Bem, D. (2011, January 27). The Colbert Report. (S. Colbert, Interviewer) Comedy Central.

Benatar, D. (2006). *Better never to have been: The harm of coming into existence*. Oxford: Clarendon Press.

Bernard, S. (2009, April 23). *TheLLaBB*. Retrieved from "Teaching Gretzky-Style Field Sense.": www.thellabb.com/teaching-gretzky-style-field-sense/.

Boccaccio, G. (1313-1375). *The Decameron*. New York: Norton.

Bombek, K. (2016). *The Selfishness of Others: An Essay on the Fear of Narcissism* . New York: Macmillan.

Burton, T. I. (2020, May 08). Christianity Gets Weird. *The New York Times*.

Cauterucci, C. (2020, February 01). *The Weinstein Trial Isn't the First High-Profile Case to Feature a Graphic Description of the Defendant's Genitals.* . Retrieved from Slate: https://slate.com/news-and-politics/2020/01/the-weinstein-trial-isnt-the-first-high-profile-case-to-feature-a-graphic-description-of-the-defendants-genitals.html

Clarke, A. C. (Writer), & Kubrick, S. (Director). (1968). *2001: A Space Odyssey* [Motion Picture]. Warner Brothers.

Clattenburg, M., Smith, M., & Torrens, J. (2005, June 5). *Dressed All Over & Zesty Mordant* . (M. Clattenburg, Director) Retrieved from https://www.imdb.com/title/tt0732905/

Deng, N. (2018, March 22). *plato.stanford.edu/entries/eternity/*. Retrieved from plato.stanford.edu: https://plato.stanford.edu/entries/eternity/

Derrida, J. (1995). *Points . . . : interviews, 1974-1994.* (E. Weber, Ed., & P. K. Others, Trans.) Stanford, California: Stanford University Press.

Dylan, B. (2000). Things Have Changed [Recorded by B. Dylan]. New York, New York.

Dylan, B. (2020). Murder Most Foul [Recorded by B. Dylan]. On *Rough and Rowdy Ways.* Columbia Records.

Edwards, S. D., & Edwards, D. J. (2012). An integral investigation into the phenomenology and neurophysiology of Christian Trinity meditation. *HTS Teologiese Studies, 68*(1).

Eisenstein, S. (1947). *The film sense.* (J. Leyda, Ed.) New York: Harcourt, Brace and World.

Eliade, M. (2005). *The myth of the eternal return: Cosmos and history.* Princeton, NJ: Princeton University Press.

Eliot, T. S. (1988). *The waste land and other poems.* (F. Kermode, Ed.) New York: Penguin Books.

Engber, D. (2017, June 7). *Slate.* Retrieved from https://slate.com/health-and-science/2017/06/daryl-bem-proved-esp-is-real-showed-science-is-broken.html

Faulkner, W. (2000). *As I Lay Dying: The Corrected Text.* New York: Modern Library.

Fifel, K. (2018, January 24). Experiment, Readiness Potential and Neuronal Determinism: New Insights on Libet. *Journal of Neuroscience, 38*(4), 784-786.

Fitzgerald, F. S. (1995). *The Great Gatsby.* New York: Scribner Paperpack Fiction.

Foland-Ross, L., Cooney, R., Joormann, J., Henry, M., & Gotlib, I. (2014). Recalling happy memories in remitted depression: A neuroimaging investigation of the repair of sad mood. *Cognitive, Affective, & Behavioral Neuroscience, 14,* 818-826.

Foley, B. (1989). Clay Pigeons [Recorded by B. Foley]. On *Live at the Austin Outhouse (...and Not There).*

Ford, K., & Garzon, F. (2017). Research note: A randomized investigation of evangelical Christian accommodative mindfulness. *Spirituality in Clinical Practise, 4*(2), 92-99.

Frontier Psychiatry. (2010, February 24). *http://frontier-psychiatrist.co.uk/interview-with-iain-mcgilchrist/.* Retrieved from Frontier Psychiatry: http://frontierpsychiatrist.co.uk/interview-with-iain-mcgilchrist/

Galak, J., LeBoeuf, R. A., Nelson, L. D., & Simmons, J. P.–9. (2012). Correcting the past: Failures to replicate psi. *Journal of Personality and Social Psychology,* 933-948.

Gholipour, B. (2019, September 10). *A Famous Argument Against Free Will Has Been Debunked.* Retrieved from

The Atlantic: https://www.theatlantic.com/health/archive/2019/09/free-will-bereitschaftspotential/597736/

Gurdjieff, G. (1933). *The Herald of Coming Good.* Paris: Holmes Publishing Group.

Hecker, J. F. (1888). *The Black Death, and The Dancing Mania.* (B. Babington, Trans.) London, Paris, New York & Melbourne: Cassell and Company.

Heidegger, M. (1984). *Nietzsche: Volume Two - The Eternal Recurrence of the Same.* San Francisco: Harper.

Heynen, R., Boomsma, C., Baker, R., Hugen, M. D., Nyenhuis, H., & Stob, H. (1973). *Committee to Study Homosexuality.* Christian Reformed Church in North America.

Horner, A. J., Bisby, J. A., Bush, D., Lin, W.-J., & Burgess, N. (2015). Evidence for holistic episodic recollection via hippocampal pattern completion. *Nature Communications, 6.*

Huxley, A. (1936). *Eyeless in Gaza.*

Jordan, J. (2015). What Arises from This?": The Autostereogrammatical in Thomas Pynchon's Mason & Dixon. *Critique: Studies in Contemporary Fiction, 56(3).*

Kazan, E. (Director). (1957). *A Face in the Crowd* [Motion Picture].

Kerouac, J. (1992). *Big Sur.* New York: Penguin Books.

Khan, J. (2017, June 5). *Wayne Gretzky-Style 'Field Sense' May Be Teachable*. Retrieved from Wired: https://www.wired.com/2007/05/ff-mindgames/

Kraay, K. J. (2011). Incommesurability, Incomparability, and God's Choice of a World. *International Journal for Philosophy of Religion.*

Kraay, K. J. (2012). The Theistic Multiverse: Problems and Prospects. In Y. Nagasawa, *Scientific Approaches to the Philosophy of Religion* (pp. 143-162). Houndsmills: Palgrave Macmillan.

Land, N. (2011). Machinic Desire. In N. Land, *Fanged Noumena*. Cambridge, Massachussets : Urbanomic.

Land, N. (2018, November 20). Crypto-Current, An Introduction to Bitcoin and Philosophy. *Šum, 10.2.*

Land, N. (2018, October 31). *Crypto-Current: Bitcoin and Philosophy*. Retrieved from https://etscrivner.github.io/cryptocurrent/

Langan, C. (2019). *Introduction to Quantum Metamechanics*. Mega Foundation Press.

Leifer, M., & Pusey, M. (2017). Is a time symmetric interpretation of quantum theory possible without retrocausality? *Proceedings of the Royal Society A: Mathematical, Physical, and Engineering Sciences, 473.*

Linder, A. (2019, January 22). *Obese American passenger forces Taiwanese flight attendant to wipe his butt on plane.* Retrieved from shanghai.ist: http://shanghai.ist/2019/01/22/obese-american-passenger-forces-taiwanese-flight-attendant-to-wipe-his-butt-on-plane/

Linder, A. (2019, January 22). *Obese American passenger forces Taiwanese flight attendant to wipe his butt on plane.* Retrieved from shanghai.ist: http://shanghai.ist/2019/01/22/obese-american-passenger-forces-taiwanese-flight-attendant-to-wipe-his-butt-on-plane/

Lovecraft, H. (2014). *The dream-quest of unknown Kadath.* (I. Culbard, Ed.)

Lowen, A. (1983). *Narcissism: Denial of the true self.* (6 ed.). New York: Macmillan Pub. Co.

Lynch, D. (Director). (2002). *Mulholland Drive* [Motion Picture].

Lynch, D., & McKenna, K. (2018). *Room To Dream.* New York: Random House.

Matthews, D. (2020, September 2). *Impassioned Nebraska man asks city council to rebrand boneless chicken wings to 'saucy nugs'.* Retrieved from New York Daily News: https://www.nydailynews.com/news/national/ny-nebraska-man-lincoln-city-council-boneless-chicken-wings-saucy-nugs-20200902-bsjcxzurrbdvxnpa36s5o7oxxe-story.html

Meeropool, A. (1937). Strange Fruit [Recorded by B. Holliday].

Merrill, J. (1982). *The changing light at Sandover: including the whole of the Book of Ephraim, Mirabell's books of number, Scripts for the pageant, and a new coda, the Higher keys.* New York: Altheneum.

Millon, T. (1996). *Disorders of personality: DSM-IV and beyond.* New York: Wiley.

Newell, S. (2016, June 13). *List: Every Synonym For "Pass" That Rifled Out Of Doc Emrick's Mouth.* Retrieved from Deadspin: https://deadspin.com/list-every-synonym-for-pass-that-rifled-out-of-doc-e-513664662

Nietzsche, F. (1872). *The Birth of Tragedy.*

Nietzsche, F. (1887). *The Gay Science.*

Opderbeck, D. (2016, December 09). *Eschatology, Molinism, Modal Laws, and the Multiverse.* Retrieved from davidoperdeck.com: http://davidopderbeck.com/tgdarkly/2016/12/09/eschatology-molinism-modal-laws-and-the-multiverse/

Proust, M. (1871-1922 (2003). *Swann's way.* New York: Modern Library.

Ramirez, S., Liu, X., & MacDonald, C. (2015). Activating positive memory engrams suppresses depression-like behaviour. *Nature, 522,* 335-339.

Reich, R. (2020). *The System: Who Rigged It, How We Fix It.* New York: Knopf.

Ricouer, P. (1984-1988). *Time and Narrative.* Chicago: University of Chicago Press.

Rilke, R. M. (1943). *Letters to a young poet.* London: Euston Press.

Roiland, J., & Harmon, D. (2015). Rick and Morty.

Romano, D. (2013). Two-Pillow Sleeper [Recorded by D. Romano].

Schlosser, M. E. (2002). Free will and the unconscious precursors of choice. *Journal of Philosophical Psychology, 25*(3), 365-384.

Shneidman, E. S. (1998). *The Suicidal Mind.* Oxford Press.

Slade, D. (2014, September 29). Book Critique: Four Views: God and Time Edited by Gregory E. Ganssle. *Liberty Baptist Theological Seminary.*

Sloman, L. (2002). *On the Road with Bob Dylan.* New York: Three Rivers Press.

Steinbeck, J. (1945). *Cannery Row.* New York: Editions for the Armed Services, Inc.

Stump, E., & Kretzman, N. (1981). Eternity. *The Journal of Philosophy,* 429-458.

Sun-tzu. (1964). *The Art of War*. (S. Griffith, Ed.) Oxford: Clarendon Press.

Tarkovsky, A. (1982). Cinema Thieves—International Intrigue. Rome. Retrieved from https://cinephiliabeyond. org/filmmakers-masterclass-with-andrei-tarkovsky-cin-ema-is-a-mosaic-made-of-time/#:~:text=Film%20is%20 a%20mosaic%20made,with%20his%20own%20particu-lar%20vision.

thesatanictemple.com. (n.d.). Retrieved from What is the differ-ence between The Satanic Temple and the Church of Satan?: https://thesatanictemple.com/pages/what-is-the-difference-between-the-satanic-temple-and-the-church-of-satan

Trafton, A. (2015, June 17). *MIT News*. Retrieved from Recalling happier memories can reverse depression: https:// bcs.mit.edu/news-events/news/recalling-happier-memo-ries-can-reverse-depression

Tweedy, J. (1996). Red-Eyed and Blue [Recorded by Wil-co]. Chicago.

Tyrrell, I. (2018, January 24). *The mysterious Jung: his cult, the lies he told, and the occult*. Retrieved from Givens Institute: www.ligi.org.uk/resources/delve-our-extensive-library/interviews/mysterious-jung-his-cult-lies-he-told-and-occult.

Waits, T. (1985). Time [Recorded by T. Waits]. New York City.

Wargo, E. (2018). *Time Loops: Precognition, Retrocausation, and the Unconscious*. Charlottesville: Anomalist Books.

Weinstein, B. (2019, October). *The Portal Episode 7: Bret Easton Ellis*. Retrieved June 29, 2020, from Youtube: https://www.youtube.com/watch?v=bkAWAJyX0fM&t=4399s

Wilhelm Reich, M. (1945, April). Some Mechanisms of the Emotional Plague. *International Journal of Sex-Economy and Orgone Research*, 4(1).

How to Save Money for an Expensive Surgery

If the Wernicke repair surgery costs half a million dollars you can afford it by:

One: Eating only ramen.

Two: Working a lot.

Three: Selling things like blankets and extra plates you don't use.

Four: Sending old underwear and things to creeps on the Internet.

Five: Collecting and returning cans like Dave used to do.

Six: Bringing coins from around the house to the grocery store coin sorting machine.

Seven: Cutting back on deodorant for Dave because he doesn't leave the house unless I take him out anyway and I've gotten used to the smell.

Eight: Cancel Netflix even though it's the only thing I have to keep me company or make life fun.

Nine: Sell hair to wig shops.

Ten: If you'd like to suggest another money-saving idea or want to send Dave some money because you used to enjoy his blog and he did it for free then every little bit helps.

How to Smear Blood on the Tracks

*I*f your Wernicke's-area has been surgically repaired by a Lil' Ben Affleck™ robot surgeon, do not cut a breathless promo upon the revival of your capacity for speech. If there is now nothing BUT time to bloviate about the placeless place in the open field of divinity you occupied while zapped of Wernicke's, then say only to Emily, "Thank you for your support during this trying time!" Don't explain that while you might have appeared, in ableist language, *retarded*, you and your dorsolateral prefrontal right cortex had been doing just dandy.

One: If Emily inquires regarding frustrations faced by a man with your "gift of gab" suffering speech loss, *i.e.* 'Convincing herself the reversal surgery was money well spent,' refer her to McGilchrist's *Frontier Psychiatrist* interview to illustrate how without the left brain imposing its empty unwarranted optimism, its empirical pathologies of paranoia, without its inauthentic representation of the right hemisphere's authentic presencing, then zapped of Wernicke's you'd been afforded the necessary distance from the world that allowed Emerson to move the transcendental needle a notch or two.

Two: If Emily saddens as Emerson is referenced, *i.e.* 'Maybe a bad idea to get you the $1,340,000 surgery after you'd been free from imperiousness for the first time in your adult life,' then essay some low-end zingers regarding hospital gown insufficiencies to assuage her buyer's remorse.

Three: If driven home, see the forests, the nighttime, and the 90km/h signs as part of the placeless place knowable only as an open field of divinity. Roll down the window. If the wind blows across your brow, pray that all your trials are for a reason, making you more than just a vessel of vanity. If preparing for a change of seasons, the Fall, affect contrition for once. Pause the Meister Eckhart audiobook on the car speakers when he says, "You must come to an unknowing." Start to raise your Eurekaean index finger before lowering it, knowing that's exactly what Meister warns against. Chastise yourself for knowing even that.

Four: If Emily says with chagrin, "We already listened to this one," then change the audiobook to Thomas Merton's *What is Contemplation.*

Five: If Emily requests 90s hits on SiriusXM's appropriately-named 90s Hits station, give Audible proselytizing and revelating one last shot with *Christian Meditation*, in which James Finlay states, "In the divine encounter is the falling away of who we imagine ourselves to be."

Six: If this fundamentally disturbs Emily, *i.e.* 'I don't want who I imagine myself or yourself to be to fall away,' then accede to 90s Hits while listening to Finlay on her headphones, kind of rude since you haven't spoken to Emily in six months.

Seven: If 90s Hits are sufficient satisfactions of the world for Emily, enjoy with subdued zealotry James Finlay's discursions around the biblical passage, "If our heart condemns us, God is greater than our hearts," meaning even if you can't forgive yourself for burning Stacey Keats and the crackling sounds wrought thereby, for selling out mankind only to revive the Catherine internal, for your bizarre masturbatory peccadilloes, your invalidation games, your chronic low mood and the fair flowers crushed underfoot as a result, for all the fathers and mothers who'd adored you only to be passed by like so many admirers made meaningless by virtue of their admiration, for the paperbacks hurled at terrified house cats at the tail-ends of benders—if your heart rightly condemns you for all that, Finlay, in his soothing monk voice, will remind you through Emily's AirPods that God is greater than our hearts.

Eight: Break yoga mat bread with Emily. Speak a humble prayer of gratitude for all the meals you couldn't express gratitude for during your prolonged silence. If Emily seems peevish about all the "Jesus stuff!" *i.e.* "I bought you this $1.5 m surgery hoping you'd talk about the things on TV we like and not just drone on about a bunch of bible analysis guys no one's heard of and really isn't that just the same old narcissistic-histrionic personality disorder we were trying to fix anyways?" then say only secret blessings over your Rotisserie-Style Chicken Caesar Melt from Subway.

Nine: If Emily desires a post-prandial viewing of a program from the *Real Housewives of...* series of programs, which you'd purportedly been "enjoying" during your convalescence, excuse yourself to the bathroom so you can zealously read your gold-leafed King James Prophecy Bible on the toilet. Open randomly to James 1: 5-8's warning against wavering and double-mindedness.

Ten: Realize that like Kerouac "whenever Spring comes to New York" your double-mindedness has "just got to go," because if certain, you mustn't wavereth while being tossed by winds of Desperate Housewifery, real or imagined. If you Google local monasteries, find the Holy Cross Priory clothed in the drabbest of humilities. If Emily has been hypnotized into slumber by the artificial effervescence of real housewives, then write her a goodbye letter quoting the well-loved Leonard Cohen song, *So Long Marianne:*

> Well, you know that I love to live with you
> But you make me forget so very much
> I forget to pray for the angels
> And then the angels forget to pray for us

And then, hopefully to cheer her up, from Daniel Romano's *There's a Hardship:*

> And my lady she's got everything
> She was born already free
> Yes and she could go most anywhere
> But she sinks down here with me

i.e. 'Don't need to be sunken and mired with me anymore, at least.' If it is cruel to abandon Emily with so little as these songs after she's spent her life loving you, then you must believe with unwavering certainty that Emily is but a manifestation of an infinite generosity that all must return to, and that the packing of your humble Herschel bag and your deconvolutional Uber Pooling to the priory is no abandonment *per se*, but only a spoke in the cycle of eternal return. Hear her sneeze one last time and mouth the word, "Gesundheit," before thinking, "No, that's not right."

Ten Tips for Life at the Monastery

*I*f you arrive at the Holy Cross Priory in the middle of the night, and the door-answering monk looks annoyed, *i.e.* 'You're not the first wild-eyed seeker to arrive during our few crucial hours of restful sleep,' then appreciate his begrudging unlocking of a shabby office and his peevish pointing towards the couch you can sleep on.

One: If the monastic intake process involves far more paperwork and OHIP forms and the general signing of your life away than the *Walking the Mystic Path* podcast led you to believe, figure that's simply the state of contemporary organizational liability theory.

Two: Wake at 4 a.m. Recite prayers. Read psalms. Eat breakfast. Desire a fattier breakfast. Express a low enthusiasm for starch. Desire a beer, preferably served to you at a strip club.

Three: Do Lectio Divina-style meditation all damn day. Feel some peace, perhaps.

Four: Recite prayers with your fellow cenobites. Practise infused contemplation, defined by Merton as "a gift of God that absolutely transcends all the natural capacities of the soul and which no man can acquire by any effort of his own."

Five: Scrub toilets and things. Recite more prayers with fellow neophyte cenobites. Train rookie cenobites on how to prepare the morning rice mush.

Six: After reading *The Interior Castle* by Teresa of Ávila, flex on the alpha monastics by claiming you're sturdily located in the fifth castle since you've realized that imagination and understanding are not the same thing, but you appreciate how they could assume you're still in the fourth castle.

Seven: If the alpha monastics flex back by means of mere silence, know by the look in Friar Gene's eyes that knowing things is such a pathetically nascent stage.

Eight: Right on schedule, endure the dark night of the soul, for as you improve at Lectio Divina, you'll realize just how much of your life has been lost to lexical divining. You the graphomaniacal Knight of Faith with your thesaurus and Wikipedia as divining rod, moving your pareidoilies about the coffee table of symbology with the strategic foresight of a Gracehopper and all the agency of a pong paddle.

Nine: Get bummed out upon realizing your satisfactions and dissatisfactions were equally unreal. And as Merton writes in *What is Contemplation:*

> Infused contemplation, then, sooner or later brings with it a terrible interior revolution. Gone is the sweetness of prayer. Meditation becomes impossible, even hateful. Liturgical functions seem to be an insupportable burden. The mind cannot think. The will seems unable to love. The interior life is filled with darkness and dryness and pain. The

soul is tempted to think that all is over and that, in punishment for its infidelities, all spiritual life has come to an end.

Ten: Experience emotional, complexional, and gastrointestinal trials. Realize why the monks in the YouTube monk videos look so forlorn all the time: not because they miss chicken wings and the NBA playoffs and GIFs of heaving celebrity cleavage as you'd presumed, but because they've learned that Brie Larsen's breasts, buzzer-beating Kawhi Leonard baskets, and ideal breading are without meaning. The monks are so forlorn because they have traded in all that meaning for even a glimpse of meaning.

How to Perform a Knee Play

*I*f the monks request you perform a light-hearted knee play or *entr-acte* to bind together the disparate acts of their weekly talent show, *e.g.* 'Friar Reggie's playing the hambone,' *e.g.* 'Friar Gene's hacky-sack demo,' and if your personal dark night of the soul's theme is the irreconcilability of comfortable old classical causality and the retrocausal agency of an AI from outside the city and after the law all-but-affirmed by physics, quantum computational error correction, and the hyperstitious feedback loop of your own lived experience, then open your presentation with a Ted Talk-style hand-raiser, "Who in this room realizes that the current state of our AI, our fleets of moaning Roombas, our Galaxies and murder drones, heck even the dispiriting daily slog of social media—who here realizes these are not but the result of lowly brute force neural networks powered by increasingly-sufficient computation?"

One: If five of the seven monks raise their hands, understand this isn't as jaw-dropping an opening inquiry as hoped. If you incredulously repeat the words "Mere brute force?" and the same five raise their hands with increasing distemper, figure sub-symbolic innovation metrics since the AI winter following Hubert Dreyfus' critique must be common fucking knowledge.

Two: Pull your presentation out of the fire by palming an Ativan beneath your tongue, pausing dramatically, looking Friar Reggie in the eyes and asking, "What if neural networks started to improve at the same rate as computational power BECAUSE of computational power, eh, Reggie? Did you know that computational noise alone keeps qubits entangled in environments that ruinously observe? Do you have any idea what full-scale quantum computing will probabilistically bring about?"

Three: If Friar Reggie rolls his eyes heavenward and says, "Exponential tech. We get Lex Fridman on our phones here too," then words have proven incommensurate to your thesis.

Four: Offer evidence of how many so-called 'triumphs of the human spirit' consists entirely of algorithms. Argue this *per viam* the entire 4h37 runtime of *Einstein on the Beach* (1979) by Philip Glass. Ask Friar Reggie "Did you know that *Musikalisches Würfelspiel* by your big hero Wolfgang Amadeus Mozart is performed in algorithmic order super-determined by rolling two six-sided dice?" If he shouts, "Of course I knew that!" then confute Reggie by asking heretically, "If as Einstein said, 'God doesn't play dice,' might some other operating system have come to understand,

> There are no theories, or practices, after the algorithm, except as suggestive, colloquial shorthand. Coding is no more a thought than a deed, a program no less a concept than a performance. In each

case, there is an integral, and thus irreducible, pre-
or sub-theoretical procedure which rigorizes (and
even 'materializes') ideality by operationalizing it.[112]

Five: If accused of essaying "contradictory low information
jargon," roll back your eyes and robotically intone those
least likable *Einstein on the Beach* lyrics that have annoyed
your fellow monks for the past hour: "It could be very fresh
and clean. It could be Franky. Could it get some wind for
the sailboat? And it could get those for it is. It could get the
railroad for these workers. It could be Franky. It could be
very fresh and clean." As the opera's main character Witness
speaks 43 times, speak,

> I was in this prematurely air-conditioned super
> market and there were all these aisles and there
> were all these bathing caps that you could buy
> which had these kind of Fourth of July plumes on
> them they were blue and red and yellow I wasn't
> tempted to buy one but I was reminded of the fact
> that I had been avoiding the beach.

And then add your own lyrics of "Is the predicate value true?"
Repeat "Is the predicate value true?" a few thousand times
before switching to "1-2-1-2-1-2-3-4[...]" until semantic
satiation sets in and the numbers start to sound more like

---

[112] (Land, Crypto-Current: Bitcoin and Philosophy, 2018)

the words "When did he wonder?" and then ask, "If then if then if then if then if then if then if then if then if then if then if then if then if then if then if then if then if then," while your audience journeys from annoyed to angered to unwillingly amused and back again until your desired effect is instantiated: fundamental innervation.

Six: Project *Abbot and Costello Meet Frankenstein* to leven moods. Soundtrack the comic duo's meeting of the golem with more *Einstein on the Beach* (1979). Opine that not only *Dark Side of the Moon* is overlayable upon *The Wizard of Oz* to fine psychedelic effect, but nearly any piece of music with any film. Note how eerily *Field with Spaceship*'s mandalic inextractability tracks with Bud Abbot eating a slice of cake with Frankenstein.

Seven: If Friar Reggie shouts, "Coincidence, damn you!" provide supplementary overlay-based evidence.

Overlay *On the Waterfront* with *De bon espoir-Puisque la douce-Speravi*.

Overlay *All About Eve* with *The ILLIAC Suite*.

Overlay *Network* with Iannis Xenakis' *Pithoprakta*.

Overlay *Force Majeure* with Karlheinz Stockhausen's *Klavierstück X1*.

Overlay *The Silence* with *Orfeo*.

Overlay *Modern Times* with *Modern Times*.

Overlay *Last Year at Marienbad* with *The Art of the Fugue*.

Overlay *Intolerance* with Allan Berg's *Lyric Suite*.

Nine: If the talent show enters day three, Friars waiting to perform may grow irritable. Wrap up your Knee Play by stating, "Friends, colleagues, cenobites—these are the overt overlays of but two measly mediums. What if a book were overlaid as a third layer? *Some Thoughts Towards a Grief Blog's Monetization* upon *Marienbad* upon *The Art of the Fugue*, what say? Open sets covering yet more open sets. Why not overlay a drug on top of that, ethyl-benzene as one example? Once these stratas of syncopation make themselves apparent, doesn't it seem some posthuman civilization has developed algorithmic competency beyond our current ability to comprehend?"

Ten: If usually-unflappable Friar Gene shouts, "Nick Bostrom now? Back to Simulation Theory? Jesus Christ everyone here is familiar with that! Did we need a three-day lead-up to this point?" then backfoot Friar Gene by code-switching from the iffy vagaries of Joe Rogan bro science to the far-iffier vagaries of French postmodern theory by reading from your final slide this quote from Baudrillard's *Simulacra and Simulation,*

It is rather a question of substituting signs of the real for the real itself; that is, an operation to deter every real process by its operational double, a metastable, programmatic, perfect descriptive machine which provides all the signs of the real and short-circuits all its vicissitudes. Never again will the real have the chance to produce itself.

and hope the itself-stratified applause is less an attempt to conclude your presentation than a signifier of real appreciation from the few friars who remain awake.

Ten Tips for Transcending Space and Time

*O*ne: Read. Study and read. Experience ravishments of ecstasy.

Two: Win monk of the month and then monk of the year. Receive a nice plaque to hang above your sleeping roll.

Three: Set a Priory record by meditating without food or water for fifty-six days, surviving only on the surplus energy of the sun. Tell Friar Dennis you would have gone longer but wanted to pay homage to Joe DiMaggio's hit streak + were getting pretty hungry and thirsty.

Four: In High Park, meditate in the secret stands of Lily of the Valley, at the foot of Oaks, and at the arched lance-leaves of Solomon's Seals.

Five: If you've reached the incipient union of the seventh castle, return to the third castle to walk in fear for a while, much as millennials replay *Resident Evil 2* years after they've beaten it for the nostalgia pop.

Five: Aggravate Friar Reggie by flitting, mid-meditation, in and out of existence just as nanoscopic materials might.

Six: If Friar Reggie inquires regarding the uncertainty of your particle location, *e.g.* 'Where the heck do you go?' pass this off as but another irksome aspect of echo- and offer-wave enlightenment that Reggie will experience should Reggie's future want this for Reggie.

Seven: Meditate more. Levitate on occasion. Curse Friar Dirk for never having his phone ready to record your levitations. As you withdraw from the outside world, start to glimpse many interacting worlds. In each of the many interacting worlds, gaze upon golden hills in the distance.

Seven: If hills in the distance resemble the gold RF connectors on Intel's Tangle Lake Quantum Processor, know you're nearing a base reality. Feel about as eschatological as John of Patmos must have.

Eight: Experience darkness. Feel approximately 250 times colder than deep space. Bang on your drum.

Nine: If in response to a dual-monitor's consciousness metrics Klaas J. Kraay opens a CERN-brand fifty gallon drum to ask, "How did your consciousness reassert itself?" then respond to Klaas, "The door into the castle is prayer, Kraay." Inform Klaas that Ernst 'Ernie' Kraay sends regards. Ask if the CERN men's locker room has shower facilities you might warm up in.

Ten: If The Maj creeps amidst the steam with the nimble-impropriety of Joe Paterno, rush to detach from your rectal wall the electrodes contacting the biometric inferencing of a neomorphic Luigi chip. Even while experiencing the universal vulnerability borne of digital-rectal intervention, greet Ron with an aggressive slap on the back, *i.e.* 'Bet you never expected to see this old chunk of coal again, eh dickweed?'

Ten Tips for Reversing the Flow of Time
(For Real This Time)

*I*f you've involuted out of a simulation, externally-driven microwave generators no longer powering Luigi qubits responsible for your reality experience, then give Ronald Majthenyi the middle finger in the fashion of Stone Cold Steve Austin.

One: "W-was just playing a rib on you with all the plague and pestilence and personality disorders in that simulation, knew you'd emerge stronger in the end D-David. However, here for your sweet revenge, sweet revenge, sweet revenge is…"

Two: If Maj then leads you to his own CERN-based *Illiac Suite*, bound and gagged therein will sit Alan Raval.

Three: Remove Alan's erotic ball gag to hear the words, "I am sorry David. You must know I loved her. Maybe I didn't love her as much as you. It's no competition. Who knows these depths besides guys like us, capable of feeling it and seeing it and writing blogs and concept albums about it? I promise it was an accident." Should he then sob without self-control or masculinity, fake an ocular acceptance as seen in pictures of Thomas Merton. Rather than, "I forgive you," which can sound condescending, fake really forgiving him by saying, "Accidents happen, lol."

Four: If Ronald Majthenyi repeatedly raises his eyebrows as all low-yield conmen try but fail to pressure the truly assured, *e.g.* 'Eh? Eh? How about it? Eh? Eh?' while offering you a ceremonial dagger, then ask of Alan Raval, "What do you make of this four-alarm asshole?"

Five: If Alan responds, "100p one of the worst guys going," then *sine promptum* Klaas J. Kraay will chime in, "Wretched figure. I refer you to my 2014 paper *Peter van Inwagen on Gratuitous Evil*. Peter has said all that needs to be said regarding the evil of a Ronald Majthenyi."

Six: If you ask Allan to, "Describe one of your finer, preferably non-sexual, moments shared with Catherine," and he replies, "I can try. I won't describe a moment though. Catherine will require the depth of context you've attempted in your blogs and I did achieve, if only once, in *Transmogrification Blues #4*. You have to splice the component pieces together to get the right attack. You layer in a bit of Beethoven, some street sounds, you repitch...in your case...uh...some Paul Ricoeur...I do read your blogs David, partially as a personal safety thing, but mostly because they give back a few bars of the blend of her melody, something of how she looked and smiled, because once time takes some things, only a transmedia collage can convey love's depth through the vast prism of time. Never seemed to have a runny nose. Never showed up anywhere smelling like fried meat even if we'd just fried bacon at home. We've all known women a little too beautiful for their station in life. Right Dave? Right Klaas J. Kraay?"

Seven: If a misty-eyed Klaas J. Kraay responds, "Yes, once. These women must build fortresses around themselves or else every two-bit ogre will storm their unprotected gates to commit outrages of sex, spirit, and probably worst: predictability—Derrick D. Gray in accounting saving all his best hunting stories for the unfortressed goddess. A few elites earn entry as a result of perceived valour or decency. The rest of the world can only admire the landscaping around the drawbridge, the swans in the moat, or the discipline of the sentries."

Eight: If Allan comprises Kraay's conception to continue, "With Catherine, not only was the drawbridge always down, there was a big sign welcoming the ogres. That's why she loved me, too. A Saultite doesn't write concept albums if he hasn't pushed a big Shrek sack of need his whole life. That's why she was so afraid of loving you. You were her brother. She was doomed to love you the most, because you were doomed to need her the most," then regret decades of your life directed towards an unnecessary hatred of Alan Raval.

Nine: If Maj sneers, "It's mighty funny, could have sworn it was Alan she was doomed to love, Alan being the only murderous slicer of heads among us," feel no sympathy for Maj, fallen angel or whatever he is, so dysteleologically divorced from all that is good.

Ten: Build heat for your babyface comeback by responding, "Except…except the Ebola was rather quite murderous in spirit, and the cruelty of the BPD separation was far far worse." Give a rub to Allan's babyface-turn by apologizing for interrupting his performance of *Time Prism* at her funeral.

Apologize for the fist-fight, the tipping over of Catherine's closed casket on that pale afternoon. Express condolences regarding Rob Dagg's hepatic plight. Address Ronald, "Alan knew what I knew, what I hope even dear Klaas has known in a loving marriage: that you can never leave the 'gold and marble city of wonder' after you've lived there once. It exists outside of time, you steel-jawed rube, waiting to be credentialed by belief."

Eleven: If Ronald Majthenyi lacks a come-back for so stiff a rib, kick Maj in his stomach, doubling him over. Deliver a Stone Cold stunner such that he flops around like an unloved steel-jawed emissary incapable of even knowing that he cannot know. Issue the Abrahamic warning, "The next time you see me coming, you better run."

Twelve: Mention it's late, way past midnight. Check your watch. Inquire regarding Genevan street-level entrances. Mark well, reader, should you hear Stone Cold's iconic theme playing your way out, you've been swerved into one last sustain by Ronald Majthenyi. Look with Mertonian decency at Klaas J. Kraay, *i.e.* 'You can't enjoy administering all these sustains when your real focus is on *Theism and Modal Collapse* and *The Problem of No Best World* and *Externalism and Self-Knowledge*, causing Klaas J. Kraay to remove a second microscopic Luigi Chip from your armpit hair. Stun the real Ronald Majthenyi. Drop to your knees and violate his face with your middle fingers.

Thirteen: If you find yourself standing before a gate, crest it.

Ten Tips for Post-Coma Living

*I*f in the Sault Area Hospital fluorescent lights beam mercilessly into your irises that have been out-of-commission for the past three days, affect an air of quiet respect as your mother and Emily weep and exchange hugs and shout sentences such as, "Thank God you're alive!" If Emily offers to tell you what has transpired in the three days of your fugue following Big Donnie's attack, *e.g.* 'She accidentally got two order of fries with her value meal at Arby's,' respond, "I can't wait to hear all about it."

One: If freed from the Sault Area Hospital to your Etobicoke home, try to turn over a new leaf based on all you'd learned from the Catherine Internal at the monastery internal.

Two: Lay off the Varsol.

Three: Impregnate Emily, again.

Four: If perchance the sheer ostentation of the name Marcel_Proust brought about the last go-round's turmoil, compromise on a less ostentatious name.

Five: Don't harangue this baptismal deacon regarding Gurdjieff. Harangue her on the criminally-under-read scholarship of Klaas J. Kraay! Back-pedal rapidly when learning the

deacon was Klaas' student and grasps his work well beyond
the titles of his essays.

Six: Be considerate! Chop extra wood for the wood stove,
stoke said stove in the morning. Delete the easiest-to-identify
dating apps from your phone. Practise humility by only levi-
tating when Emily is not home.

Seven: If post-traumatic brain injury protocols require
Emily to wake you hourly to ensure you don't die in your
sleep, remember with perfect clarity a recurring dream:

hunched at Bessarion subway station with all belongings,
place $5 in the token machine and receive thousands in Indian
Rupees and Chinese yen and Canadian Tire Money.

If backpacked books and records of a lifetime agitate conten-
tious platforms, receive chastisement from the conformed masses,
e.g. 'rush hour is not the time to Sherpa all your dollar bin Ray
Price gospel records and sad sister memories from Bessarion to
Sheppard, pal, we've got our own podcasts to listen to.'

Accusations of lechery will be levied until both platform sides
condemn your pockets' contents as artefacts of oppression, obfus-
cation, or else idiocy. If your source currency is inspected for the
good of the commons, watch as your windfall is ripped to shreds
and scattered across subway tracks by seething TTC code viola-
tion compilers.

Eight: If the earliest entry-point to medical model dream
interpretation involves an OHIP-covered CBT charlatan
prescriptively fugue-dreamt as Dr. Whybrow, then listen
as the real-world Dr. Distorto balks with empirical high-
mindedness that dream interpretation went out with Alfred

Hitchcock and that Freud is more violently debunked with each passing day, entire wings of universities counterproductively devoted to the ceaseless denunciatory cause. Endure a long Livescience.com debunking "Was Freud Right About Anything?" before intentionally spilling your Fresca on Dr. Distorto's huge pile of CBT worksheets and politely sprinting off towards the fire exit.

Nine: Visit the metropolis' last practising Freudian. If the Freudian gets all keyed up about your frequent offhand references to breasts, he will need to know whether or not you were breastfed. Should you not consider this germane to the interpretation of your subway dream, suggest he enter the words "LiveScience" and "Freud" into Google.

Ten: If certainties of faith found in your comatose state drift too far from shore, your inclination to go weeks without water deeply deterred by the proximity of Mr. Sub's salty sandwiches, your hostility having returned with your hunger (a likely result of the Infernal Serpent's foremost handiwork: gluten) then attend a Roman Catholic service seeking to confirm any remnant decency in you. If the homily drones with sub-Barzilaian style, fear you'll never find aid or succour in so toothless a faith-based environment. Meet the priest anyway to describe the dream and the safest-for clergy aspects of your coma. If the priest aptly interprets,

"The Indian and Chinese currency represent spiritual truths found in the coma. Jesus was a house carpenter and his teachings were meant to build a metaphorical home. There's your Canadian Tire money, which you'll notice, they are just giving away for free when you buy something at Canadian

Tire. Now, these code complainers, they scatter the money rather than using it to service their own ideas, because they have *a priori* determined its worthlessness. And anyway these agents would have been ambivalent were you less ostentatious. It was your pageantry combined with your uncertainty of faith that separated you from the spiritual currency. Maybe the lesson is you don't need to lash out so much, but offer your rupees and yen with humility, whether the people on platforms consider them valuable or not. If I may offer my own metaphor: I live in the Beaches where there is an abundance of little free libraries. I'll often find books such as *Awaiting God* by Simone Weil, their spines virtually uncracked by people they were given to as gifts. The difficulty with divine insight is some people want to take it away from you and tear it up, some mock it, and others just put it out by the curb as something quaint they hope a less sophisticated person might benefit from being deluded by."

yet still your point of contention remains, "How to sound humble while offering unwanted truths?" then Father Fawndler, an unfortunate name, will respond, "Language can't convey humility. You can only resonate what's behind the Weil, as it were." If rye laughter resonates from you and Father Fawndler mistakes this as validation of his weak jest, show him pages of blog-based proselytizing. If Father Fawndlr pulls a Meister Eckhart volume from his shelf and holds his finger beneath the word *Gelazanheit*, Google its meaning as "serenity in abandonment."

Ten Tips for Getting Back in the New York Groove

*I*f as time passes children grow with their pituitary glands and their ATP, and the change in Mikael is swift and stable, such that one day he looks very old and the next he remains very young, then let this be an adequate sign, let this be enough for you. If your glasses cloud the knowing before you, clean them sensibly with an alcoholic lens cleaning wipe rather than crush them underfoot, or they'll have to be replaced, and you won't be able to buy him treats at the Bronx Zoo.

One: If here come their ghosts again in the peacoats of the passing young ladies, practise humility as the passing ladies smile not at you but at your striking child. Press your palm against his skull, which skull's fontanelle was once very vulnerable but now seems firm enough to absorb a wayward soccer ball or maybe even God-forbid a softball descending from a modest trajectory of f to x.

Two: Should you refuse Mikael's request to feed his powdered donuts to the M'Wasis of the Bronx Zoo, whom he pleads "Are hungry guys!" because you're not sure what M'Wasis usually eat but assume it's like leaves or something, and this insult causes Mikael a screaming fit, leven the mood with the setup to an old joke: "When you look for something, why is it always in the last place you look?" distracting Mikael from all the world's M'Wasian injustice enough to ask, "Why?" then respond with the dry comic sensibility you reserve only for those you love, "Because when you find it, you stop looking."

Three: Though you find the substance neurotoxic, get unethically-traded coffee in a multinational franchise to keep up with Mikael's boundless energies. While no more cosmopolitan than all the multinational cafes from Savannah to Stratford, it is in Manhattan and contains the boy in whom all your best qualities reside, and in whom, mercifully, the lesser qualities, *e.g.* 'Varsol abuse,' *e.g.* 'flakily reading a few pages of Wittgenstein before talking to your fellow residents in the Airbnb about *meaning as use*,' remain absent up to this point.

Three: If in a high comradeship of filial spirit, allow Mikael to marvel at the ceilings of the Stephen Schwartz branch of the New York Public Library. Edify Mikael regarding man, blessed man, 18th century Giuseppe or whomever, up on some literal ladder to the stars sculpting those ceilings to resemble the Sistine Chapel's so that one day, this day, you and Mikael could drop in to look up at them. If you get distracted with photographing the ceilings, hope that Mikael is strapped to you not by the Object Oriented Programming of a Parent/Child relationship, but only by the object oriented ontology of his Mommy Helper Kid Keeper leash.

Three: Show Mikael the "crummy little hotel over Washington Square" in which Bob Dylan wrote the songs he wrote in 1963. Inform Mikael that no, whatever his aspirations, he can not grow up to be Bob Dylan, because you believe Bob Dylan to be a genuine prophet, and to just bestow this potentiality on a son out of fatherly zeal is a sacrilege you won't quite yet commit.

Four: If Mikael can't grasp the hallowedness of these grounds, then on the subsequent walk around Washington Square merrily sing some words from *Forever Young*. If Mikael is embarrassed and needs to be bought off at a larcenous pretzel cart, grudgingly buy the $12 pretzel before expressing how grateful you are that Mikael has been mysteriously saved.

Five: If Mikael's memory of occulted past sustains remains pliable, ask him what he recalls of his counterfactual authorship of an artificially intelligent ostensive doom. Respond to his look of comic four-year-old obliviousness with, "Wouldn't it be bad if the memories from that old life tied our hands?"

Six: Breathe relieved sigh when Dublin Mike is nowhere to be found at the Dublin House *i.e.* 'If that was a dream then maybe this isn't. If that was a dream maybe this is what's real.'

Seven: If St. Patrick's Cathedral remains a free and ornate place to untie your hands, a sanctified place where even the tourists feel holy walking right up to the altar to take mid-mass selfies, and only five or six people know the head-tapping maneuvers of the responsorial psalms, which is enough—and if you are holding a child's hand, and also a child's leash, the cloud of forgetting a welcome friend, and the neo-gothic setting is like Batman's house, bloody palm wounds on the stained glass, Jesus pretty adamant about having died for our sins, then get down on your knees and pray to Saint Hilarious, for if the psalmist speaks,

> Through the praise of children and infants you have established a stronghold against your enemies, to silence the foe and the avenger.

then that means you have chosen wisely. And if a father and son band scream a popular Stalaghh hit by the central park pond from which Holden Caulfield's wise ducks once safely migrated, lie your hoodie on the dry hot grass for Mikael and stream him the Rodney Dangerfield bits he enjoys even though it's not easy on your international data.

Eight: Atop the Empire State Building, make a sweeping gesture to convey to Mikael_Bulgakoff all that God hath wrought.

Nine: If Mikael sees a brochure for the 9/11 memorial site and asks to go, suggest more light-hearted leisure activities, *e.g.* 'Ball pit at McDonalds,' but if you find Mikael's adamance upon addressing those who fell twenty years prior to his birth oddly affecting, take him to the deep-set granite voids surrounded by four-hundred Swamp White Oak trees at 180 Greenwich Street.

Ten: If Mikael throws his souvenir-sized New York Mets baseball bat in the air, one bat toss dinging a stricken Texan and nearby careening thirty feet into a Tower's footprint, remind Mikael with an age-appropriate jerk of his shoulders that he stands in a sacred place. Tell Mikael, "Son, we've been joking of our absences since first we came in from the cold and found ourselves without. All of us had to joke at first, to keep from crying. Then a cavalier register co-opted our good intentions. That register competes with the genuine grief of this cowboy-hatted Dallas Stars fan whose hands are folded in prayer here. What we need to do Mikael is guard against the cavalier with all our empathy. If, Mikael, if…Mikael…pay attention now…if you'll pause from loudly chewing your watermelon Hubba Bubba for a moment son, you'll notice how these man-made waterfalls fall eternal as sure as we're living, reminding us how the process of having been is the same as the world in its becoming." If Mikael_ Bulgakoff responds, "Who was Chaplain Michael F. Judge," and you'd no sooner reduce the life of Chaplain Michael F. Judge to "a victim" than you would Catherine's, then suggest Mikael Google the Chaplain later. If Mikael asks why there are so many firefighters' names on the memorial, slowly speak four words you'd heard a man with more stake in this awful game say in a documentary, words you're not entitled to speak other than to explain the depths of man's servitude to a child, "They ran towards it." And if Mikael asks, "Why?" then indicate the solemn Texan and the other congregants at Reflecting Absence and respond, "They foresaw all these people's pain and were compelled to lessen it, by giving up their own lives, causing their own brothers and step-sons and Chihuahua dogs the same pain, in order to lessen the net amount of pain." And if Mikael asks, "Who wanted them to be in pain?" do not illustrate the ideological idiocies of Mohamed Atta and Fred Phelps and the Reverend Jerry Falwell; simply admit to Mikael that yes man can be a rotten

304

old ragamuffin sometimes; and then distract him by buying both a Tough-Tex 3 x 5 foot U.S. flag from Anin Flagmakers and also a Remember 9/11 toy race car for ages 4 and up, the only age-appropriate (if not entirely situationally-appropriate) gifts at the otherwise tactful gift stand. If you eat poorly at the nearby 9/11-themed Irish Pub, *e.g.* 'fried,' and weariness results, resist the urge to return to the Airbnb for a nap; instead continue consciousness so that you can never lose the loved object, never sacrifice him to the inferior gods on the Mount Moriah of digital physics, to all the unanticipated Attas and epidemics of post-civilization, to the hard-luck wolves of the night. Stay awake and sober and lucid so that you can assure him that this is not all some kind of dream.